CITYSCAPE
AFFAIR
BOOK ONE

COME Undone

JESSICA HAWKINS

USA TODAY BESTSELLING AUTHOR

Olivia Germaine has already found love. Devoted wife,
loyal friend, determined career woman—she's created the
life she always envisioned…until she locks eyes with a
handsome stranger across a crowded room.

David Dylan—alleged playboy and Chicago's most eligible
bachelor—awakens a passion in Olivia she buried long
ago. He challenges her to confront the perfect life she's
built and to ask herself questions that could lead to either
happiness…or regret.

Because David knows who she is. He knows what she
wants. And he can give it to her. If only she'll give in…

Praise for The Cityscape Affair Series

"Wanna talk about alpha? Wanna discuss STEAM? Wanna chat about chemistry and angst and total obsession? [David] Dylan is the answer to all of it. And more. If you've been dying for what us OG's call "old school trilogies" that just consume you like FSOG, This Man, and Driven did back in the day, I present to you this trilogy."

—USA Today Bestselling Author Adriana Locke

"The writing is fantastic, the emotional detail, involved, and the connections are so well explored, that we get to LIVE this story (the good, the bad and the ugly). Thoroughly. Intensely. Honestly."

—Maryse's Book Blog

"This series is incredible. It belongs on every best-seller list. Hell, it belongs on the big screen. FIVE STARS."

—Amazon Reviewer

Come Undone is also available in:
Audiobook
Ebook

2nd edition © 2020 Jessica Hawkins

1st edition © 2013 Jessica Hawkins

Editing by Elizabeth London Editing

Beta by Underline This Editing

Proofreading by Paige Maroney Smith

Cover Designed by Najla Qamber Designs

Chapter One

Sophistication perfumed the lobby of the downtown performance art center as if it'd been bottled and sold to Chicago's elite. It clung to red velvet drapes with gold tassels and spiraled up to where I waited on marble steps.

A pair of large male hands slipped my coat from my shoulders. "Does your husband know you're here alone?"

I nearly shivered despite the warm breath on my skin. "Ask him yourself. He'll be here any moment."

"Then I'd better make this quick." I heard the smile in his voice as his tone lightened. "Is this a new dress?"

"I've worn it before," I said, glancing back at my husband. "Dinner with your sister."

"The green suits you."

"Your favorite color."

He pecked me quickly on the mouth. "Because it matches your eyes."

Having come straight from his office, the day wore on him. The sagging knot of his tie and dark circles under his eyes were evidence of many consecutive late nights at the

office. But Bill's smile never failed to comfort me with its familiarity. "How was work?" I asked.

"The usual."

"Did you defend any criminals?"

"They're not criminals," he said, draping my coat over his elbow. "They're people accused of committing crimes."

"Spoken like a true lawyer." I tucked my hair behind my ear. "You're fitting in more at that firm every week."

An early-evening spring breeze passed over us as more people shuffled in the theater doors. Smartly dressed women carefully stepped down scarlet-carpeted steps, passing beneath elaborate chandeliers that cast shadowy corners.

I scanned the room for our friends as Bill slipped an arm around my waist, pulling my back to his front. "We can still skip out before anyone notices."

"That wouldn't be fair to Lucy," I said. "She and Andrew are expecting us."

"I'm sure they'd understand."

Of course they would. My best friend's sweet-as-sugar personality didn't lend itself to guilt trips—and she might've found the one man on the planet more amiable than her. Still, Bill and I needed this. Aside from a client dinner last week and a charity function hosted by one of Bill's bosses, we'd each been spending more time at our respective offices than with each other.

"It's good for us to be social," I said.

Bill slid his hand up my hip, over my dress, to the elastic of my tights. "We could always be social with each other."

We hadn't had sex in weeks. Why was he suddenly frisky *now*, at the most inopportune time, while friends waited on us? The answer was obvious—to get out of sitting through the ballet tonight.

Fortunately, I had a topic on hand equivalent to *down, boy.*

"I talked to my dad today," I said. "He'll be in Chicago for a night next month and wants to have dinner."

Bill released me with a groan. "Great."

"It's only one night," I said as we checked our coats.

He pocketed the claim ticket, arching an eyebrow at me. "And you're so thrilled when my parents drive in."

"Touché." But while my dad was conservative, nobody would dare call him stuffy like the Wilsons. I flipped my hair over my shoulder. "You don't have to come, but I know he'd like to see you."

"Sure he would," Bill said. "Where else would he get free legal advice?"

As we navigated through clusters of murmuring theatergoers, I kept a lookout for Lucy. "You're exaggerating. Dad's too prideful to ask for free things. Anyway, he has plenty of corporate lawyer friends he can go to."

"I'm not talking about work, Olivia. I mean his divorce from Gina. Lawyer friends don't put up with that shit—they charge you for it."

"Luckily, his divorce is almost finalized anyway," I pointed out. "And I'm sure if you ever need advice on how to win over girls half your age, he'll be happy to repay the favor."

"Half my age? Are you trying to get me locked up?" he asked. "I'd say I've got my hands full as it is."

I turned, reached up to my six-foot-one husband, and pushed a lock of brown hair out of his eyes—while making a mental note to schedule him a haircut.

This time, when he hugged me and ran his hands up the hem of my dress, over my backside, I didn't stop him. Public foreplay was, at least, one thing we hadn't tried. Maybe it was what we needed. What *I* needed.

After all, Bill wasn't the one with an issue, but it wasn't as if he'd come up with a solution, either. I'd have thought our sex life would be sorted five years into our marriage, but here I was, wondering if getting revved in front of a well-to-do crowd might help bring me to orgasm when nothing else with Bill—or any partner— had worked.

"Oh, there's Lucy," Bill said, walking past me. "Did you know Gretchen was coming, too?"

My two best friends stood at the center of a group of men and women. From behind, they looked about as different as their personalities actually were. Gretchen, boosted by spiky heels, stood tall in a revealing pink dress. Her long platinum hair bounced in signature curls as she gestured wildly with everyone's eyes glued to her.

Next to her, petite Lucy dodged Gretchen's flailing limbs. She wore a boat-neck black dress, her short chestnut-colored hair fashioned into a perfect chignon as she clasped her hands in front of her.

Lucy's boyfriend spotted us first. Standing off to the side, wringing a program, Andrew grinned toothily and beckoned us over. "Sorry, Gretch," he interrupted her midsentence. "Everyone, this is Bill and Liv Wilson."

I shook hands with one of Andrew's associates. Since I'd never officially taken Bill's last name, I was still technically Olivia *Germaine*, but I didn't bother correcting Andrew.

"Liv is Lucy's other best friend," Andrew said. "They met in college."

"Now I'm the *other* best friend?" I joked. I'd only introduced Lucy, my college roommate, to Gretchen, who'd befriended me my first day at a new elementary school. We'd stuck the same magazine tear-out of Andrew Keegan in the plastic covers of our respective binders while everyone else in our class fawned over Jonathan Taylor Thomas.

Lucy showed me her YSL pumps. "Look, we're the same height tonight."

"I don't know, shrimp," Bill said. "Liv's still got some inches on you."

She scowled playfully. "I'm glad you guys are here, by the way. To celebrate the tax season ending, Andrew's boss practically bought out the theater for clients, accountants, and the rest of the staff. Plus, I know Liv has been wanting to see this."

"Have you?" Bill looked down at me. "I would've brought you if I'd known."

"We've been busy," I said. Bill spent more time at the office than at home lately, but I regularly worked eight-to-ten-hour days, too, so I couldn't complain.

"*Anyway*," Gretchen said, picking up whatever story we'd interrupted, "the plane lands, and I rush to the station, barely making the train. Since it's now one in the morning and I've been traveling for fourteen hours, I immediately pass out. When I wake up, the stewardess says, 'Welcome to *Chile*.'"

"Chile?" one of the women cried.

"I'd gotten on the wrong train, slept through the entire ride, and ended up in Santiago."

I politely joined in everyone's laughter, though I'd heard the story of her travel blunder twice before.

"To make matters worse," Gretchen continued, "it was fifty-something degrees outside, and I was wearing shorts and a tank top."

The man next to me guffawed. He was the only one who'd been introduced without a partner—Gretchen's lure was cast. "What do you do that you can take off to Chile whenever you like?" he asked.

She turned her megawatt smile on him. "I'm in enter-tainment PR."

"Hook, line, and sinker," Bill muttered, reading my mind. When I giggled, Gretchen shot us a dirty look, her blue eyes as playful as they were piercing. I couldn't blame the man for falling under her spell.

Bill raised his chin over the crowd. "I see an old colleague. Mind if I go say hi?"

"Make it quick," I said. "It's almost curtain."

Lucy, ever the hostess, turned sideways to include me in a conversation about mutual funds and expense ratios.

As I watched Bill walk away, my gaze lingered on different people. Their stiff, deliberate movements coun-tered the elegance of ballet dancers. Strangers. An older woman slid an olive from a spear with her teeth. A busi-nessman checked his cell during a conversation. A couple stood shoulder to shoulder, flipping through their programs. Not a genuine smile in sight. Sometimes it seemed as if everyone was just operating instead of living. Or maybe I was, and it was me who didn't belong here. Or anywhere.

A feeling that'd haunted me for sixteen years.

Since my parents' abrupt divorce when I was a teenager, I'd never figured out exactly where I was supposed to be. Large crowds heightened that insecurity, as if they were all in on something I wasn't. I had the unfortu-nate ability of feeling spectacularly alone in a crowd, even when surrounded by friends and family.

Or was I alone?

I had the sensation of being watched seconds before I met a man's unfamiliar stare across the room. Dark and narrowed intensely in my direction, the handsome stranger seemed to either try to place me—or strip me bare. My toes curled in my high heels. He stood taller than anyone else around him, his hair and eyes midnight-black like his tuxedo. His furrowed brow and frown exaggerated a long, angular jawline. Something about the way he looked at me slowed time, everything going fuzzy—except my heartbeat, which whipped into a rapid flutter.

My body only buzzed this way when I'd had just the right amount of wine. I held his gaze longer than I should've. My pounding heart echoed in my ears. It wasn't his immense, tall frame or darkly handsome face that struck me, but a draw so strong that it didn't break, even when I finally blinked away.

I moved my hair off my clammy neck. The hem of my dress ghosted the tops of my tight-clad thighs. I didn't have to look back to know he was still watching me. *Staring* at me. Goose bumps started a slow crawl over my skin, up my arms and legs.

I knew I shouldn't look again, but I started to raise my eyes just as Lucy linked her arm through mine. "It's starting," she said, pulling me away as the lobby lights pulsed. "Let's go to our seats."

Bill found us in the auditorium, making his way down the row, apologizing when his elbow struck a woman in the back of the head.

He took his seat, shifting to get comfortable. His long legs knocked against the seat in front of us, and its occupant turned to purse her lips.

When she looked forward again, he shrugged and said under his breath, "I'm tall, sue me."

I suppressed a laugh.

"So, are you familiar with the tale of Odette and Prince Siegfried?" he asked.

I furrowed my brows, taking the *Swan Lake* program from him. "Yes. Are *you?*"

He chuckled at my expression. "Of course. I, uh, probably never mentioned how my parents forced me to audition for the play in high school." He rubbed his chin. "One more desperate attempt to round out my college applications."

"You *danced* in high school?" I asked.

"Well, you already know my parents forced me to take ballroom lessons—but no, not ballet. The play was a modern-day retelling minus the ballet. Huge disaster. Plus, they changed it to a happy ending to appease the parents. I prefer the original."

"The tragedy?"

"Yep." As the conductor lifted his arms, Bill winked. "Just another love story gone wrong."

Before long, the stage was awhirl with white tulle, hard muscles, pretty and perfect pink slippers that curled and arched and lengthened unnaturally. Everything about the ballet appeared smooth and blemish-free, from the dancers to the patrons. The graceful precision was one thing, but the flawlessness of the performance awed me.

Everything in life should be so clean.

A bewitching Odette mournfully enthralled the crowd as her story unfolded. Why did it feel as if she focused on me?

Like the black-haired man from earlier. With the memory of his dark and stirring gaze, the velvety red seat under my thighs suddenly pricked me. I couldn't remember exactly what he looked like. Hard as I tried, the details of his face remained hazy—I could only feel him. I tried to sit still, but the heat in his stare enveloped me now. What had made him look at me that way? Like he'd been seconds away from tearing across the packed room and dragging me into a dark corner. Pushing me up against a wall. Shoving my dress around my hips and ripping through my tights.

I gasped as I released the breath I'd been holding.

He was probably somewhere close by. Maybe even watching me now. Was he also thinking about fucking a married stranger, shielded by elegant curtains with sophistication-reek? I turned my head over my shoulder just as the curtain fell for intermission. It took me a moment to catch my breath and clap along with the crowd.

We spilled into the lobby as Lucy excitedly reviewed the first half. "I can't believe my mother let me quit ballet when I was seven," she said. "I could've been a star."

"You might be reaching with that one," I said.

She shook her head. "Can't you just imagine me as a professional ballerina?"

I laughed at her sincere expression.

"Fine, don't believe me." She sighed, then perked up. "Should we hit the restroom?"

"I need to touch up," Gretchen said, nodding, then tapped her bottom lip with a pink manicured nail. "Then again, I also need wine, and there's a line for both. We only have fifteen minutes."

"I'll get drinks," I volunteered.

Since Bill was entrenched in conversation with Andrew's colleagues, I made my way through the crowd to the bar. As I waited to order, I pulled a lipstick from my clutch and popped open my compact.

Ever so slowly, I glided Ruby Red on my parted mouth and smoothed my lips together. I drew away from the mirror to admire my work. I looked . . . poised. Perfectly coiffed hair, teased and styled into a long bob, floated just at my shoulders, every shiny, golden-brown lock cooperating. My eyeliner swelled over my almond-shaped eyes, winging at the corner. I'd chosen lipstick just the right shade of red to complement my emerald dress and my olive skin—not too rich, not too subtle.

Everything looked just right.

But that was the problem with perfection. The slightest tremble could send it all tumbling down. A sense I'd been experiencing more as of late.

A bartender slipped a black cocktail napkin in front of me. "What can I get you?" he asked.

I quickly dismissed my unease and snapped my compact closed. "Three glasses of your house chardonnay."

He nodded, turning away as I tossed the mirror in my handbag.

"Chardonnay?" A deep, steady voice rumbled beside me, the single word rolling off his tongue. "Not what I would've chosen for you."

The din of the crowd faded as I looked up and met the same dark gaze from earlier that both pierced right through me and begged me closer. Only, the man's eyes weren't dark, but an indisputable light chestnut brown, intensified a thousand times by jet-black lashes and thick eyebrows.

I drew a sharp breath at the magnitude of his beauty, the kind that turned heads. All I could do was stare back and ask, "Excuse me?"

A woman trying to place her drink order bumped into me. I steadied myself on the bar but never broke the stranger's gaze. I couldn't take my eyes off him. Hair blackest black, short and unruly but long enough to run my hands through. A naturally suntanned complexion, as if he regularly spent time outdoors. A freshly shaven, angular jawline that ended with a cleft chin, the only soft curve amongst otherwise chiseled features.

The bartender's voice cut into my consciousness as he set three glasses in front of me. "That'll be twenty—"

With an elbow on the counter, the man passed over cash without even glancing away from me. "Thank you."

I opened my mouth to protest, but the bartender was already gone with the money.

"Merlot," the man in front of me said, tilting his head. "Or Malbec. Plump and dark, with a smoky finish."

As my mind raced to catch up, I resisted from touching my lips, suddenly aware of their color, grapes ripening on the vine. "That's the wine you would've picked for me," I figured.

"Chardonnay isn't complex enough." He gave me a once-over as he added, "Maybe even something rich and flavorful like aged scotch."

There was nothing inappropriate about his words, but the way his voice deepened with the sexy clip of his voice, my insides quivered.

He took the lipstick I'd forgotten I was holding, his fingers brushing mine. My nipples pebbled as he checked the bottom of the tube and glanced up at me. "Ruby Red," he mused. "So, which are you?"

"Which one what?" I asked.

"Dry and goes down easy? Or full-bodied . . ." He wet his lips. "With an aftertaste that sticks on my tongue."

My heart beat in my stomach with his probing question. "You seem to think you already know the answer."

"Maybe it's both. Chardonnay on the outside." He moved a little closer. Something about the lean in his posture was intimate and easy, yet the space between us physically warmed, fire flickering under my skin. "But with those green-olive eyes of yours, *easy* isn't the first word that comes to mind. Neither is dry."

If he kept this up, he'd be right about that—my body was already responding, the tender place between my legs pulsing as it grew wet. "Do I know you?" I asked. Something about him felt familiar, comfortable, as if our eye contact earlier had been equivalent to a first date, sweeping dull small talk out of the way and pushing us past formalities.

"No." Another man tried to get between us to order, but the god in front of me moved closer, shooting him a dagger of a look I'd never seen. The intruder fell back into the crowd.

Shit. Bill might be looking for me. Gretchen and Lucy would be here any second, on the hunt for their alcohol. I didn't want them to find me here, entranced by another man, but I couldn't tear myself away. "Are you sure we haven't met?"

He palmed the lipstick and said frankly, "I'd remember."

The thing was, I didn't particularly like or dislike chardonnay. Bill had sounded so sophisticated ordering it for me on our first date, and I hadn't really been much of a wine drinker before him. It was fine. Lucy and Gretchen both drank white wine most of the time, and it'd grown on me.

Kind of the way Bill had. We'd worked in the same building and it'd taken him more than six months to ask me out. Even then, I'd said no. At first.

"There you are," came a woman's lilting voice from behind the man.

His expression closed a moment before he looked over his shoulder. "What—"

The break in whatever spell he held over me allowed me to regain my sense. I picked up all three of my drinks and ducked away.

I'd barely had time to exhale before I nearly collided with Bill. "Where are the girls?" he asked, taking a glass from me.

Andrew appeared, boxing me in. "What do you think of the performance, Liv?"

Bill took a sip before I could tell him the drink wasn't for him.

Gretchen appeared, taking the other glass. "Finally," she said. "As much as I'm enjoying the battle of the bulges on stage, I can't sit through an entire ballet sober."

Bill wrinkled his nose. "Battle of the *what*?"

"Male dancers in tights," Lucy said, a seasoned translator of Gretchen's innuendo. She touched my elbow. "Are you okay?"

"I . . ." I looked back toward the bar. The man's eyes roamed over the head of the woman in front of him, scanning the crowd. I moved a little closer to Bill, hiding in his shadow, both spellbound and a little terrified by what I'd just felt.

"Liv?" Lucy asked.

I blinked a few times, trying to focus on my friend. "I'm sorry," I said, offering her my wine. "Bill took yours."

"It's okay." She smiled warmly. "I don't need it."

Sweet little Lucy wouldn't admit if she did. She always made sure others were comfortable before her. "Please," I said, pushing the wineglass into her hand. "The truth is . . . I really don't like chardonnay anyway."

The heavy door of our Lincoln Park apartment threatened to slam behind me, but at the last second, I caught the knob and eased it shut. With a yawn, I hung my coat, stepped out of my pumps, and peeled off my restrictive tights. In the next room, Bill flipped on the television while I sorted through the day's mail, tossing half of it into the recycle bin.

I found Bill in his boxers, already stripped of his suit and tie, on the brown polyester couch his mother had given us some years ago. Replays of tonight's basketball game that he'd grudgingly missed flashed across the screen.

After the ballet, we'd all gone out for dinner and drinks. Three dirty martinis and a smoldering, penetrating stare coursed through me.

Flavorful, rich, complex.

The man's presence spread warmth from my neck down in a way I'd never experienced—and had told myself many times was impossible for me.

Plump, dark, smoky.

I stripped off my emerald-green dress in one sinuous motion and let it drop to the floor. When Bill didn't look up, I shimmied over and settled myself onto his lap.

"Hi," I said in my sultriest voice. He righted a stray strand of my hair, glancing between the screen and me.

I wet my lips and kissed him full on the mouth. I'd hummed with electricity since intermission, impatient to recapture that stranger's invading eyes, to feel hungry hands all over me, to disappear into dark corners for inappropriate reasons.

"Well, well," Bill said when we broke. "What's gotten into you?"

"It's late. Take me to bed."

His eyebrow rose, and his mouth popped open as if connected by an invisible string. He looked about to protest and then, in one move, stood and carried me to the bedroom.

I fell back on the mattress. He caressed the outsides of my thighs, hovering over me.

As his face dipped to meet mine, I shot up in a panic, forcing him to sit back. "Shit, wait," I said. "I forgot to pick up condoms."

"It's fine."

I frowned. "It is not fine. I told you I forgot to take a birth control pill last week. We need to be extra careful."

"Come on, babe." He nuzzled my neck. "You're not going to get pregnant because you missed *one*—"

"I'm not taking the chance."

"Yeah, I get it." He flopped onto his back, blowing out a breath. "There's a condom in the drawer under the sink."

I shuffled to the bathroom and rifled through hairbands, bobby pins, deodorant, and eye drops until I uncovered a small foil packet.

"What're you doing in there?" he called. "I'm falling asleep."

"One second." After checking the expiration date, I went and jumped onto the bed. "I'm sorry. Where were we?"

Frown lines faded as he rolled over and propped himself above me. I touched his pecs, trailing my fingers down to a flat, slightly soft midsection. Goose bumps sprang to attention across his skin.

"My, my, Mrs. Wilson," he said. The designation always made me think of Bill's mom, but I'd managed to control my grimace over the years. It remained one of the reasons I hadn't given up my maiden name. "What big green eyes you have." He touched his lips just above my cheekbone and brushed a lock from my forehead. "And such pretty blonde hair."

"Not blonde, just plain brown," I said with a pout.

"What?" He feigned surprise and ground his hips against me. "You must be colorblind. I see some blonde strands in there."

"Highlights fade." I cocked my head to the side. "You just want to tell people you married a blonde."

"Agree to disagree then." His smile creased his adorably crooked nose. He loved to say he'd broken it during one-on-one, but the truth was that despite getting hit in the face with a basketball once, the bridge of his nose had always been that way.

He unhooked my bra swiftly and gently cupped my breast in one of his hands. I didn't quite fill up his palm. The unmistakable sounds of a heated basketball game blared from the television.

The motions were familiar. Over time, his touch had become defter, more confident, and his natural woodenness more fluid. He groaned my name as he pushed into me, pulling my hips closer. I echoed his movements, my arousal growing with his satisfaction. Beads of sweat formed on his brow, more apparent when his face screwed up with pleasure. He didn't kiss me again, but I was fine with that. Make-out sessions were better suited to the adolescent and sexually frustrated.

I inhaled his natural scent, enhanced by a salty concoction of shampoo and perspiration—it was always sharper when we made love. I gasped with a twinge between my legs, but it faded like a soft sigh on a breeze.

It wasn't long before he came, squeezing his eyes shut as he collapsed onto me.

"Sorry," he breathed after a moment. "Do you want—"

"I'm good," I reassured him, suddenly tired from the alcohol. "It was nice."

It took him less than two minutes to fall asleep—I knew because I often watched the clock as I waited. Untangling myself from his clutches, I tiptoed out of the room.

Most nights, sex was quick, and that was fine. Not even a marathon session could get an orgasm out of me. It wasn't that I didn't get pleasure from our lovemaking—I did. Feeling physically connected to Bill wasn't a problem; I just couldn't climax with a partner. I'd never been able to with Bill or anyone else. And the harder he tried, the more self-conscious I got, which only frustrated him. When it came to sex, something inside me was fundamentally out of order.

Once the apartment was dark and still, and I'd washed my face of the day, I returned to cocoon myself in our cotton sheets. Bill stirred, unconsciously reaching for me. When he and I had started dating, I'd had to learn to find the comfort in post-coital cuddling. I never passed out like him, so I was the one left with tingling limbs, hot breath in my hair, and sweaty skin as I tried to turn off my brain and sleep.

Tonight, I wasn't in the mood to play bedroom Twister, so after a few minutes, once he was out cold, I moved to my side of the bed.

A twinge.

It wasn't much of anything. I rolled my head to the side, toward my husband. At one point he'd wanted my orgasm as much as I had, but it was the one thing I couldn't give him. We'd experimented in the beginning, including with toys, but neither of us was comfortable with them. There were times when we'd been close, when stars and body parts had aligned, and I'd shuddered in response, climbing the mountain to the peak. But when it came time for the grand finale, I always buckled under the pressure. Every time.

Bill had found comfort in the fact that it wasn't just him —I'd been with other men, mostly in college—but I had yet to find peace in any of it. My incapacity to give Bill all of myself was my eternal flaw—and as a wife, my greatest inadequacy. If things were the other way around, could I live with the fact that I couldn't pleasure Bill?

I *was* happy, though. I knew how to get myself off when I was alone. And I had a husband who loved me. My life was pretty much as perfect as a night of good friends, evocative art, strong drinks, and satisfying sex.

I lay in bed and watched the ceiling, waiting for sleep.

And I reminded myself that yes—I was happy.

Chapter Two

The pungency of self-tanner was an eye-stinging welcome at eight in the morning. The lingering scent meant I couldn't be arriving to work that far behind my boss.

As I passed through the reception area of *Chicago Metropolitan Magazine*'s fourteenth floor offices, Jenny waved at me from behind the front desk and put a call on hold. "Good morning," she sang, lowering the phone receiver to her shoulder. "Know what I love more than Fridays?"

I headed past her toward the office's glass doors. "Gossip."

"You know me so well," she said. "Mr. Beman wants to see you first thing."

I paused with my palm on the door handle and glanced back at her. "About what?"

Her eyes twinkled. "If my sources are right, something to do with Diane . . . who isn't coming in today."

Odd. It wasn't unusual for Diane, my direct superior, to come in late or take a long weekend, but I was usually the first to know.

I went by my cubicle to drop my things at my desk.

"Hey," I said to my co-worker Lisa. The office would be mostly empty for a few more minutes, but with her heels off and coffee cup nearly empty, it was entirely possible she'd slept here.

She removed her earbud. "What?"

"Nothing, just saying *good morning*."

She kept her eyes trained on her computer screen but smiled as she replaced the headphone. "It is, isn't it?"

Something was going on. Even though Lisa hadn't technically smiled *at* me, she rarely showed any positive emotions in my presence. I picked up the *Keep it Sassy* mug Gretchen had given me for my birthday and stopped by the kitchen for fuel on my way to my boss's office.

I knocked on his door gently, nodding at some of my colleagues as they filtered in for the day.

"Come in," Mr. Beman called.

I entered his office and shut the door behind me before turning to him. "Jenny said—"

"Nice to see you here early." He gestured at the chair across from his desk. "Have a seat."

As always, his back was too straight, the part in his white hair too perfect, his face bordering on orange—and his compliments backhanded. I arrived at this time every day, same as everyone else—except brown-nosing Lisa. But he knew that.

I sat and sipped from my mug while he tidied his desk. "I let Diane go last night," he said.

I only just stopped myself from spitting out my coffee. I'd worked under Diane for years. "What? But she . . ." I set the mug on his desk, and he glared at it until I picked it up again. "Why?"

"We need new ideas. Fresh perspective. She was getting too complacent."

He wasn't entirely off base. I'd been carrying her workload for some time while she took long "client" lunches and expensed "necessities" like manicures and an espresso machine for her apartment.

"I've been very pleased with your work as her editorial assistant," Beman said. "Don't think I haven't noticed how you've been covering for Diane. As the magazine skewed younger, her writing style grew older. Until you came along."

"I—oh, um. Thank you, Mr. Beman." By his pinched expression, I wasn't doing a good job of hiding my shock at the rare compliment. "Your opinion means a great deal to me."

"As it should."

The meaning of Diane's sudden absence began to sink in. That would free up the position for senior editor. I wasn't next in line, but why else had Beman called me in? My heart skipped as opportunity opened up in front of me. Some people didn't consider what I did a real job—*some people* being my dad. Our magazine covered the latest and hottest news around Chicago culture—hotel, gallery, and restaurant openings, art and fashion shows, local celebrity and socialite sightings, and more. My father joked that I worked on "fluff pieces for people who didn't care about important current events,"—but he wasn't kidding. Unfortunately for him, I loved my job—people needed fluff in their lives as much as hard-hitting news—but maybe swapping the title *assistant* for *senior*, along with a substantial raise, would help change his perspective a bit.

"I can do it," I said.

"I know you can." Beman straightened his already rod-like back. "You'll make a great associate editor to Lisa. We'll have her transitioned into Diane's position by the end of the month."

Associate editor. A step up from assistant, but not the

giant leap I'd just psyched myself up for by any means. I rested my coffee in my lap, the tops of my thighs warming like my face. "Oh. I . . . I thought maybe—"

"You're welcome. Send Lisa in to see me, please."

I hesitated. I'd only dared to dream of having the position a few minutes, so my disappointment surprised me. Lisa had worked hard for this, but so had I. Diane had told me many times that unlike Lisa, journalism came naturally to me, and that was why Lisa had to put in extra hours. I should've at least been considered for the job.

Plus, there was no way in hell being Lisa's subordinate would turn out well for me.

"With all due respect," I said, staying seated, "I've worked closely with Diane for a while now. I think it's only fair to let me interview for her position."

Mr. Beman eyed me carefully. "As associate editor, Lisa is technically next in line."

"If the goal is to combat complacency, competition is one way to do that," I pointed out. "It would force each of us to step up our game."

"Indeed." His fingertips drummed the desk. "You believe you're ready?"

My dad—a businessman to his core—had been drilling the same motto into my head since I was a girl:

"Say yes to anything asked of you, Olivia. Never pass up an opportunity to excel."

"I'm ready," I said.

Beman sat forward, his leather seat creaking. "I hadn't really planned for that, but a little competition in the workplace never hurt anyone." I followed his gaze to a pile of past issues at the edge of his desk. He picked up the top magazine with a cover I recognized from last spring and read the headline. "'Chicago's Most Eligible Bachelors and Bachelorettes.' Our most popular issue of the year, and it's coming up. It's got potential to cover a good chunk of our annual ad quota."

"Diane and I already started the interview process." I shifted in my seat. "However . . ."

"Go on."

"The selection is largely underwhelming. If I were in charge, I'd throw it out and start over."

He arched an eyebrow. "With the issue coming up so soon?"

I nodded. "I can handle it. We need fresh faces on the pages."

"Unlike that slimy promoter Lester Cartwright, who's been featured multiple times," he said, "or Diane's free-loading cousin she snuck in at the final hour last year."

"Exactly. Consider them—and everyone else who's been featured before—yesterday's news," I said, even though we hadn't ever published the list without overlap. I had no idea how we'd go about finding fifty new bachelors and bachelorettes in a matter of weeks, only that it could be the leg up I needed.

"Work with Lisa on the article, along with whatever other assignments Diane had coming up," he said. "You two can use Diane's office when necessary. I'll decide who I'd like to promote after the issue hits."

I nodded and stood to shake his hand. "Thank you, sir."

While moving a few items into Diane's office, Lisa appeared in the doorway after her meeting with Beman, her arms crossed. "Already taking over, I see," she said.

"They're things we can both use," I said, showing her a stapler. "You *do* sometimes need to fasten two or more papers together, don't you?"

"Very funny."

"So let's have a brainstorm session, just the two of us,

and go over what needs to be done. Since I normally do the grunt work for these issues, I've got some ideas."

"Hmm." Lisa pursed her lips. "I'll see if I can squeeze you in this afternoon."

I gave her a tight smile, but she was already rolling her eyes on her way out the door.

I finished my coffee and headed across the office to the intern station, a room stuffed between the Samples closet full of swag and Conference Room A. Only one girl sat at a computer, her short blonde bob bouncing as she typed furiously.

"Are you Serena?" I asked.

A young girl just out of college whirled around, and her hair *swished*, longer in the front and tipped with soft pink. "Oh, yes, hi. Hello, Mrs. Germaine."

"Call me Liv," I said and offered a smile. Diane had mentioned once that while focused, I could come off a bit stiff. "About the article you e-mailed me last night—you sent it pretty late."

"I know, I'm sorry," she said, her light eyes widening. "I was feeling so, like, inspired, and I didn't want to stop so I was up all night working on it. Next time I can wait to send it till the morning."

"No, don't worry about that," I said, waving my hand. "I'm just glad you got it in early. Makes everyone's job easier."

"Oh." She covered her mouth and giggled. "I thought I was in trouble."

"Anyway, it was good, but there are some revisions I'd like you to make. I'll e-mail my notes. In the meantime, we're gearing up for Chicago's 'Most Eligible' issue, and this year, we don't want any repeats on the list so we're starting over. Can you help gather new prospects?"

"Sounds good," Serena said as she made notes on a

yellow pad. "How do I know what to look for? Attractiveness? Personality? Occupation?"

"All of that. Grab the last several issues to get an idea. Everyone who works here will have a suggestion, but I only want the best of the best. No friends of friends or relatives. Set up interviews with the top picks so Lisa and I can decide from there."

"K," she said. Even though it was just a letter, her voice wavered, and her eyebrows met in the middle.

"I was an intern once, too," I said reassuringly. "You'll figure it out."

At an Italian restaurant uptown, my godparents, Mack and Davena Donovan, greeted me with more energy than friends my own age could ever seem to muster. I accepted their strong hugs by the hostess stand.

"How are you, dear?" Mack said, kissing my cheek.

"I'm well." My heels made us the same height, putting me face to face with the salt-and-pepper flecks in his hair.

His wife's Texan drawl starkly contrasted Mack's clean, seasoned British accent as she added, "We want to hear everything new with you."

"Bill should be here any minute," I said. "He's been at work late most nights since he started this job, but he's on his way."

"No problem." Mack's smile deepened the wrinkles by his eyes. "Let's sit and get a drink."

I let them go ahead on our way to the table. Mack and Davena's hands stayed linked while they maneuvered through the restaurant after the hostess.

"How's work?" Davena asked once we were seated.

"Great," I said. "I just found out I'm up for a promotion. My colleague, Lisa, is more qualified on paper, but I know I can handle more responsibility than I have now."

"I knew you'd work your way up," Davena said. "Didn't I say so, sugar? I recommended you for that internship years ago because I believe in you."

I grinned. "I still owe you. You never let us pay when we go out to dinner."

"And you won't tonight," Mack said, "or any night we eat together."

"Don't waste your energy worrying about the competition." Davena took out her reading glasses. "If I know you, she's the one who should be worried."

"And your mother?" Mack asked, his tone softening. "How's she?"

I opened my menu. "She's my mother."

"Anything in the works?"

"Sure," I said lightly. "Isn't there always?"

"I always brag about what an outstanding writer she is," Mack mused. "Brilliant artist when she's on her game."

"Certainly has an artist's temperament," I muttered.

"You know that Max, from her first novel, was based on me?" He straightened up. "A sprightly British detective come to steal all the young American ladies away from their quarterbacks."

"Of course she knows that," Davena teased. "You remind her constantly."

"Rubbish." He snuck me a devious smile. "She was quite the girl, your mother. Walked right into the university's newspaper office and demanded they print her piece on corporate sexism when nobody else wanted to touch the topic. I knew then we'd be great friends. No surprise she became editor of that paper soon after." Mack covered the back of my hand with his palm. "A real go-getter, like our Liv here."

Maybe my mother had been once. That was before I'd gotten old enough to really know her, though.

The sight of Bill maneuvering through diners was a relief in that moment. He'd save me from this topic.

"I was here on time," he said as he approached. The restaurant's lighting turned his gold shirt mustard. "Parking is damn impossible." He leaned over and gave me a lingering kiss on the cheek. "Got your text. Congrats on Diane's job."

"I didn't get it yet," I said.

"You will." He turned to Mack and Davena, dragging his chair from the table. "What'd I miss?"

"Not too much." Mack signaled a passing waiter. "Bring a bottle of your finest Cab for the table," he said, winking at me. "We're celebrating Liv's news."

Cabernet Sauvignon: rich, full-bodied wine. Chosen by someone who knew me as well as anyone. Maybe even as well as my dark stranger. At the memory of deep, bold words rolling off his tongue weeks ago, I buried my face in my menu to hide my blush.

"Mack was just reminiscing about old times," I answered Bill.

"Old times, huh?" Bill asked. He understood that meant my mom. He cleared his throat, turning back to the table. "Hey, don't you two have a big trip coming up?"

I cast Bill a grateful glance for saving me a trip down memory lane.

"Amalfi Coast," Davena replied. "We've been shopping ourselves silly."

"Correction—*she* has been shopping herself silly," Mack said. "I'm just the human credit card."

Davena waved him off. "I only needed a bathing suit that'd cover my new scar." She put a hand over her side. "No more bikinis for me. Just old lady one-pieces."

Mack took her hand from her ribcage, lacing their fingers as he brought her knuckles to his mouth. "Careful. That's my beautiful, vivacious wife you're talking about."

With a petite but athletic body, fair skin, and cropped, curly, blonde hair, Davena was the picture of health, her fiery eyes only surpassed by her sassy attitude. Even with the discovery of her breast cancer years earlier, I'd never seen Davena without a twinkle in her eye. The word *pity* did not weigh down her vocabulary.

Tempted as I was to ask about her health, I knew I'd get a brush-off. I'd learned long ago that for her, normalcy was the best medicine.

"You really should go see Lucy," I said as the waiter arrived with the wine bottle. "She'll set you up with a fabulous new wardrobe."

"Which one is Lucy again?" Mack asked, holding up his glass to taste.

"That precious little stylist Liv has known since college," Davena said. "You've met her at least three times. Try to keep up."

"Lucy works just across the street from me," I said to Davena. "We can all get lunch, and then she can help you find something cute and conservative."

"Me, *conservative*?" Davena made a gagging noise. "Can't stand that word."

Mack took a sip and nodded at the waiter. "Why do you think she made us move from Texas?" he joked.

Bill unfurled his napkin onto his lap, humming. "You know, we just wrapped up a case against a doctor who nearly killed a woman when he botched a double mastectomy."

"*Bill*," I scolded. Sometimes, my husband's emotional detachment could be a good thing. His straightforward approach to most situations had initially drawn me to him, and his intuition to back off when I needed to be left alone had saved our relationship many times. But in social situations, it sometimes left me apologizing for his behavior—like now. "I'm sorry, Davena," I said. "Of course you don't want to hear that."

"Cancer kills," she said, adjusting her eyeglasses to read the menu. "It's not groundbreaking news or anything."

Once we'd ordered our meals, Mack leaned into me, lowering his voice. "How's Mum?" he asked. "Really."

"I haven't spoken to her much lately," I confessed. "She says she's working on her next bestseller, but she won't share details. Since Dad no longer owes her alimony, she claims she's broke and can't focus. But between a successful publishing career and my father's support all those years, I just don't see how that can be."

Because of Mack's history with my mother, he knew her in a way Bill didn't. I could talk frankly without worrying Mack might discount my feelings, take her side, or accuse me of overreacting. Not that I could blame Bill for sometimes doing those things—he didn't know all the details. I worried if he did, though, he still wouldn't understand.

"She'll survive," Mack said. "She's a fighter, like her daughter."

"Me?" I asked.

"Aren't you?" With a paternal smile, he nudged my ribcage with his elbow and said, "You and Davena have matching scars now. Must be the mark of someone special."

I squeezed his forearm as a show of gratitude for his reassurance. The scar wasn't special, and being touched by most people generally *wasn't* a comfort, but no matter how tense things had gotten between my parents, Mack had always been on my side.

"Bill offered to lend her money," I continued as Mack sat back and picked up his Cabernet. "I think it's a bad idea. And we really don't have it to spare, since we're house hunting."

"Are you?" Mack's face brightened. "I'm so happy for you. You really are all grown up, little Liv. I still remember your first birthday—such a fabulous event your mother threw—and you, hardly able to enjoy it. She had that party for herself."

"What's so funny?" Davena asked when we both laughed.

"These two are looking to buy a house," Mack said.

Bill perked up, launching into his favorite topic as of late. I let him talk about neighborhoods, comps, and interest rates, nodding at all the right times. Davena, a natural know-it-all, especially when it came to buying and selling real estate, interjected when she disagreed.

"Go easy on him," Mack said to her, most likely noticing Bill's frustrated sighs with each interruption. "They're new at this."

"Which is exactly why they need our guidance," she pointed out. "So they don't make the mistakes we did."

"Mistakes?" Mack asked, leaning in to peck her on the lips between bites of his *cacio e pepe*. "I'd say we did all right in the end."

Her shoulders eased as she wiped the corner of his mouth with her thumb. "Oh, I suppose."

I glanced over at Bill as he checked his phone and rubbed the bridge of his nose.

"What's wrong?" I asked, leaning over to read a text from his boss.

"They want me back at the office."

"But it's Friday night," I said.

"I know—it's ridiculous. I'm sorry. I'll stay through

dessert and make it up to you tomorrow. I'll come help out at the animal shelter."

"Really?" I'd been volunteering there for years, and Bill had only tagged along a few times. "I'd like that," I said, "but I'm not worried about myself." I took his phone, set it on the dinner table, and laced our fingers the way Mack and Davena did. "I just don't want you to burn out."

Bill and I each looked at our hands. As with sex, it wasn't like me to initiate intimacy. It wasn't that I never did it or didn't want to feel close to Bill—physical touch just wasn't how I expressed love. Affection didn't come naturally like it did for the couple across the table from us.

"All my hard work will pay off when we buy our new home," Bill said, squeezing my hand. "Just stay focused on the peace and quiet we'll get in the suburbs. It'll be so nice to finally get out of the city."

My palm began to sweat. I took my hand back as a busser cleared our empty dishes. *Peace and quiet.* It would be hard for me to adjust to that after a decade living in or near fast-paced Chicago—which I wasn't sure I wanted to leave behind yet. It'd been our plan for a while, though. Bill had been saying for years that once he was settled at a private practice, we'd start looking for a home to raise a family. Back then, that life had sounded far off. I thought I'd be more on board when the time came. And the time was here.

Was I ready? Was I on board?

As my thirtieth birthday loomed in less than a month, I couldn't envision for myself the things I was supposed to— a house, children, and an existence free of surprises. Lucy made no secret she was ready for that. Gretchen valued her single life too much. I landed somewhere in the middle, so maybe I was just transitioning. Why *not* try to get excited about what was ahead of us?

Bill worked hard and deserved a spacious home in a calm neighborhood like he wanted. Picturing that life didn't exactly send my heart racing, but maybe that was the point. Settling down was just that—building a life on a firm, solid foundation. Wasn't that one of the things I loved most about Bill, the fact that he brought a sense of normalcy back to my life that my parents had taken away years ago?

Maybe I didn't feel ready, but I'd get there soon enough.

Chapter Three

Lucy and Andrew's pristine River North apartment proved the perfect backdrop for their upscale friends. Snow-white plush carpet spanned the living room where guests congregated. Large windows framed Chicago's dotted cityscape and starless sky while dim lighting illuminated the overstuffed cream leather couches, a glowing fireplace, and abstract art. As I crossed the living room to where Gretchen stood alone at a makeshift bar, I idly wondered how Lucy seemed to repel mess.

My heels steadied as I stepped from carpet to white oak hardwood. Gretchen set her elbows on the bar to smile at a cute, young bartender. "Cosmo, please," she said.

"You should try the pomegranate martini," he said.

She bit her lip. "How come?"

With a shrug, he grabbed a bottle of triple sec. "Pretty girls always love pomegranate."

Chardonnay isn't complex enough for you.

Ever since the ballet, the man from the theater's warm presence had stuck to my skin like static cling. What had he seen in my eyes that had made him approach me?

"I'll take a Merlot," I told the bartender.

Gretchen whirled around. "You're here," she exclaimed, pulling me into a hug. "Thank *God*. This crowd is beyond boring."

It was easy to go unnoticed amongst the high-society, supposedly interesting social circle Andrew had brought Lucy into. Since arriving a few minutes earlier, I'd over-heard tidbits here and there such as investment portfolio advice, private school laments, market projections, and vacation home upkeep.

I didn't fit in here. So where *did* I belong? I stopped the thought in its tracks. It was that kind of thinking that got people into trouble. That had put me in the orbit of a mystery stranger who'd seemed to cut through my defenses with a single look.

"Lucy's come a long way from a few years ago," I said.

"We all have." Gretchen accepted her pomegranate martini from the bartender. "Remember that first shitty apartment the three of us shared after college?"

"I wish I could forget it," I said as I got my wine next. "I still don't know how I survived stumbling up five flights of stairs drunk at three a.m. Or the rat poison we had to put out every few weeks. Or the moldy shower."

"But there were more good times than bad," Gretchen said.

I smiled to myself. "We'd meet at home after work, change outfits, and stay out until the early morning hours without even realizing it." *Responsibility* had been just another word in the dictionary. Where had the time gone? Things were different now, there was no doubt. But some-thing in particular felt amiss. With the onset of a new season, change seemed imminent, although I couldn't identify why that might be.

"I love this," Gretchen said, admiring my very fitted

white dress that hugged my slight curves and dipped just off my shoulders. "Where's Bill?"

"He's in New York for work."

"Damn. Why didn't I think of that excuse?" She laughed as I sipped my Merlot. "Lucy shot down all my attempts to get out of this."

"What *is* this anyway?" I asked, glancing around the room.

"No idea."

"I've never known Lucy to throw a party for no reason," I said. "It's always something—housewarming, job promotion, election night. She didn't even send a formal invitation."

"How long do you think we have to stay?" Gretchen tapped her black strappy heel on the floor. "I've been here twenty minutes and haven't even seen Lucy yet."

I craned my neck but only spotted Andrew talking to a group of his friends. "Should we go find her?"

As the words left my mouth, Lucy appeared from the hallway leading to the master bedroom. She looked over the crowd as best she could at her height until she spotted Gretchen and me. With her chin raised, she made a beeline for us, smiling politely at her guests but not stopping for anyone.

"Where have you been?" Gretchen asked when she neared.

Lucy inhaled deeply through her nose. "I was waiting for you both to get here. I wanted you to be the first to know."

Gretchen and I both leaned in. "To know *what*?" I asked.

Lucy took Gretchen's martini from her and sipped.

"Hey!" Gretchen complained.

Lucy's face turned several shades of red as she watched

us over the rim, her eyes sparkling. She raised the glass to us—and nearly blinded me with the rock on her finger.

Gretchen and I gasped at the same moment. "Andrew *proposed?*" I asked.

"You have *no* idea how hard it's been to keep it to myself," she said with a squeal, "but I wanted to announce it in front of all our friends."

"So this is an engagement party?" Gretchen asked.

"Um, no," Lucy said. "This is just to celebrate the engagement *announcement.*"

Lucy and I each set our drinks on the bar. She wiggled her fingers as I took her hand and admired the three oval-cut diamonds, centered on a smooth platinum band. I was certain I'd seen some version of this ring before on the "Dream Wedding" collage she'd made in college. Lucy could've designed it herself.

"Tell us the story," Gretchen said, nearly vibrating with excitement. "How'd he do it?"

"You know how Andrew and I set aside Sundays for each other, right?" Lucy asked. "Well, last weekend, he was acting strange all afternoon and then said we were going to a movie. Normally we stay in on Sunday nights, but there was some superhero blockbuster he said everyone had been talking about at work."

Gretchen twisted her lips. "How'd he get *you* to an action movie?"

"He promised me tiramisu at Bruna's afterward." She waved her hand, her gaze catching on the glint of diamonds. "So he takes me out of the way to this small theater in Lincoln Square, that's totally not our regular place, and when we arrive, he waltzes right in without paying or anything. I'm like, 'Andrew, *what* is going on? We're nowhere near Bruna's!' But he won't tell me." She put her hand over her heart, sighing. "The theater was empty except for an attendant holding a tray of two champagne flutes. Instantly, the screen lights up, and I recognize the first bars of 'Moon River.'"

"*Breakfast at Tiffany's*," I said, nearly swooning. "Your favorite movie."

She nodded. "The clerk led us to a row in the center. On my seat was that famous little blue bag. I begin to cry right away. Andrew pulled out the box, told me how much he loved me, and asked me to marry him."

A wave of emotion surprised me. I wasn't easily moved, but the ring and the proposal were so *Lucy*. It showed just how well Andrew knew her, and I wanted that for my friend.

I took my Merlot from the bar, glancing at my own ring. The gold and diamond solitaire stone was an heirloom Bill had inherited from his grandmother. Family was important to Bill—as was saving money. Since his grandmother had passed before we'd met, I couldn't say it held much sentimental value to me aside from representing our love. Bill's proposal had happened at one of his family reunions with everyone looking on, waiting for the magic word from me.

Yes.

More distracted by the crowd than excited about the proposal, I'd had to say it once more, with enthusiasm, for the people in the back.

Yes!

"You'll be my bridesmaids, right?" Lucy asked, taking each of our free hands. "My sister's around here somewhere, and she agreed to be maid of honor. Andrew and I have already started making plans."

"Yeah, aren't his parents going on some huge trip soon?" Gretchen asked.

"The timing isn't ideal." Lucy's smile faltered.

"They've been working with a travel agent on their trip around the world for years, and they leave in fall, so either we have the wedding before then or we'll have to wait over a year until they come home."

"*Fall?* We have our work cut out for us," Gretchen said to me. "And, yes. Of course we'll be there for you, Luce."

"I can't believe I'll be Lucy Greene soon." She sighed longingly. "I've wanted this for so long, to be a wife and a mother."

I tried for my best supportive smile. I'd never aspired to be either of those things the way I'd focused on my career. Early in our marriage, Bill had gotten on my case frequently about changing my last name, but he rarely brought it up anymore. With distance, I could admit—I didn't have that same desire as Lucy to *belong* to Bill. I told anyone who asked about my surname that I was a modern woman without the need to follow antiquated traditions, but the truth was—ridiculous as it sounded—the designation didn't fit me. Olivia Wilson had always felt like some other woman trying to overshadow my identity.

"I better go make the announcement before someone notices my ring." Lucy bit her bottom lip and backed away as she said, "Wish me luck."

"Can you believe it?" I asked Gretchen when we were alone again.

"Um, I definitely can," Gretchen said under her breath. "Lucy has wanted this as long as I've known her."

I frowned as Gretchen nearly chugged the rest of her martini. If I didn't know Gretchen as well as I did, I'd almost think she was jealous of Lucy's announcement. Gretchen thrived on meeting men and socializing, though —she wasn't interested in settling down.

"What's wrong?" I asked.

She looked into her empty drink. "Nothing."

"Liar," I said. "Spill it."

After a light sigh, she looked up again. "I got a voice-mail from Greg the other night."

"*What?*" I asked. "Why didn't you say anything?"

"I didn't know how to feel about it. I still don't. He wants me to call him."

I'd introduced Gretchen to her current ex after he and I had become fast friends at Notre Dame. During our first class of Introductory Biology, we were the only people who seemed to notice how crazy the professor was. We'd looked at each other across the room and made the same face. Greg, Lucy, and I would discuss lectures over cold pizza in the dining hall or stay up late drinking Kahlua hot chocolates under the fleece *Fighting Irish* blanket my dad had sent me.

Thinking Greg was the perfect guy, I'd set him up with Gretchen years later and they'd hit it off immediately—until he'd mercilessly dumped her two days before graduation.

He'd accepted a job in Japan, an offer we'd heard nothing about, and was moving to start a new life. It'd been obvious to everyone but him and Gretchen that he'd been terrified of how intense things had become with her. Regardless, he'd gotten on the plane and none of us had heard from him since. Until now.

"Aren't you curious about what Greg has to say?" I asked.

She shook her head vigorously, blonde curls bouncing over her shoulders. "Nope," she said with finality. "It's done."

"Wow." I lifted the wineglass to my mouth. "I can't believe, after all this time—" I started and promptly spilled wine down my front.

"Oh, Jesus," Gretchen said, taking my drink from me. "Put club soda on that. Now."

"But Lucy's about to make her announcement—"

"That dress is too sexy to get ruined," she said. "And too *white*."

I cursed my clumsiness and hurried into Lucy's kitchen to search her refrigerator, finding only Perrier. I poured some onto a dishtowel and pressed it against the impurity on my breast. At a noise behind me, I turned.

My lips parted. Hooded golden eyes, darkened with hunger, stared back at me. A hot thrill pulsed somewhere deep in me. My body remembered him first with the impulse to arch toward him. I froze, back in the theater, mesmerized by the handsome, mysterious stranger, under his spell again as if no time had passed since that night.

When we'd met eyes across a crowded room.

When he'd suggested ordering me something *flavorful*.

When I'd momentarily lost all sense of my surroundings.

I'd almost convinced myself it'd all been a dream.

He flattened his hands on the surface of the kitchen island, the only thing separating us. "You disappeared on me."

I hadn't disappeared so much as run away. Standing in front of him again, I was hit with the same dueling urges as I'd had during our first encounter.

Go to him.

Stay away.

"Tell me your name." His thick voice was my desire manifested.

My draw to him was so strong, it seemed the only thing to do was back away from it. So I did, retreating one step. "I . . ."

He straightened up. "Don't run again. What's your

fucking name?" he repeated. It didn't occur to me to question the intensity of his question or the urgency in his voice —not malicious but *pleading*.

"Olivia," I said, hardly recognizing my own voice.

"Olivia," he said with reverence, momentarily satisfied.

He rounded the island toward me, his eyes never leaving mine as he took the towel I'd been holding —*clutching*. The hair on my arm rose over me as his skin brushed mine, the look in his eyes growing hungrier.

"Olivia," he said softly. "I'm desperate to know you."

My lids fluttered. A man like this wasn't desperate for anything, but in that moment, *I* held his full attention. And his golden-brown gaze, fringed by long, unblinking lashes that softened strong, carved-from-marble features.

He raised the dishrag as if to press it against my breast. I swallowed, urging myself to protest such brazenness despite my body's urge to move against him.

"Red wine," he noted.

Merlot, I almost said. *Like you wanted. Like I wanted.*

Boisterous laughter came from the next room. I half-leaped back as Lucy's boyfriend—now *fiancé*—waltzed into the kitchen with a leftover smile on his face.

"Liv! Where've you been?" Andrew asked, rounding the island. As he spotted the man, Andrew laughed, shaking his head. "*Aha*. David. Of course," he said, popping a few mini cupcakes into a red cocktail napkin. "I should've known you'd be the one keeping her from the party. Always one with the ladies."

David, I thought. A common name—nothing out of the ordinary. But now, I repeated it to myself behind sealed lips, as though I'd never heard that name in my life.

"Actually, she spilled wine. I was just getting her a towel," David said, pushing up the sleeves of his black V-neck sweater. He watched me from under his eyelashes.

"We haven't had the pleasure of meeting yet. But I'll certainly take an introduction."

His face gave *everything* away, even though he casually rolled the cuffs of the white button down under his sweater. I glared at him, willing him to turn down the intensity in his gaze.

Andrew paused with a cupcake halfway to his mouth. "Oh, yeah. Sure," he said, looking at it longingly, as if we were keeping him from his dessert. "Sorry about that. Lots of crossover between work and personal life." He nodded between us. "Liv, this is David. He's the lead architect on our new office building in the Loop."

For some reason, I dropped my eyes to David's enormous hands. I could too easily picture them drafting blueprints, then bringing them to life.

Nice to meet you, I thought, but I stayed silent. Why? I was acting as if I'd done something wrong. I attempted to mimic David's relaxed stance, loosening my shoulders and releasing my death grip on the counter.

"Anyway," Andrew said, thumbing over his shoulder, "I'm hoping if I hang around this guy enough, some of his charm will rub off. The ladies in my office can't get enough of him." Andrew glanced around the kitchen before turning back to David. "Where's your date?"

"I . . ." David crossed his arms, showing off brawny forearms that only confirmed my theory he was the *hands-on* kind of architect. "I didn't bring one."

Andrew pulled back. "No date?" He finally took a bite of cupcake, chewing. "That's a first for you."

David released a short laugh as he scratched his brow. "Not true."

"Don't be modest. You couldn't pay me to be single again," Andrew said, "but I'd love to spend a day in your shoes, women throwing themselves at me left and right."

"I don't . . ." David's expression closed. He looked at me. "That's not my life."

I shot my tongue into my cheek as I returned his stare. He was downplaying what was surely true. No doubt women tripped over themselves to get to him. Someone that confident—who could relax on command, who was *that* smoldering—he knew what he was doing. How foolish of me to think he'd picked me out of a crowd. That draw between us? It was just the effect he had on women. The question was how *many* women?

And did he think I was one of them?

I wasn't. Not even if I were single. I couldn't believe I'd almost fallen for his act. Flavorful? Complex? He was *desperate* to know me? I couldn't really blame myself, though. Apparently, the man had plenty of willing subjects on which to practice.

I stepped back, distancing myself. "Well, looks like I'm all cleaned up. I'd better go find Lucy."

"Sorry Bill couldn't make it," Andrew said. "I should've had you put him on speakerphone for the announcement."

The air in the room thinned. "*Bill?*" David asked.

Here was my chance to make it clear that David could take his *desperation* elsewhere. I was *married*. I swallowed, my instincts warring between pushing him away for good and spending just a few more innocent moments with him.

David's gaze slowly traveled the length of my left arm until it came to rest on my hand. I only had a second to try to comprehend the way his face fell before he asked, "Who's Bill?"

"Olivia's husband," Andrew said. "Great guy. You'll meet him eventually."

That was it. This was over, not that anything had even begun. I continued backing away as David watched.

"David, was it?" I said. "Nice to meet you. Enjoy the party."

I turned and strode into the next room, finding Lucy within a few steps.

"Hey," she said, touching my arm as she noticed my expression. "Are you all right?"

My voice came out unnaturally high. "Fine," I quipped. "Totally fine."

"Found some champagne," Gretchen cried over the crowd, squeezing her way toward us while juggling three flutes. She held two out as she approached. "We have to toast the bride-to-be."

I followed Gretchen's lead and raised a glass. Lucy was getting married, and that was more important than anything tonight. She'd memorized all the different types of veils before most girls had even thought about their wedding day. "To Lucy," I said.

"And her *fiancé*," Gretchen added.

"And to the best bridesmaids a girl could ask for," Lucy finished.

I had a mouthful of fizz when Gretchen sucked in a breath. "Whoa. Who is *that*?"

I didn't need to turn to know who she was referring to.

Lucy rose onto the balls of her feet and followed Gretchen's gaze over my shoulder. "Ohh," she said, nodding with a knowing look. "Yep. That, my friend, is the infamous *David the architect*. He's doing work for Andrew's firm. They've bonded over sailing." Noticing Gretchen's raised eyebrows she said, "I know. He's absolutely *dreamy*."

I lowered my glass as bubbles tickled my nose. I didn't know what to say, but staying quiet made me feel strangely guilty. "Since when is Andrew a sailor?" I asked.

"Oh, didn't I tell you?" Lucy half-rolled her eyes. "Andrew wants to buy a boat."

Gretchen's eyes fixated behind me. She shook her head slowly. "David," she repeated to herself. "My God. He is just so . . ."

As her eyes shifted and a deceptively innocent smile touched her lips, I realized he must be coming toward us. The hair on the nape of my neck rose, and I straightened my back, trying to think of something to say when he reached us. Something that wouldn't give me away—something to dispel the electricity that passed between us whenever we were close.

But then, he breezed right by the three of us. Lucy and Gretchen turned to watch him go, making no secret of the fact that they were staring at him. I averted my eyes in case he looked back. The last thing I needed was for him to think I'd given him a second thought. The last thing *he* needed was another woman—especially a married one—fawning over him.

"Look at that ass," Gretchen said, her mouth twisting into an appreciative smirk.

Lucy clucked. "Don't be vulgar."

"I'm just stating the obvious," she said with a shrug. "Don't tell me you weren't thinking the *exact same thing*, Lucille Marie."

Lucy blushed crimson and looked away. "Don't let Andrew hear that. He already has a complex about men like David."

"Men like David?" I asked and bit my lip to shut myself up. I shouldn't be inviting more on this topic.

"Well, true—I doubt very many like him exist," she said with a laugh. "Maybe it just applies to David."

"That's not what I meant," I said. "I was asking what Andrew's complex is."

"He thinks I'd leave him in a heartbeat for someone

45

like David." She tapped her chin. "Handsome as sin, wealthy, and a genuinely nice guy."

Gretchen looked skeptical. "Nice?"

"He's always been very polite to me," Lucy said. "And as far as I know, he's single."

My fingertips cooled around my champagne glass. Just because David was single didn't mean he wasn't dating—yet the prospect of him unattached still gave me butterflies. Until, that is, I noticed Gretchen's sharp eyes narrowed in his direction. For the first time in a long time, I missed the excitement born of possibility and anticipation that came from meeting someone new.

"Gretch," Lucy said, "why don't I intro—"

"I met him in the kitchen," I blurted, panic descending at the thought of Gretchen luring him in. She was a female version of David—impossibly beautiful, impossible to resist, impossible to tie down. Just *impossible*—that's what David was to me, and yet I found myself continuing, warning her off him. "I wouldn't call him *nice*. He seemed like a jerk to me. Andrew practically said, flat out, that David's a playboy. I wouldn't bother."

I wouldn't bother with that arrestingly dark face, that smooth cleft chin, those milk-chocolate eyes. How many girls had he suckered in with just a look?

Gretchen gave me a curious glance, but she shrugged. "I'm not looking to marry the guy."

Lucy waved down a passing cater waiter and handed us each a mini tuna tartare. "Well, Liv's right. Andrew says since he's met David, he's seen him with several different women, and each one was more striking than the last. Andrew actually said *striking*."

"I can be striking," Gretchen said and rejected the appetizer with a flick of her wrist. "I'm not eating any more tonight."

"Don't tell me you're on another diet," Lucy said.

I pivoted slightly to see David better. He gestured with purpose as he spoke to another man, his voice endlessly deep, vibrating in me, although I couldn't make out what he was saying. His audience nodded along. Did David make every man and woman feel as if he or she were the only person in the room? That was how I'd felt the moment we'd locked eyes—as if he'd been looking for me all along. Craved me. Hungered for me.

"I'm desperate to know you."

As I stared at him, it was all I heard—the grave rumble of his voice, and words I should never want from anyone but my husband.

"Olivia," Lucy snapped, sounding exasperated. "What is *with* you? You've been acting strange all night."

"What?" I asked, blinking back to reality. "What'd I do?"

"Gretchen and I are talking about having lunch at Park Grill on Monday. She asked you twice if that works for you."

I swallowed, my throat dry as I tried to refocus on the conversation. "Lunch? Why?"

Gretchen scoffed. "So we need a reason to spend the afternoon with you?"

"We have a reason: bridal magazine bonanza," Lucy said. "You have no idea the amount of work ahead of us just picking out a dress style alone."

"Oh," I said, tugging on my earring, still shamelessly trying to eavesdrop while also answering Lucy. "That should be fine, yes. Where?"

"*Park Grill*," they said in unison, clearly growing frustrated with me.

"Right. Yes. Let's do it." What was wrong with me? I was letting a complete stranger get under my skin and interrupt an important night for Lucy. And it wasn't even the first time David had invaded my private moments. The memory of stripping for my husband while I'd thought of David washed over me, followed by a flood of guilt.

David stopped speaking and looked directly at me. There wasn't even a hint of uneasiness or surprise in his face, yet my body buzzed, as if coming to life just for him.

He had a fucking spell on me.

Me, and every other woman in the room.

I had to break it or escape it.

With a mumbled apology to my friends, I ducked away, keeping my gaze anywhere but on David as I forced myself away in search of fresh air.

Break it. Escape it.

Those were the only two options. They had to be.

Chapter Four

I cooled my palms on the iron railing of Lucy and Andrew's spacious eighth-floor balcony. Sharp-edged buildings of varying heights surrounded their downtown apartment, some towering, some short enough that I caught glimpses of the Chicago River.

A city full of people, and then me, looking in from the outside.

I wasn't alone, though. Like at the theater weeks ago, I was surrounded by friends. Bill was just a phone call away. I'd met, at some point or another, many of the people in the apartment. But it didn't seem to matter how many smiles and greetings I'd avoided as I'd made my way through the crowd. I *was* alone. I had been for a long time without giving it much thought, but the mysterious stranger—*David*—his presence heightened that feeling, as if he'd shown up to poke at old wounds.

His eyes on me made everything in my life feel like it belonged to another woman. As if I'd been playing a role, biding my time until he would come along. With him, there was a connection I couldn't explain—the feeling of being wanted, loved, desired.

When we were in the same room, I was anything but alone.

And that was dangerous. I had every reason to be terrified.

I took a lungful of fresh air—and coughed as smoke filled my throat. I glanced over my shoulder. Two lit cigarettes floated in the opposite corner of the balcony. I recognized one smoker as Andrew's receptionist and nodded at her. She looked about to speak, but I turned forward again.

Every time I took in the city, it was like the first time I'd visited as a girl. Holding my dad's hand on the sidewalk outside our hotel while trying to soak in everything at once. The grandness of downtown Chicago had a way of humbling me, and that was oddly more comforting than trying to hide in a roomful of people. Out here, I was free. Nobody expected anything from me or disappointed me. Tiny blocks of light scattered randomly into the patterns of buildings, and I wondered about the inhabitants—what they were doing at that very moment.

Leaning over the barrier, I examined the people walking the streets below. It wasn't a long drop from the eighth floor, but it was enough to accelerate my heartbeat and take me back to that first visit some twenty years ago.

"Do you have any idea how that makes me feel?" my mother screamed from inside the hotel room. On the balcony, I hid behind the stucco wall and peered through the glass door.

My father raised his hands in exasperation. "Leanore, you're being ridiculous," he said. "Do you have any idea how your accusations make me feel? Like you don't trust me."

"How can I when you're flirting with every woman in the hotel lobby? And in front of your daughter."

"Don't bring Olivia into this," he said, sticking his finger in her face. "This is your *problem. You* are *ruining our vacation."*

I turned away from the door and grasped the bars until my knuckles whitened. Lifting onto the balls of my feet, I wondered what it might be like to fly. Had anyone ever tried? Perhaps it was possible and nobody knew it. We'd learned about evolution in school. Maybe we had secret wings that would know the difference between flying and falling.

"Olivia." I jumped at the voice behind me. "Come inside. And fix your hair," my dad said. "I'll take you out for a milkshake, but not until you brush those tangles out."

I shivered, wrapping my arms around myself. My dad had made a career of handling and redeeming failing businesses and the men who ran them. It took a lot to get under his skin, but that was the power my mom possessed. She knew just how to get the reaction she wanted. Back then, I hadn't understood why they yelled so much, but that naiveté hadn't lasted long. In the years following that trip, I became familiar with my mom's manipulations and came face to face with the dangers—and sometimes violence—of loving someone too much.

The sliding glass door opened behind me, and the hair on the back of my neck prickled, but not from the cold or harrowing memories. I didn't have to turn to know who it was, but every second I resisted looking, his gaze grew hotter. More persistent. If I'd learned anything about the man from the theater, it was that his presence said more than words could.

He waited. I fought myself. I'd come out here to catch my breath, not to lose it again. To regain control when every glance, every word, felt like a submission to him. To break a spell that could only lead to the kinds of things that destroyed families and turned *trust* into a dirty word.

And yet I knew, David wasn't going anywhere. The best way to get rid of him was to tell him to leave me alone. I turned my head over my shoulder. He filled the doorway to the balcony, his hands fixed against the jamb, his head cocked as he watched me.

The smokers had stopped talking to gawk at him. David stepped out onto the terrace. He wore an open, black pea coat over his sweater as if he'd been on his way out. I opened my mouth to tell him to go, but the thought that he'd actually leave, and that I'd never see him again, halted my words. It made me panicky.

As he walked toward me, I turned back to the skyline. My mouth dried, and my heart thumped. I couldn't let him know how he affected me.

"You're married," he said to my back.

I drew a breath and with it, inhaled his spicy after-shave. "Happily."

When he didn't respond, I glanced back to find his expression solemn, pensive. Why? It'd been made clear to me that he could—and *did*—have any woman he wanted. Foolishly, I'd assumed for a few moments that connection was unique to us. That it was different—special. That *he and I* had something special.

And here he was, pretending to be crestfallen over the fact that I was taken. Marveling at the believability of his act, I twisted, facing him as I squared my shoulders. I lifted my hands to the railing behind me, partly to steel myself while attempting to appear casual. "And you're quite the playboy."

He drew back at the comment, but then a small smile touched his lips. "You look cold. Take my jacket."

"I'm fine." I shook my head as he moved to take it off. Never mind that I was wearing a coat of goose bumps.

He paused before shrugging it back on. "Actually, being a playboy takes a lot of time," he said, "and with my career, that's something I don't have much of. Maybe if I kept more regular hours, I could be a proper womanizer."

Was he teasing me? I couldn't tell if his tone was sarcastic, serious, or something else. I lifted a shoulder to show my indifference. "It's not really my business."

"I suppose it's not, but . . ."

From my gut, I wished he'd finish his sentence—tell me why he thought it might be my business. The fact that I wanted him to meant he shouldn't. "But nothing," I said. "I don't even know you."

He sniffed, looking over the top of my head at the skyline. "I have to get going."

My heart fell a millimeter before I stopped it. He had to go. He *had* to. Nothing good could come from spending more time with him. The women in the corner had resumed their conversation but kept glancing at us. Almost . . . accusingly? Could they see how badly I wanted this moment to last?

The next time Andrew's secretary looked over, her eyes trailing David head to toe, I admitted her interest had nothing to do with me.

She wanted *him*.

And that was almost worse than feeling like I'd been caught.

"I'd like to see you again," David said.

I whipped my eyes back to his. "What?"

"I attended the ballet with Andrew's firm. I'm here tonight by his invitation. I'm not waiting for Andrew to decide when we meet again."

"We're *not* meeting again," I said. "There's no reason to."

"Where's your husband?"

"He's not here tonight."

"I gathered. Where is he?"

"Out of town," I said.

"How'd you meet him?" he asked. "And don't say it's not my business, Olivia. Just answer me."

My breathing sped. He said my name as if it belonged to him, a collar around my neck to which only he held the key. And he made demands the same way, as if he knew without a shadow of a doubt that I'd answer. And I did.

"We met at work," I said. "Kind of. Our offices were in the same building, and we'd take our breaks in the court-yard at the same time."

"And he asked you to marry him?"

The absurdity of the question made me laugh. "Not right away. We were friends for a while."

"How long?"

I shook my head. It wasn't as if these were intimate details about my relationship—anyone who knew us had heard the story of how we'd met. Yet I felt as if I was doing something wrong. Sharing intel with the enemy, however harmless. "I don't know," I said. "Six months maybe."

He grunted. "Six months. Six fucking months he waited to ask you out."

I drew my eyebrows together. "Plus one day. Since you want to get specific."

"I *do* want to get specific. Very specific." He stepped closer to me, and my heart rate kicked up. "Why one day?"

"I . . . I had to think it over."

He dropped his eyes to my lips. "What made you say yes?"

"I realized he'd become more than a friend." I watched

the way David watched my mouth. "Do I have something in my teeth?"

David seemed to be getting closer. He was so tall, so wide, I couldn't even see if the other women were still on the balcony. I couldn't see the door. He raised his eyes from my mouth. "So you took pity on him. That's why you agreed to go out with him?"

"*No*," I said. "It was more than that. I was attracted to him."

"Was?"

"*Am*."

"You were attracted to him." David tilted his head. "And it took him six months to notice."

Now, we were getting into gray area, into the details only Lucy and Gretchen knew. I hadn't even shared this with Bill. But the deeper David probed, the more uncomfortable I was—and that was something I hadn't felt in a while. My friends and family knew my limits.

Discomfort meant things were too real.

"Answer me, Olivia," he said, leaving no room for argument.

"The attraction wasn't . . . it didn't build. It just happened. I didn't see Bill that way. But the day he asked me out, that night, I had this dream . . ."

David put one hand on the railing next to me. After a few moments of silence, he said, "I don't think I need to hear the dream."

"We made love." It came out unbidden, but I got a sense of satisfaction with the way David's jaw ticked. He'd made me squirm, and now it was his turn. "And it seemed so real, the sex. Even to this day, it feels more like a memory than a dream. And after that, he was no longer a friend in my eyes."

David took another step. He was so close now, I had to

tilt my head back to look up at him. "You've been married for . . . how long?"

"Five years."

"In that time, have you ever had an extramarital affair?"

I sucked in a breath at his boldness. "That's private. I should slap you for even asking."

"So slap me," he said. "Then answer the question."

I swallowed. The longer he waited, the warmer the space between us grew. I licked wine from the inside of my lips. I had the sudden urge to see what he'd taste like, to put my mouth on his. "No. I've never cheated on my husband."

"Ever been tempted?"

"*No*," I said. "I love him. I've never so much as fantasized about another man since I met him. I wouldn't even be out here with you if—" I stopped myself, my heart pounding.

"If?"

If I'd ever felt anything close to this before.

The reason I wanted to stay and the reason I needed to go was the same. I couldn't voice my attraction, but he understood. By the way he flicked his tongue over his bottom lip, by the satisfied half-smile that followed—he understood.

"Sorry to disappoint you," I said wryly, "but I'm not that kind of person. I'm not going to sleep with you."

"I'm not disappointed."

My face warmed. I certainly hadn't misunderstood his intentions—for God's sake, he'd practically asked me to have an affair—but maybe I'd made our attraction bigger in my mind. "I don't believe you."

"I'm not disappointed you won't sleep with me—I wouldn't sleep with you, either. Not tonight."

"Not any night," I said, but my voice faltered, and my declaration came out sounding more like a question.

"And I'm sure as hell not disappointed you've never had an affair. That only confirms my suspicion."

The railing dug into my back. He had me cornered. Trapped. I could set myself free if I wanted. Yet not even the fear that Lucy or Gretchen, or God forbid Andrew, Bill's closest friend, might come out and find us this close was enough to get me to move. "What suspicion?" I asked.

"This is about you. It's about me. There's something here, between us, that goes deeper than sexual attraction."

No. It was the first response that came to mind, but not because I didn't agree. I didn't want to recognize anything *deeper*. Emotions I'd been suppressing for years threatened to surface. Everything in my life was how I wanted it, and Bill respected that. He didn't push my boundaries like David was doing now, because he knew I'd withdraw. "I'm married, David."

"I know. Believe me—if you weren't, we'd be having a different conversation."

"You can't say things like that."

"I *am* disappointed about one thing," he said, ignoring me. "That I didn't meet you first. If I had, all bets would be off."

The intensity between us had never left, but it grew thicker in that moment. I didn't want to ask myself if I felt the same. I barely knew this man. I didn't regret meeting or marrying Bill—he was exactly what I needed. A good man. Someone who accepted me as I was and didn't take pleasure in making me uncomfortable.

The thought of this being my last meeting with David sent a wave of dread through me, but I needed to put a stop to this. I gripped the railing and lowered my voice to a whisper. "There are plenty of women here—*single* women.

If you're looking for company, I'm sure they'd be much obliged."

"You're right—they would."

I gaped. "Cocky much?"

"You don't think I could find someone else tonight?" he asked.

I wasn't about to answer that. Of course he could. Gretchen, for one. And I realized that was why I was still standing there. David could be paying this kind of attention to anyone at the party, but he'd chosen me. He'd followed me out here knowing I was married and that he couldn't have me.

"Find someone else," I dared him. "This city is littered with available women. If an affair is what gets you off, there are plenty of married women who'd go home with you tonight. You shouldn't have any problem finding someone—"

His nostrils flared. "I don't want *someone*."

The women chatting in the corner quieted with his raised voice.

"Are you even single?" I asked.

He cocked his head and made me wait. In the silent seconds that followed, I knew I should take the question back. "I'm available, yes," he said finally. "Thanks for asking."

"I'm just making conversation."

He shifted his gaze. "Something wrong with your earring?"

I realized I was fidgeting with it. "No," I said, lowering my hand to my side.

"You were doing that earlier. Inside. Nervous habit?"

It was, but I wasn't about to give him any more than I had. How had he even noticed? "If you're asking if you make me nervous, you don't. I'm long past the butterflies-in-my-tummy stage of my life."

"That's a shame," he murmured.

"No, it isn't. I hate that feeling of . . ."

He raised his chin, looking intrigued. "Of what, *Olivia?*"

He drew out my name the way he might run a fingertip down my side. More goose bumps sprung over my skin, and David's eyes jumped to my bare shoulder. The man noticed everything, every little way he affected me. I hated *that* feeling, too, as much as it intoxicated me—that sense that he could read my thoughts, my fears and desires.

I didn't want to be that vulnerable to anyone—not even my husband.

Especially not my husband.

That was how people got hurt. Their walls came down, and they stopped protecting themselves—and divorce took down everything and everyone in its path.

I needed to walk away—if not out of respect for Bill, then to save myself from getting any closer to David.

"Take my coat," David said, but made no move to take it off. "You're nearly shivering."

"I'm going back inside."

"I should warn you—I'm not good at taking no for an answer. I can be very persistent."

I leaned in until we were almost touching. "No."

"You'd rather freeze?"

"How many other girls have you offered your coat to tonight?"

His eyes narrowed a fraction. A possible sore spot? "None."

"I don't believe that."

"I'm not what you think."

"You don't have women falling at your feet wherever

59

you go? Endless dates on your arm like Andrew said? You're *not* a total playboy?"

He gritted his teeth. "I've never, not once, described myself as a playboy."

"But have other people?"

He inhaled a short breath. "What do you want me to say?" he asked. "That I've waited my whole life for you?"

Even though he was being sarcastic, my annoying heart skipped a beat. We'd met twice, and he was already very much under my skin. "Excuse me," I said, ducking out from under him.

"Wait." He caught my elbow so swiftly, I was too stunned to do anything but let him pull me back to him. "Have dinner with me tomorrow night."

"No."

"Lunch then."

"Are you serious?"

"I'll be on my best behavior." His eyes scanned my face, and for a moment, his bravado seemed to give way to a hint of that desperation he'd mentioned earlier. "You said your husband's out of town."

For the first time tonight, real anger rose in me. Not just for what he was insinuating, but at myself. Why couldn't I just walk away? Why did I let him get to me—and why did I consider accepting his invitation? I knew, no matter what, how something like this could end. Just the *threat* of infidelity—the accusations leveled on both sides, the vulnerabilities exposed and exploited—not even the act, had eroded my parents' marriage.

"How dare you?" I asked.

He sighed, his minty breath tempting me closer. "I'm not asking for anything more than a meal."

"Ask *someone else*," I said sharply.

"I don't *want* someone else," he shot back. "Haven't you heard anything I've been trying to tell you?"

He was angry now, too, but *he* had no reason to be. I delivered my good-bye slowly so he'd hear every word. "If my husband knew what you were suggesting . . ."

David loosened his grip a little. "What?" he challenged. "What would he do?"

Nothing. Bill would be hurt, but he wouldn't take action. And David seemed to know that somehow.

"Being away this weekend was his mistake," David said. "If you were mine, I'd never let you out of my sight unless I absolutely fucking had to. And if I did, no man would make the same mistake I did and presume you were single. Every person within a mile radius would know you were *mine*."

His. His words, his cool breath, his firm but reverent grip on my arm—it all made me want to let him kiss me. Because there was no question in my mind that he ached for it. And me?

Ache was too mild a word.

I need to know how he tastes.

That terrifying thought spurred me to take my arm back and hurry inside. I should never have let David think he had even a chance of kissing me.

I was the one who'd made a mistake. Not Bill.

Chapter Five

Lucy's engagement-announcement party remained in full swing. I found her and Gretchen right where I'd left them, talking to Andrew as if the earth hadn't shifted in the twenty minutes I'd been on the balcony with David. As if everything was *normal*.

While Andrew and Gretchen argued over the reasons she needed to get into the stock market, I tried to remove my heart from my throat. With every second that passed, guilt ate at me. I'd let David say too much. We'd gone too far and nowhere at all. There was nowhere *to* go.

As he reentered the party, I took him in for the last time. There was no reason we should ever see each other again and every reason we shouldn't.

He towered over everyone as he made his way in my direction, then stopped a few feet away, holding my gaze as he rubbed his jaw. Finally, he took a breath and said in his endlessly deep voice, "*There's* the bride-to-be."

Lucy looked over, and her face lit up. "Hi, David. I've been meaning to find you."

He spread his arms. "Here I am," he said, dazzling her

with a large smile, one that was almost too big for his face. A knee-weakening smile that I hadn't yet seen.

She stuck out her bottom lip. "Why do you have your coat on?"

"I'm sorry to swoop in and out, but I've got somewhere to be."

Andrew settled his arm around Lucy. "We're glad you could make it. And I'll be taking you up on that offer to go out on the water."

"Oh, I don't know about that." Lucy patted her fiancé's chest. "We're in trouble if Andrew falls in love with your sailboat, David."

"Why don't you come, Luce?" David asked. "I'll take you both out."

"We could bring Dani, too." Lucy glanced from Andrew back to David. "Do you have to go right now? I was hoping to introduce you to my sister."

"Well, hang on," Gretchen said, masking a glare at Lucy by batting her lashes. "What about your friend *Gretchen?*"

My heart pounded from holding my breath. Dani and Gretchen were both single, both beautiful and smart—and while Gretchen wasn't looking to settle down, Lucy'd had her heart set on setting up her sister for a while.

"Oh, I'm so rude," Lucy said, ever the hostess. She turned in our direction. "David, these are my best friends, Gretchen and Olivia."

David held out his hand, but Gretchen shooed it away. "I'm a hugger," she said, crossing the circle.

It only lasted a second, but I tensed as he bent so she could put her arms around his neck. "Pleasure," he said.

"Pleasure's all mine," she replied.

He hugged Lucy next, which normally would've made me laugh considering she barely came up to his chest. "I *do* have to go," he said, "but thank you for having me." He nodded at Andrew. "Congratulations. I'd tell you how lucky you are, but I think you already know."

Andrew grinned. "That's for damn sure."

When Lucy had tucked herself back into Andrew's side, David turned to me.

"We already met," I said, my tone a little too defensive, as I was sure everyone could sense the connection between us.

David shrugged, opening his arms. "What can I say? I'm a hugger."

Lucy and Gretchen giggled. I needed to look away, to focus on anything but the impossible-to-ignore man in front of me. But rejecting him would look more suspicious than giving in.

David didn't make a move, his intent clear—*I* was to go to *him*. Time slowed as I took one step toward him and then another. He slipped his arms around my waist, pressing my front to his with a strong squeeze. He lowered his mouth to my ear for a warm, silky whisper. "Maybe tonight, you'll dream of someone new."

I had no breath to respond, and not a second, either. He released me as time caught up with us.

"It was nice to meet you," Gretchen said as David buttoned his coat.

"You too," he said, but his eyes were fixed on me.

David lit a fire in me that left my skin hot long after he'd left Lucy's. Once the party died down, I hailed a cab, but a few blocks from my apartment, I got out to walk.

I couldn't shake the tiny knot at the pit of my stomach. Something had been planted inside of me that I was finding hard to escape. I needed to cool down and shake David's presence. To rid my mind of dangerous thoughts and questions I should let lie.

Such as . . . *why*?

If composure had been a subject in school, I would've aced the class. I'd grown up with a mother whose emotions turned on a dime. She'd regularly threatened my dad that she'd disappear with me in the middle of the night for offenses ranging from him missing dinner to leaving on a work trip to being assigned a female secretary. After every episode, she'd apologize and beg his forgiveness. Some nights, my dad would take the bait; others, he'd let her wear herself out. Until the one time she'd gone too far.

Why had my father stayed so long? There were good times, too—stretches of a normal, white-picket-fence existence. Weekends where Mom and Dad had barbecued together, then canoodled after dessert on warm Texan nights. But her episodes sometimes had happy endings, too. Dad was the only one who got her worked up that way —and the only one who could calm her down. Once I was old enough, I understood how their all-out fights could lead to something else behind closed doors.

If my parents had taught me nothing else, I'd learned how to stay in control from them. How to take my mom's hysterics in stride. I'd learned when love became more dangerous than anything. And when to let go.

Tonight, I'd almost let a complete stranger undo all that work.

Why?

What made him think it was okay to push against not just socially acceptable boundaries, but the walls I had in place for a reason? And why did I let him, when nobody else got to? Gretchen was the only person who tried anymore, and that was because we'd grown up together.

She'd known me before it all, knew my parents and my history, because she'd lived it.

Glass shattered on the pavement, jarring me from my thoughts. I checked my watch as I passed under an open window blaring the Grateful Dead. It was well after eleven. Readjusting my purse strap, I took a crosswalk toward my apartment building.

I looked forward to crawling into bed alone. I didn't want to keep thinking about *him*, but I wasn't sure I could help it. The brazen way he'd demanded details about my marriage, had asked me to dinner, had suggested I *dream* about him—it was equally unsettling and intoxicating to have my limits pushed so unapologetically.

"Hey," I heard as I tuned into footsteps behind me. "Hold up," a man said. "You got a light?"

I'd been completely wrapped up in my thoughts, not paying attention to my surroundings. I rarely felt unsafe in my neighborhood, but that didn't mean there wasn't crime. "Sorry, I don't smoke," I said over my shoulder.

"Wait up."

I quickened my stride as the footsteps bore down on me.

"Hang on—" Fishy fingers grasped at my elbow. With an adrenaline spike, I yanked away to run, but the man grabbed my arm and jerked me back into a cloud reeking of alcohol and stale cigarettes. "I told you to wait, bitch."

Having my head in the clouds one moment and my elbow in an unforgiving grip the next, shock immobilized me. "Wh-what do you want?" I asked.

He whirled me around to a face I didn't recognize. Dark-haired and blurry-eyed, he wasn't much taller than me and swam in an oversized sweatshirt and sagging jeans.

"The name Lou Alvarez mean anything to you?" he slurred.

What? He was clearly on something and thought I was someone else. My heart skipped, panic closing in with the way he restrained me. I struggled to free myself. "Let go of me."

He leaned in and put his cheek to mine. "You smell like flowers."

With my free hand, I smacked my handbag into the side of his head. He cursed, and his hold on my elbow tightened so hard that my knees buckled.

As I sank to the sidewalk, he bared his teeth at me, his misty eyes clearing. "I'm here about my brother Lou."

"I don't know who that is." I labored for breath as pain radiated up my arm. "I swear."

He pulled me to my feet. "Get up."

I flinched. "You have the wrong person."

"Yeah, you're right," he said. "But since Bill's not here, you'll do. You're his wife, right? Olivia?"

At the sound of my name, the street lamp behind him got blindingly bright. Everything around us sharpened. This wasn't an accident? "Who the hell are you?"

"You tell your husband I know what he did, and if he doesn't get my brother out of prison—"

"That's not what Bill does."

"He better find a way, and fast." He released me with an emphatic push. "Or my friends and me will pay him a visit."

I backed away, watching him. When it became evident he wasn't going to follow, I ran to my building. Once in my apartment, I bolted the lock and leaned against the door, exhaling my relief.

The name *Lou Alvarez* didn't ring any bells. Before Bill's current position at a private law firm, he'd been a prosecutor. Back then, he'd sent criminals to jail. Now, he mostly kept them out of it. But as far as I knew, he didn't spring prisoners free.

I dug my cell phone out of my handbag to call him. With my thumb hovering over Bill's name, I paused. David should've been the last thing on my mind, but since he'd dominated my thoughts up until five minutes ago, he felt like a secret. One I was keeping from Bill.

This had nothing to do with David, though.

I had to call my husband.

I stared at the screen until it went black. My heart pounded. Too shaken up to control my thoughts, they fixated on David. I wanted to be back in his presence, trapped by his body. Or had he been shielding me from the world?

I imagined him at home, wherever home was, replaying our conversation in his mind. One moment he'd had me in a corner, asking for more time—and the next he'd been gone. What had stolen him away? Or who?

Did he assign her a drink order, too? Make her feel like she belonged to him with just a glance? Did she make it easy for him when I had made it hard?

No—I hadn't made it anything. That implied he had a chance when he didn't. He and I, we weren't easy, hard, or anything in between. We were impossible. Non-existent.

I didn't exist to him nor him to me, and I had no plans to ever see him again. And as it turned out—I had bigger problems than the fleeting attention of a persistent bachelor.

Chapter Six

Serena followed me to my new shared office with two cups of steaming coffee. The intern I'd tasked with helping out on the "Most Eligible" feature had kept me well-caffeinated while also completing most tasks almost immediately. I had a feeling she was gunning to get hired as an assistant.

As we navigated through cubicles, Serena gave me the lowdown on her weekend, spent in her boyfriend's studio apartment binge-watching TV.

"What's *Enter the Dragon*?" I interrupted as she covered the highlights of their movie marathon.

Her eyes doubled in size. "Only a martial arts *classic*," she said, handing me a mug as I sat behind my desk. "Brock and I could lose days just on Chinese cinema."

"Sounds like you did," I said with a grin. "What's the latest with the bachelors and bachelorettes?"

She pulled a folder from under her arm and handed it to me. "One of the guys wants to meet with you today. He's interested but has some concerns he wouldn't address with me."

"*He* has concerns? We haven't even narrowed our selections yet." I opened the file, glancing over a one-page typed sheet Serena had obviously cobbled together. *Thirty-four, employed, single.* "Did Lisa call him?"

"He came to us. Apparently, he's been asked to participate in the past but turned it down. Now he's reconsidering."

"Well, that's bold of him. What makes him think we still want him?"

"Trust me," she said in a low tone that made me look up. "We want him. He's the *definition* of handsome. Like, if you Google the word, he'll come up."

I frowned. Attraction was subjective, and it wasn't the defining quality on which we'd make our final selections. "There's no photo here."

"The printer's out of ink, but it wouldn't do him justice anyway. He literally called a half hour ago, so I threw the file together. Just look him up."

"I trust your judgment to at least meet with him." I checked my watch. "As if I don't have enough to do first thing Monday morning."

"I can ask Lisa," Serena said, holding out her hand for the file. Her eyes glinted. "But since he's a likely finalist, I thought you might want to reel him in."

She had a point there. If I knew Lisa, she'd already been plotting ways to edge me out of the promotion. "I'll make time," I said.

"Great. He'll be here at eleven."

"Who'll be here at eleven?" my boss asked from the doorway.

Serena whipped her head over her shoulder as I straightened up. Despite Mr. Beman's small frame, the office shrank when he was in it. "A highly promising potential bachelor," I said, doing my best to sound convincing even though this guy could've been repulsive for all I knew. I opened the file and squinted as I read off, "Lucas Dylan."

Beman raised his eyebrows. "From Pierson/Greer?"

Serena subtly nodded at me.

"Er, yes," I said. "That's the one."

"Incredible. Nice work," Beman said but wagged a finger at me. "He doesn't go by Lucas, though. I'm sure you knew that?"

"Of course," I said.

Luke it is.

"He's a bit private," Beman continued. "Only does work-related interviews. Diane tried for years to score him, but she wasn't even able to get him on the phone. An in-person interview is promising."

I smiled, silently thanking Serena for coming to me with this before Lisa could get her hands on it. Clearly, I had to do whatever necessary to land this guy.

"I believe Liv is all set on coffee," Beman said to Serena, dismissing her with a nod.

"Oh, right." She shrugged at me. "Let me know if you need a refill."

"Have a fresh pot ready for Mr. Dylan," I said.

She nodded on her way out, barely squeezing by Beman as he fixed his tie. "This would be a huge coup, Liv," he said. "If you manage to get Mr. Dylan in the issue, well . . ." Beman tilted his head as if presenting a challenge. "He'll sell magazines. And I like to sell magazines."

So did I. Especially since that would be the key to unlocking my promotion. "I'll do my best."

"Do better than your best," he said. "Make it happen. Any other updates?"

"I'd actually love to run an idea by you," I said, setting

aside Lucas—*Luke's*—file and opening a spreadsheet on my computer. With Bill out of town, I'd spent my weekend brainstorming fresh ideas to set myself apart from Lisa. "As you know, the issue's launch party is perhaps the magazine's biggest event of the year. Why not capitalize on the buzz? We could throw an invite-only exclusive pre-party, like a meet and greet for the finalists. Since many of them are local celebrities, it would drum up some publicity before we go to press."

"Publicity is good," he agreed. "I've already promised Russ it'll be our best-selling issue of the year, and since I *also* assured him this would be our most profitable quarter yet, that would make this our best-selling issue *of all time*."

Beman made no secret of his great expectations each year—each *issue*—and as an easy sell to the public, "Most Eligible" had a target on its back. Especially when making promises to the CEO of our parent company. Beman had just never directed those expectations at me since I'd had Diane as a buffer in the past.

I swallowed, trying not to look spooked. "It *will* be," I said. "That's why we're pulling out all the stops."

He worked his jaw side to side before nodding. "Get me your projected costs for this pre-party by Wednesday. I'll see if there's a budget. We'll need sponsors to foot the majority of the bill."

"I'll get started now."

"Oh, and might I suggest a little touch-up before meeting with Mr. Dylan?" he asked, gesturing around his pursed lips. "No harm in trying to look nice for guests."

I held my fake smile until he blustered out. I wouldn't have put it past Beman to pimp us out to guarantee a best-selling issue, but how bad did I look? I'd slept fitfully all weekend, tossing and turning over my encounter with the

Alvarez brother—and worse, the one with David. Maybe it wasn't my fears that kept me up, but my guilt. Bill didn't know anything yet. Every time I went to call him, or respond to his texts, the wrong man flashed across my mind.

David.

I shouldn't get a thrill when I thought of his eyes on me. I shouldn't wonder if I'd ever see him again. When it came to David, I shouldn't feel or do anything—except forget.

My desk phone buzzed, jarring me out of a virtual black hole of research on alcohol sponsors for the Meet and Greet event. I dropped my pen on my open notebook and grabbed the receiver.

"Mr. Dylan's at the front," Jenny said breathlessly. "Should I show him to your office? I'd be happy to."

"Have Serena bring him back," I said, closing out of the browser. "She'll be assisting me with the feature and should get to know the candidates."

"*Candidates?*" Jenny asked, lowering her voice. "If you don't pick this man for the feature, you'll be joining Diane in the unemployment line. Beman's out here flirting so hard, I'm afraid he's going to pull a muscle."

I raised my eyebrows, pleased. "Is Mr. Dylan gay?" I asked, also whispering but for no reason. One thing Lisa and I agreed on—Diane's selections over the years had been too homogenous.

"*No,*" Jenny said. "And he looks uncomfortable."

"Then get off the phone and call Serena," I said, hanging up.

A surge of panic hit me. I hadn't expected to conduct any interviews this early on in the process, and everything I knew about Luke Dylan was in a folder I'd barely peeked at. I hadn't forgotten Beman's unsubtle threat about fixing myself up, either.

I peeled off my borderline homely wool cardigan and took an emergency makeup kit from my handbag. Fortunately, Diane had hung a mirror on the back of the door. Balancing my cosmetic bag on the arm of the couch, I chose raspberry-colored lip gloss that left threads of goop when I smoothed my lips together. I had just enough time to comb my fingers through my hair when Serena's voice came from the hall.

"It's just right back this way, Mr. Dylan," she said. "So, are you, like, from Chicago?"

"Born and raised in Illinois."

I reached behind myself for the makeup bag and knocked it over, spilling products all over the floor.

Shit.

I squatted, threw everything back in record time, and went to stand when a green Clinique tube caught my eye. I squatted to slip my arm to where it had rolled between the wall and couch as the door opened.

"Olivia," a man said as I grasped the lipstick.

Not just any man. I recognized that chest-rumbling voice that had been reverberating through me for days.

Palming the tube, I turned. Burnished, brandy-colored leather brogues stared back at me. My eyes drifted up a long body and landed on a familiar face that managed to be both intense and expressionless.

My mystery man. Sultry, penetrating eyes from the theater. Broad, walled-off shoulders that had shielded us on Lucy's balcony.

David.

He'd parted his hair off to the side and gelled it into a soft, cohesive wave. His sharp, navy suit followed every edge of his body, from the cliffs his shoulders created to his trim waist to the hem that hit just the right spot of his shoes despite his height. He wore his collar open with no tie, and the exposed skin of his collarbone made my breath catch.

How long had I been staring, kneeling at his feet like his disciple? Why couldn't I speak? If the office had seemed smaller before, it became a shoebox now, especially from my current position. His presence could barely be contained.

"David?" I asked.

"Were you expecting someone else?"

"Yes." I rocked off my heels and finally stood, smoothing my hands over my dress. "Luke Dylan."

"Do you always do this much research before an interview?" By the quirk of his mouth, I assumed he was teasing me, though I couldn't be sure. "Lucas is my first name. I've always gone by my middle, though."

"David," I said. "David . . . Dylan."

"David Dylan," he confirmed with a nod.

Serena hadn't taken her eyes off of David, clearly starstruck. "You *know* each other?"

"Not really, no," I said quickly, holding out my hand. What else could I do? It was best that I *didn't* know him, and so I'd pretend that was the case. "I'm so sorry for the mix-up. Nice to meet you."

David glanced down, seeming to debate whether to call out my lie or to go along with it. After a moment, he took my hand and squeezed it. "Your hand is cold," he said.

"I'm sorry," I said and tried to take it back, but he kept

it in a firm grip. As we held each other's gaze, his palm warmed mine. Heat crept up my arm to my chest. By the time he released me, I was half-thawed, half-chilled, my nipples hardening in my bra.

Serena broke the silence. "I can bring coffee," she quipped. "How do you take it, Mr. Dylan?"

How do you take it?

How do you like it, Mr. Dylan?

I didn't even really know the man, but I thought I knew the answer.

He liked it *his* way.

I wiped excess lip gloss from the corner of my mouth.

He didn't even blink. "Black is fine."

"I'll be back in a jiff," Serena said.

Once alone, I returned to my spot behind the desk. "Have a seat, Mr. Dylan," I said, gesturing to a chair.

"Call me David."

"I wasn't expecting to see you again." I avoided his eyes and picked up a pen, unclicked it, and put it in a pencil holder before rearranging its contents.

He laughed softly as he sat. "I should think not after the way you ran away from me on the balcony."

I straightened up, looking across the desk at him. "*I* didn't run away," I said. "*You* left the party—you were the one . . ." I stopped at the slight smirk on his face. If he'd been trying to get a rise out of me, he'd succeeded in no time at all—again. "Nobody ran away from anyone," I said. "We had a normal conversation, that's all."

"You've had conversations like that before?"

"Me? No," I said without missing a beat. "I meant normal for you."

His expression eased. He gripped the arms of the chair and looked around. "I love what you've done with your office," he said wryly. "It's . . . inviting."

As if the bare walls weren't bland enough, the brown carpet was the matted and grimy type that I never wanted to touch with bare feet. The only personal thing I had was a photo of myself with Gretchen and Lucy that Lucy had taken, printed, framed, and brought over my first week at the magazine.

"It's not mine," I said. "I'm just borrowing it."

He glanced around the room. In the daylight, his mysteriousness persisted. But in an office, with the desk between us, he somehow seemed less threatening. And if possible, more handsome.

"Is Diane coming back?" he asked, turning back to me.

"Oh—well, no." It shouldn't have surprised me that he knew Diane, except that Mr. Beman had made it sound as if they'd never spoken. I shifted in my seat. "Weirdly, I'm the new point person on the 'Most Eligible Bachelors and Bachelorettes' feature. Well, one of them."

"Why is that weird?"

"First, I run into you at Lucy's. Two days later, we're meeting again. It's just a weird coincidence is all."

He nodded slowly, as if processing for the first time that this might be out of the ordinary. And then, he shook his head. "You think this is a coincidence?"

More teasing. Wasn't it? I frowned. "I mean, yes . . .?"

"Isn't there a chance I came here looking for you?" he asked.

In the few minutes he'd been here, that possibility hadn't crossed my mind, yet he didn't laugh or even smirk. "You don't know anything about me, but you and Diane have discussed putting you in the feature. So it makes more sense you'd come here to see her and found me instead."

"Or maybe it's fate?" He raised his chin. "That's a nice way of looking at it."

"Not fate, Mr. Dylan. This isn't a John Cusack film."

He chuckled. "Diane and I never discussed my participation. I don't even know who she is beyond the fact that an editor at this magazine has left me several messages over the years that I've never returned." David leaned his elbows on his knees, his eyes dancing. "I came here for you, Olivia Germaine. I warned you I could be persistent."

Chapter Seven

Persistent bachelor David Dylan sat across the desk from me, a magnificent sight in a bland room. He'd come for me, he said, but I heard the alternate meaning in his words.

I see you, Olivia Germaine.

As it had on our first introduction, my heart skipped hearing my name from his mouth. My *full* name, this time —which I'd never given him. Saturday night, I'd gotten the sense he'd seen deeper in me than others. Now, that suspicion veered dangerously close to truth. "How did you find me?" I asked.

"Luckily, we have a few friends in common."

My throat dried. "You asked Andrew about me? My best friend's husband—who is also a close friend to *my* husband? What makes you think that's okay?"

"Don't worry." He winked. "I didn't give anything away."

His insinuation wasn't lost on me. He was trying to rile me again, to get me to admit there was something to give away. I sat back in my seat. "Why are you here?"

"Two reasons. First, to apologize if I made you uncomfortable the other night. I know I came on strong—I've never been one to mince words." Lowering his voice, he continued, "It wasn't my intention to . . . well. It caught me off guard, seeing you again. We can blame *that* run-in on fate."

He sounded sincere, though an apology was the last thing I'd expected.

"I appreciate that," I said carefully.

"To be clear, I'm not sorry for what I said . . . only if I alarmed you. I had the distinct feeling you might run out on me any moment, and it made me—"

Serena entered the office. "Here you are, Mr. Dylan," she said, carrying a tray to my desk. I slid my notebook out of the way to make space, and she offered us each a steaming mug.

"Thank you, Serena," I said.

As he took a sip, David stared at me over the rim, a hand cupped around his coffee. His eyes narrowed as if he was contemplating having me for his next meal.

I shuddered. In unison, we glanced at Serena. "Can I get you anything else?" she asked.

We were giving too much away. The way I looked at David couldn't have been half as bad as how he looked at me. I held out my notepad. "Can you call these places and find out the cost of event space for the Bachelor and Bachelorette Meet and Greet?"

David leaned forward and intercepted the pad, scanning my scribbled notes. "Have it at the Gryphon Hotel," he said. "The other two venues will gouge you and cut corners."

"How do you know?" I asked.

"It's part of my job to know these things." He set my notebook in his lap, slipped a black business card from the inside of his jacket, and handed it to Serena. "Here's my info. When you book the space, tell Amber to call me about the details."

"Who's *Amber*?" I alleged as if he'd made up the name off the top of his head.

"The event coordinator," he said. "Do you have the budget for a place like the Gryphon?"

I exchanged a look with Serena. "It's good publicity for them," I said. "If they're smart, they'll offer us a discount."

"They won't," David said. "But Amber will. For me."

Serena took his business card but left my notebook. "I'll get right on it," she said and spun on her heel.

Amber. I'd never cared less for a name than I did in that moment. Amber represented warmth, glow, syrupy sweetness. She had a working—and perhaps personal—relationship with the man sitting in front of me. A man offering me—what? A working relationship as well?

He was supposedly here to talk about the feature, but so far, we'd only discussed the very heated, very dangerous topic of *us*.

"Decent coffee for an office," David remarked, setting his mug on my desk.

I cleared my throat. "What's the second reason?"

"Sorry?" he asked.

"You said you were here for two reasons. The first was pointless—a harmless conversation is no reason to apologize."

"Ah." He flipped my notebook over in his lap and ran the pad of his thumb over a list of local florists. "Are you this direct with everyone?" he asked. "Or just me?"

Just you.

That seemed like the only way to handle someone as charming as David. "I'm sure you're busy. I don't want to waste your time."

He raised his eyes to mine. "How about you let *me* decide how to spend my time."

"Suit yourself," I said. "What should we talk about then? The weather? The Bulls' season?"

He massaged his jaw, closed my notebook, and slid it back onto the desk. "I came to let you know I'll do the article."

Even though that was the reason for our meeting, and it didn't exactly come as a shock, a sense of relief hit me hard enough to make me pause. Was it only because of what his participation would do for my career? It would mean more time with him, time that was not only justifiable but encouraged.

"You don't look as happy as I'd hoped," he said. "My secretary said Diane has asked me to participate four years in a row. Was I wrong to assume you'd try again?"

"No," I said carefully. "It's not that. I'm just not sure it's such a good idea."

He extended one arm to fix his cuff. "Why not, Olivia?"

I couldn't explain why, and he knew that. Admitting my fear of being alone with him was as good as acknowledging the attraction between us. "Why now?" I asked. "After four years of turning us down, what made you change your mind?"

"Do you really want me to answer that?" He stared at me. "I think you know the reason."

My face flushed under his full attention. Afraid he'd think he was making me nervous, I held his gaze instead of turning away. If we'd be working together, I couldn't let him get under my skin so easily.

As if reading my mind, he added, "I never mix business and pleasure. I'll be completely professional during working hours. You have my word."

I narrowed my eyes, once again trying to determine if he was being sincere. "I'm not sure I believe you."

"You should, Olivia," he said, sitting back in his seat. "Because I don't like repeating myself."

The deepening of his voice coupled with his candor made me believe him whether I wanted to or not. His words, his passive expression, the way he flexed and curled one hand—said it all.

I am not a man who needs to lie to get what I want.

"All right then," I said. "You're in."

"Do you need to run it by anyone?"

"No. According to everyone else, you're a shoo-in."

"And according to you?" he asked.

"I don't really have a choice," I said. "The magazine wants you. I want Diane's position. If I deliver you, it looks good for me."

He studied my face in a way that made me wonder if that wasn't the answer he'd expected. It wasn't as if I could come out and admit the prospect of getting to know him better excited me. Not to him—not even to myself.

"It's your article," he said. "If you don't want me in it, tell me now. I'll find you someone even better to fill my spot, and you'll still look good."

Someone better? He'd just lobbed the ball back to my side of the court. *Your move.* How would it look if I went back to Beman without David Dylan? Not good, that was for sure.

"Brian Ayers," David said.

"Excuse me?"

"A friend of mine. He's a local photographer, but he also freelances for *SURFER* magazine. Better looking than me, and more interesting—just don't tell him I said that. I'll get him here for you by tomorrow." David started to take his cell from inside his blazer. The sunlight from one tiny window was enough to make his eyes glint. "Just tell me you don't want me."

I wasn't a liar—even if I sensed I wasn't being completely honest with myself. "I can't tell you that."

He answered with a large, boyish grin, so pure and unassuming that I had to flex my hands against my thighs to release tension. I'd never seen a smile like that before. It made me want to laugh and hug and kiss him all at once.

"Let's get started then," I said, pushing down the troublesome impulses. I stood and reached across the desk to pick up my notebook. "If you have a few minutes now, I can cover the basics like career path and—"

He bolted up from his chair. "What the fuck is that?"

I froze. The sharpness of his tone mirrored the concern etched in his face—and his laser focus on my arm. I followed his gaze to my elbow and lower bicep, where fresh, purple bruises had bloomed.

Shit. I'd completely forgotten they were the reason I'd worn my cardigan today. Not only were they unsightly and unprofessional, they also invited questions I didn't know how to answer.

I wrapped my left hand over the marks. "It looks worse than it is."

"I . . ." His jaw set as he ran a hand through his perfectly styled hair, tousling it. He stared at my arm as if physically incapable of looking away. "Christ, Olivia. I'm —I'm so sorry."

Sorry? I cinched my eyebrows, trying to read his expression. Why did he look as if the world had suddenly come crashing down around us? Why did a few minor bruises mean anything to him?

As I waited in silence, his expression grew pained. This definitely meant something to him, as if he'd hurt me himself.

Oh.

Our argument on Lucy's terrace. He'd taken my arm and pulled me back to face him. He thought he'd done this to me?

"David," I started, shaking my head. I took my cardigan off the back of my chair. "No, no, *no*. It's not what you think."

He startled, then strode around the side of my desk and perched on the edge in front of me. "Let me see."

"David—"

"Olivia, what did I just tell you?" He took my sweater away and set it on the desk. "I hate to repeat myself."

I wasn't sure what he was asking for. I let him take my wrist, and he gently tautened my arm. His dark, heavy eyebrows met in the middle of his forehead as he examined the bruises.

Contrary to his tender hold on my wrist, he demanded, "When I'm around you, I lose all sense of—"

"Stop it," I said. "*You* didn't do this."

He was quiet for a beat as his fingers marginally tightened around my wrist. After a moment, he met my eyes. The fire behind them told me for some reason, what I'd just said was worse than letting him believe he'd done this. "Then who the fuck did?"

I drew back slightly at his curse. I'd never had someone address me with such vehemence. And over what? He had no right to worry about me—and those who did had never looked the way David did in that moment . . . teeth clenched, nostrils flared, biceps twitching. As if it took everything in him to conceal his anger.

I didn't even know where to begin or how to explain, only that I had to. "There was this man," I started. "After Lucy's party. He was drunk—"

"Olivia." David's tone softened. "Tell me the truth. Is this . . . was it him?"

"Who?"

"Your husband."

"Oh my God, *no*," I said. "Never. Bill wouldn't hurt a fly."

"That's a common response from a victim of domestic violence. You can tell me. I'll take care of—this."

Take care of it? What did that even mean? I tried to pull my arm back, but he held it steady. "I know it sounds far-fetched, but it's the truth. Bill isn't even in town. I told you —he's in New York for a case."

David frowned. "A case?"

"He's a lawyer." I managed to slip my wrist from his grip and immediately regretted it once my skin cooled, devoid of his touch. "I think it's related to Bill's work, because the man who did this was waiting for Bill outside my apartment. He found me instead."

"He knows where you live?" David's jaw looked tense enough to snap. "For Christ's sake, Olivia. I should've seen you home on Saturday."

I lowered my voice. "You should have done exactly what you did—*nothing*," I said. "I'm not your responsibility."

He lowered his hand to grip the lip of the desk. "What happened?"

"He grabbed me when I tried to get away and made some threat about getting Bill to free his brother from jail. I don't know all the details."

David massaged the bride of his nose. "Why not? What'd your husband say?"

I sighed. "I haven't told him. I didn't want to worry him while he's out of town."

"You didn't want to worry him? You don't think your

safety is of the utmost . . ." He paused. "You slept alone last night? The whole weekend? He could've come back—"

"I'm fine," I said softly and touched his forearm. When his expression eased, butterflies twittered in my tummy. Apparently, David's urge to protect me wasn't one-sided. I didn't like seeing him upset, either—but being able to soothe him fulfilled something primal in me I wasn't ready to acknowledge. "Really," I promised. "My arm doesn't hurt."

He frowned, looking skeptical, but it was true. Vivid as they were, the marks didn't bother me.

"What about tonight?" he asked, his voice somehow both gentle and gravelly. "You can't stay alone."

"I'm not," I said. "Bill flies home later this afternoon."

That seemed to be enough to separate David from his rage—and from me. He stood, taking a few steps away from my desk. "I should get going," he said.

"Oh. Okay. Sure." I rose from my chair, but he was already halfway across the room. "We can do the interview another time," I said, trying not to sound disappointed. "Unless you want to call the whole thing off."

He had his hand on the knob when he paused. Without looking back, he said, "I don't."

With my answering flood of relief, it became apparent: I didn't want that, either.

Chapter Eight

In the front seat of our realtor's car, Bill nodded along with the tick of the turn signal.

"What'd I tell you?" He pushed up the sleeves of his cream-colored pullover and glanced back at me. "The commute isn't bad at all."

In the driver's seat, Jeanine's eyes met mine in the rearview mirror. "It's practically the same as what you do now once you factor in the walk to public transportation and train delays."

"It's Saturday," I pointed out. "We're not dealing with traffic."

Jeanine watched the stoplight through her windshield. "It's not much heavier than this," she assured me.

I kept my doubts to myself. We'd been at this an hour, and neither Bill nor Jeanine could be budged from their optimism over the suburbs. The neighborhoods our realtor had for us were either "charming" or "up-and-coming," and all in a "desirable school district." The commute was "a straight shot," the location "a tradeoff for restful sleep." Bill had never had trouble sleeping in the city until recently. Now, he was suddenly fed up with noise from our upstairs neighbors, the street lamps and car horns, the long lines, impossible parking, loitering twenty-something students . . .

"Along with Evanston, this suburb has one of the lowest crime rates in the metro area," Jeanine said. She'd been spouting off facts since we'd gotten in her car. "That's why I picked it after hearing what you've been through. I have a great feeling about this next house."

Bill glanced back at me. "You'll be safe here."

I looked out my open window at quiet streets, save the almost imperceptible rustling of foliage. Grand, old-fashioned houses sat comfortably in their foundations, settled from decades of existence. Lower crime rates weren't enough to convince me I belonged here. I'd moved to the city out of college around seven years ago, and it still awed me each day. There was always some new performance to see, activity to try, cuisine to taste. I still stumbled across gems on a daily basis. Buying a home here meant less variety. It meant backyards, a second car, peaceful nights to cook dinner and fall asleep to the TV. It was as if we'd hopped a spaceship from the bustling sidewalks of Chicago to Pleasant Street, Oak Park. What did people even do out here?

Jeanine accelerated for a green light, driving us by a playground with three strollers parked at the entry gate.

Oh, right. That was what people did around here—they raised children.

If the suburbs felt like another planet to me, the concept of kids was downright alien. Bill wanted them, the sooner the better. I, on the other hand, had reservations.

This was hardly the first time Bill had tried to get me to see houses, but I'd always been able to come up with convincing excuses to get out of it.

Until Mark Alvarez.

"I still can't get over that story." Jeanine shook her head, the needle of her speedometer hovering at twenty-six miles an hour. Champagne blonde, the same color of her SUV, streaked her brown hair. "The gang violence in this city has really gotten out of hand. I don't blame you for wanting out after your attack."

How could I argue with my safety? For Bill, having Mark Alvarez—an aggrieved family member of a convict Bill had put away—show up at our apartment was the last straw. We'd never personally faced violence in the city, but as an attorney, Bill had been exposed to the worst of it. He knew what happened in Chicago's underbelly, and now that it'd reached his doorstep, he wasn't taking any chances.

Lou Alvarez had been one of Bill's final assignments before he'd left the DA's office. He'd called the double homicide one of the ugliest and most difficult cases he'd worked on—but it'd been worth it. Lou was now serving a life sentence without parole for first-degree murder. His gang affiliation had hurt his case—and it also put Bill and his former colleagues in danger of retaliation.

What would Lou's brother Mark have done if he'd encountered Bill instead? "It could've been worse," I said.

"Worse?" Bill asked. "Well, I suppose he could've shot you down right there on the sidewalk."

I grimaced. "He didn't even have a gun."

"You don't know that. The guys at my old office have a pool going over how many counts we'll nail him for, including whether he'll be carrying when we pick him up."

"It must be non-stop action over there," Jeanine said.

As Bill did his best to shock her with overblown tales from the Cook County crypt, I removed my cell from my handbag to check my e-mail. A subject line from the night before caught my eye.

Your Safety

My interest piqued, but it was the sender's name that made the world around me fall away.

David Dylan.

I hadn't talked to him since he'd walked out of my office earlier in the week, but my heart fluttered the same way it did whenever I came face to face with him.

"See something you like?" Jeanine asked.

I glanced up. "Sorry?"

"You're smiling," she said into the rearview. "If you spot any *For Sale* signs, we can pull over."

I put my phone away as Bill shifted to face me. "I knew you'd like Oak Park. It's the perfect distance. You're still close to the city, and I can finally get a decent night's rest."

Jeanine pulled over and parked in front of a house. I braced myself for disappointment, but to my surprise, its spiked, triangular roof and jagged rock exterior was nothing like what we'd seen so far. Its enormity lay in the imposing structure rather than in square footage. It wasn't turnkey like Bill had requested; it needed work. The run-down property, thick with overgrown brush, oozed with character. Hard angles, a stone path and chimney, and clean, jutting lines gave it a modern but rustic feel. Yet in an oasis of traditional homes, it somehow retained the neighborhood's atmosphere.

It was quietly *magnificent*.

I unbuckled my seatbelt and stepped out to get a better look. Dead grass crunched under my shoes as I used my hand to shield my eyes against the lowering sun.

"Olivia?"

I glanced over my shoulder.

Jeanine gestured to me as she and Bill crossed the street. "This one. Over here."

Ah. Behind her, a realtor's sign sprouted from lush, green grass that belonged to a spacious, pretty home resembling every other house on the block. Except the one where I stood.

I should've known. And it was for the best. Neither Bill nor I had time for a DIY project.

I stepped off the curb and followed Jeanine into the house we were supposed to be seeing. We climbed the front steps to a large entryway, then an empty dining room that echoed with our footsteps, making our way through a kitchen with enough room that I'd actually be able to spread out. Upstairs, a sprawling master bedroom and en suite bathroom with double sinks would be the clincher for Bill. He often complained about our cramped one-bedroom and single bathroom, especially when we had guests over.

While he and Jeanine discussed amenities, I wandered down the hall into a smaller room that faced the street.

A cracked window allowed me to breathe in the fresh, spring breeze and absorb the sunshine that graced the home's vivid lawn in all its brilliance. What was so scary about the suburbs?

From where I stood on the second floor, the home across the way seemed even more out of place. The lush backyard seemed as unkempt as the front, but what I could see looked as if it had once been a garden. With its rock exterior, contrasting rust-colored roof, and darkened windows, the house gave off a much less welcoming vibe than its neighbors. It was different. Unexpected. It didn't belong. As it stood, it was an eyesore, but I could envision bringing it to life with a weed whacker, fixing the cracks in the stone walkway, adding a fresh coat of paint . . .

Before I could finish the thought, my phone rang in my handbag. I checked the screen but didn't recognize the number. That wasn't a surprise. The weekend receptionist occasionally forwarded me calls from the office.

"This is Olivia," I answered.

"This is David."

I froze, keeping my eyes out the window. He didn't need to announce himself. I'd have easily identified David Dylan's deep voice despite my will to forget him.

He didn't need any more encouragement, though. "David who?" I asked.

"I'm sorry," he said. "I suppose you know me better as Lucas."

I glanced at the ground, smiling at the jab. I couldn't blame him for teasing me when I should've done my homework. "Oh, *that* David," I said. "How'd you get this number?"

"Serena. I'm grateful for my sake she's working over the weekend, but you should have a talk with her about giving out your personal info to charming strangers."

"Apparently." I could only imagine how David had sweet-talked the receptionist into passing him on to Serena so he could butter her up for my number.

"You never responded to my e-mail," he said.

Your Safety. I bit my bottom lip. "It's Saturday. I haven't looked yet. What'd it say?"

"I've been worried since I last saw you. What'd your husband say about the encounter with . . .?"

"Mark Alvarez," I supplied. "He was upset about his brother, Lou, who's serving a life sentence."

"For?"

I shifted on my feet. "First-degree murder."

After a moment of silence, David said, "What about this guy Mark?"

"I guess he was also on trial, but he had a better defense attorney and served minimal time with early release."

"And now that he's out, he needs someone to blame," David concluded. "I thought your husband was at a private practice."

David had just referred to Bill as "your husband" twice in a row. "*Bill* used to be a criminal prosecutor at the district attorney's office."

"And now he does criminal defense?"

I swiped a finger along the windowsill. No dust. I could picture Jeanine as a seller maniacally scrubbing the house sparkling clean like Annette Benning's character in *American Beauty*. "That's what makes Bill a good attorney," I said. "He's been on both sides."

"I see," David said. "What now?"

"Aside from filing a report, there's not much we can do."

"Did you file a report?"

I nudged the toe of my heel between where the carpet met the wall. "Not yet."

"Why not? Isn't your husband irate? I'd think he'd be ripping everyone in his path a new one."

"He was," I said, although I wasn't sure *irate* was the right word. Bill had been shocked. Fascinated by the details. Confused as to why I'd walked home. He'd called friends at his old job to tell them the story. He was grateful I was safe, and angry enough to use this as an excuse to convince me we needed out of the city. But not necessarily irate.

The truth was boring. We just hadn't gotten around to reporting Mark—not that there was much to tell. "I'm sure they were empty threats," I said.

"You don't know that, Olivia." He said my name like a

warning, but David Dylan was the real threat. I believed him more capable of overturning my life than some vengeful, drunken asshole.

"Was there anything else?" I asked him. "Maybe something work-related?"

David's presence only seemed to expand with his silence. "What are you doing right now?" he asked.

I glanced across the street. "Looking at a house."

"What house?"

"This ugly, run-down, overgrown, magnificent eyesore of a house," I said and sighed.

He chuckled. "Now you're speaking my language. What makes it magnificent?"

"It's weird—every other house on the block looks like it belongs in the suburbs. Underneath all the disrepair, this one looks like it actually could've been something special."

"I know *exactly* what you mean."

I frowned, sure I wasn't making any sense. "Are you teasing me?"

"I'm serious. I'm an architect, remember? I'll choose a magnificent eyesore over a tract home any day."

"But it requires money. Energy. Time."

"Even better. You have to get your hands dirty to unearth the good parts. That's work I love to do."

What did he mean by that? Could he fix the place up himself? I hadn't lived in an actual house since I'd left my father's at eighteen—yet I had the sudden urge to get my hands dirty with David.

"You're in the suburbs?" he asked.

"Oak Park." I twisted the stud in my earlobe. "You asked if my husband was irate—this is his answer to the attack. Moving away."

David cleared his throat. "I see."

Voices in the hallway made me turn. My fantasy

dissolved. This house was a much more reasonable place with no assembly required. Bill wasn't the type to get his hands dirty. If I was honest, I probably wasn't, either. When was the last time I'd done anything remotely close to restoring a home? Cleaning stalls at our local animal shelter was as *dirty* as my hands ever got.

"I have to go," I said.

"I called for a reason."

"I'm sorry," I said. "It's not a good time. Please don't call again."

I hung up as Bill spoke behind me. "So, what do you think?" he asked.

I knew what he wanted to hear, but I couldn't lie. "The house across the street is interesting," I said as I slid my cell into my handbag's side pocket.

After a moment of quiet, he said, "And if you were on that side of the street, you'd be saying the same thing about this one. Conveniently, that place isn't for sale."

I turned. "I didn't say I wanted it. Just that it's interesting."

"Which is more than you've said about any other property we've seen. This is the best one yet. Good neighborhood, in our price range, and more square footage than we'd hoped. And you have no comment at all?"

"It's nice," I conceded. "It is. I'm just not sure it's *right*. I can't see myself here."

"You're not even trying."

I looked at my heels as they sank into the beige carpet. I liked beige. Non-committal, unassuming, nothing-to-see-here-folks beige. Bland walls, maybe with some staged family photos, would offer our neighbors little insight into who I was, and I liked it that way. I liked my privacy, the little cage I'd built—not to lock myself in but to keep others out. Could I live in this beige house with Bill?

Maybe. But with David's phone call fresh in my mind, I wondered—what would I be giving up? What kind of life could I live toiling on the passion project across the street, and did I even want that? Unlike safe beige, white-hot passion seared anything in its path.

There was a reason I chose chardonnay.

"This isn't just about you," Bill said. "We have our *future* to think about."

"I understand that," I said, annoyed by the suggestion that I hadn't considered our *future*. "But buying a house is a huge decision, and I want it to be perfect."

He threw his arms in the air. "There's always going to be something, Livs. How many times do I have to tell you —*perfect doesn't exist*. It'll feel like home, you just have to give it time. You think that shithole across the street is perfect?"

"I have to apologize for that," Jeanine said, appearing in the doorway. She looked past me out the window. "It's appalling. The owners live in California and stopped taking care of it a while back. I think a couple neighbors have tried to report housing code violations, so perhaps one day they'll sell or tear it down. I can find out for you."

I readjusted my purse strap on my shoulder. "It's kind of charming."

"Even if it was for sale, it would need a complete over-haul," Jeanine said. "I wouldn't describe it as family-friendly, either. This room, on the other hand, would make a great nursery."

I frowned. Was *I* family-friendly? I'd asked myself some version of that countless times since meeting Bill. Here was my chance to give in to the fantasy he had for us. Standing here at the window of my would-be nursery, I imagined a tiny human in my arms. Bill's son or daughter. Before I could even complete the picture, the skin at the base of my neck began to burn, and my throat closed. "We're not looking for that yet."

"Oh, I . . ." Jeanine said. "Sorry for assuming. Most couples who move from the city—"

"We *are* looking for that," Bill said.

I forced myself to try again. I pictured myself downstairs, chicken parmesan baking in the oven. That sight came easier. Cooking soothed me. I'd wipe my hands on my apron and call "dinner's ready!" up the stairs to Bill. From the kitchen, I could see the living room and TV—all moms wanted that in a floorplan, Jeanine had said. My family within sight on Thanksgiving, watching the parade as I prepared a feast. To call out help with homework as I steamed vegetables for my growing child. To watch the Food Network or the news in the mornings as I made lunches for those who were leaving the house for the day.

And leaving me by myself.

I had to get out of the house, too. I couldn't spend my life between the kitchen and the nursery, regardless of whether I had the privilege of seeing the TV or the kids or the house across the street that had actual character.

"Not right now." The words tumbled out, and I didn't try to stop them. Voicing them was the only thing that calmed the increasingly unbearable itch under my collar. "Maybe one day we'll need all this space, but not now."

He scoffed. "What do you think we're doing here then?"

I had no answer for that. I worried if we got the nursery now, I'd be consenting to things I wasn't sure I wanted. And then, Bill's desire for children would grow, pushing and pushing until I gave in.

When I didn't respond, Bill's brows furrowed. "You think a fixer-upper is the answer?" he asked. "Do you understand the commitment that takes? You wouldn't even get in the car to come to the suburbs if I didn't push you at every turn—now you're going to take on a gut renovation?"

I bristled at the sarcasm dripping from his tone. "I want to *choose* the home I live in, and have some kind of gut feeling about it. Not settle because it's good on paper."

"Then we'd never move out of our apartment, and you know it."

Just like I never would've gotten married, I almost said, then froze, taken aback by the thought. I'd never considered Bill as someone I'd settled for. I'd chosen him and this life for many reasons. But none of them had been based on my gut—they were all good-on-paper reasons. Why, suddenly, after all these years, did it feel as if the walls were closing in and it was my last chance to inject some . . . some desire and ownership—some *passion*—into my choices?

I glanced at the house across the street again. What once would've been a risk and potentially disastrous undertaking with more potential for failure than success now seemed like raw possibility. Hope, in a way, that things weren't already set in stone.

Jeanine slipped a spec sheet into a manila file folder. "I'll give you two a moment."

"It's fine. Stay," I said. I didn't even want to have this argument alone with Bill, much less in front of someone else. Anything I said now, I might regret later. "Let's finish the tour."

"We already did the tour," Bill said.

"Half an hour and you're ready to make an offer?" I asked.

Jeanine nodded. "This place won't be on the market long."

Bill's lips drew tight across his face, but he didn't object.

"Let's get more information then," I said and walked out, leaving them both in the *great* nursery.

In a kitchen barely large enough for two people, where I definitely could not see the television or anywhere else into the apartment, I washed lettuce and did my best to distract myself from my thoughts while making dinner. As soon as Jeanine had dropped us off, Bill had turned on ESPN and hadn't emerged from the living room for more than an hour.

Until now.

He entered the kitchen and went straight for the refrigerator. "About earlier."

I had no desire to reopen the afternoon's discussion, but I suspected he wouldn't let this go. "Dinner will be ready soon," I said. "Don't snack." I passed him a knife and motioned to two tomatoes. "Can you chop those?"

As he sliced into the first one, red juice seeped onto the cutting board. "What are you thinking?"

"About what?" I asked.

"Today."

It wasn't as if I didn't know house hunting would open up a much larger discussion. But Bill and I had become pretty adept at navigating around touchy subjects. I opened the cabinet under the sink to toss romaine stalks into the trash.

"The house has a garbage disposal," Bill pointed out. "*And* a fancy dishwasher."

"Our dishwasher is fine."

"It barely fits anything."

"I don't mind handwashing the big stuff," I said.

He stayed quiet as the knife hit the wood repeatedly.

"It's as close to perfect as it's going to get," he said. "We really can't hesitate."

"I said I'd think about it."

"Don't let the nursery comment scare you off. Just because you're not ready today doesn't mean you won't be soon."

"When?" I asked. "What's soon to you?"

"I don't know. Six months?"

My lungs emptied. Six *months*? I felt even less ready today than I had six months *ago*. "I'm in the same place I was when we last discussed this," I said, tearing up the lettuce. "And especially now, if I get this promotion— honey, I just don't feel like it's the right time."

"The timing might never feel right. It's the same with the house. You just have to do it. The rest will come."

I stiffened. It wasn't just that I didn't feel ready . . . I didn't *want* it. And I worried that I never would. Before Bill had proposed, when he and I would talk about our future, I'd assured him I'd get there one day. That there'd be a right time for children. But did that mean I owed it to him?

"I need more time," I said.

"I'm ready now."

I whirled from the sink to face him. "Now?"

He went silent again and stopped chopping. His knuckles whitened from gripping the knife. "I have been for a while—you know that."

"Bill, you can't expect me to just drop everything and get pregnant." Having a baby meant devoting my life to something bigger, putting my own dreams and aspirations second—or third, even. I'd be promising away a life I sometimes worried hadn't even *begun*. "I have things I still want to do. I'm not in the place I want to be yet."

"Everything you just said was 'me' or 'I,'" he said. "*You* have things *you* want to do. What about me?"

"I meant us," I said. "We've hardly even traveled."

"Our life doesn't end with a baby."

"It will for a while. How are we going to see the world with a newborn if we can't even afford to do it now?"

"Why do you think I sold out for this shiny new job?" he asked. "I was happier working for the State. Justice above all. But I moved to this firm for the money—so we could buy the bigger home and start a college savings account."

None of that was news to me, except that he'd never laid it out quite so honestly. When he'd come home a while back and expressed interest in leaving the public sector, we'd both wanted the money that came with joining a private practice. I'd encouraged him to look into it, and maybe I'd even pushed him when it'd come time to make the leap. Did that mean I'd also committed to life in the suburbs and all that came with it?

"You're not the only one with a career." I picked up the salad bowl and held it to my stomach like a shield. "I want this promotion. I'm not ready to give it up. I'm not ready for a baby."

"I heard you the first time, but you are. We are. I want you to stop birth control."

My heart dropped. "Don't push me on this. It's too big of a decision."

"You need me to push you, Liv—you always have. To start a relationship. To move in together. To get married. You know deep down, that's what you need from me— that's why you chose me as a partner. You need me to tell you that you *are* ready—"

"Stop saying that," I said, slamming the bowl on the island between us. "You don't know what I am. What if you're wrong—what happens if we're not ready? I don't want to end up like—"

"Like your parents," he said, his expression softening. "I know that scares you." He briefly glanced at my hand, clamped on my throat, which felt tight and hot. "Why do you think I'm pushing you?" he asked. "If I don't, you'll never get past that fear."

It was true. It was all true. I was scared. I wouldn't ever put a child through a divorce, and that couldn't happen if I never had one—a child or a divorce. As things stood with Bill, we were fine. Having a baby changed *everything*. My hands shook as I picked up the pieces of romaine that'd flown out of the bowl when I'd slammed it. "You're right. I don't want to end up like them. I won't."

"Liv," he said gently. "They didn't split up because of you. They changed. They fell out of love."

No, they hadn't. They'd loved each other *too* much. Couples didn't fight as hard as they did, especially toward the end, without love. I wasn't sure my father ever would've left my mom without a catalyst. He would've stayed if he hadn't been forced to protect me.

The year leading up to the split had been the worst of it, a painful downward spiral. Bill and I were happy now, but were we solid enough to bring a child into the world? I wasn't sure, but one thing I *did* know was that fear was not the only factor at play here. I hadn't felt anything but dread since standing in that future nursery, holding an imaginary baby I'd agreed to out of obligation.

"Well?" he asked.

I stared into the undressed salad. Some of the lettuce browned at the edges, wilting under the weight of the things Bill and I had said—and what we hadn't.

After some time had passed without my response, Bill said, "Maybe you're right. Maybe you're not ready." The knife clattered on the cutting board. "We've been married for almost five years, and you still won't let me in. I don't know how else to get you to commit, Liv. I've been patient, but I want this, and that's not going to change. Promise me you'll give this some serious thought."

He left the kitchen. I pressed my hand to my side, over the small raised scar under my blouse, trying to hold off the dread rising in me. I had already given this topic serious thought, and nothing had changed. What more did he want?

What could I give him without taking everything from myself?

My cold fingers stung the warm skin around my scar. The kitchen closed in around me. I couldn't stay. I needed *out*. I dumped the salad into the trash and called the one person who was sure to have plans on a Saturday night.

Chapter Nine

As always, Gretchen had come through in a social emergency and procured us a table at the grand opening of
what she'd called "the hottest new restaurant in Chicago."
Invitations had been extended only to the who's who of the
city's social scene—plus Lucy and me. We'd only made the
cut as friends of Gretchen, who happened to be the
current love interest of the head chef.

Lucy and I gave our names at the door, and a hostess
led us to a table in the center of the restaurant where
Gretchen sat with her roommates, Ava and Bethany. A
bottle of expensive Bordeaux had already been opened,
and two empty glasses waited at two empty seats for Lucy
and me.

"You're here!" Gretchen jumped up and came around
the table. "I was worried you were playing a prank on me,"
she said, hugging Lucy. "It's no small feat to get you both
out husband-free on a Saturday night."

"I couldn't handle ESPN another moment," I said,
opening my arms to her.

Gretchen's nose twitched, her sixth sense probably

alerting her ESPN was code for Bill. Instead of hugging me, she took my forearms and spread them as her jaw dropped. "*Olivia Germaine*," she said, eyeing me up and down. "Look at you."

I shimmied in a short, glittering, gold-sequined dress that showed off one bare shoulder. "Like it?"

"Like it?" Ava asked from her seat. "You look like a fucking movie star."

"Gretchen *did* say this was the social event of the season and that the press would be here," Lucy said, who'd added a statement necklace to a modest black dress. Despite her career as a personal stylist, Lucy had always had a very predictable, simple look. Her motto—"Classic never goes out of style"—suited her perfectly.

Lucy and I took our seats and before long, we were ordering a second bottle of red along with appetizers.

"I can't wait to see what happens when you actually *sleep* with Jeff," Bethany said, finishing off her wine.

"Is Jeff the chef?" Lucy asked, giggling at her rhyme.

Gretchen nodded. "He's been asking me out, but I'm not sure I want to add another guy into the rotation."

"God, I wish I had your stamina," Ava said. "I feel like I'm working overtime just to secure a boyfriend."

"You say that like he's a bank loan," Bethany said.

"I wish he was," Ava said. "Finding a husband would be a hell of a lot easier if I just had to meet a list of requirements to apply."

"A husband?" I asked.

Ava nodded. "I want to be a young mom, but also spend quality time with my husband before we have kids. That means I should be pregnant before thirty, so I need to get engaged, like, next year."

Ah, single life. It'd been a while since I'd been in it. I blew out a sigh. "The more you stress about it, the harder it is."

"Easy for you to say." Ava puckered her lips into a pout. "You're already married."

I shrugged. "Just saying, don't put too much pressure on yourself. Some days I wish I'd enjoyed my freedom a little longer."

Ava gasped. "Don't say that. Being single in this city is *awful*."

"Um, Chicago is the *best* place to be single," Gretchen countered. "Any competition we might have is in New York and Los Angeles trying to get famous. But the men here, they're . . ."

The table went quiet just as my ears tuned to a man's voice deep enough to cut through the hum of the crowd.

I knew that voice, and I knew the expression on Gretchen's face.

"They're *that*." Gretchen finished her sentence with a nod across the room, and everyone but me turned to follow her gaze. "You can't tell me the single life sucks when there's a bachelor like that on the loose."

I shut my eyes and inhaled as my skin tingled. My nipples hardened as if a cold breeze had passed through the dining room, yet the wine had warmed me to my core. Or maybe it was his eyes on me. How David Dylan could have such an effect on me without a word, or even a glance, I didn't know. And I wasn't sure I wanted to.

"Who *is* that?" Ava asked, sitting up straighter in her seat. "More importantly, *he's* a bachelor?"

Lucy, already tipsy, broke into a smile and waved a little too hard, nearly toppling out of her chair. "David," she called. "David! Over here."

All the women's eyes stayed fixed behind me, their

heads tilting back until David spoke from next to me. "Well, if it isn't my lucky night."

I turned. The sight of him was no less devastating than any time he and I had come face to face. If possible, I might've been even more stunned by his beauty in this unexpected setting. His eyes met mine, especially gold against his jet-black hair and in the warm light of the restaurant. "Hello, Olivia," he said.

A second later, a woman slipped her arm into his pea coat, which hung open over a black sweater that looked as if it were made of the softest cashmere in the world. She hugged his waist too intimately for a friend or family member, stunning me into silence and stealing any response I might've had to his very personal greeting.

It took me a second before I recognized her from pictures I'd seen online while researching David. She came up to his chin in sky-high heels that lengthened already long legs. Caramel-colored hair fell in waves over her bronzed shoulders, and her skin-tight red dress showed off an athletic figure with a great ass.

I dug my nails into the seat cushion. She was one of the most beautiful women I'd ever seen, her rich, dark complexion melding flawlessly with David's olive skin. They were the epitome of a glamorous couple.

Envy flooded out my shock. I looked David straight in the eyes.

Playboy.

He swallowed, having the decency to look sheepish.

"Lucky night, indeed," said another man I hadn't noticed. His French accent lingered the way his eyes traveled over each of us, leering in a way that made me tug on my earlobe.

David cocked his head, and I pulled my hand away,

mortified that I'd even *thought* I could hold his interest when he was clearly spoken for by someone like her.

"What're you doing here, David?" Lucy asked, her voice pitching into my thoughts.

"This is my associate, Arnaud," David said, gesturing to the shorter man next to him. "He worked on this project."

"The space is *beautiful*," Lucy said. "Congratulations."

"*Merci, mademoiselle*," Arnaud said.

"What brings you ladies out?" David asked.

I turned forward and clasped my hands in my lap, my back unnaturally straight as I refused to look at him. Or the beauty on his arm.

"Gretchen's dating the head chef," Lucy explained.

"Geez, Luce, Jeff is just a friend," Gretchen said quickly. "We've never even been on a date."

"Sor-*ry*," Lucy said.

"David?" The woman's whispered *Dah-veed* turned his name even sexier. "My feet hurt."

"Hmm?" he asked, sounding distracted. "Oh. Just another second—"

"The hostess is waiting for us," she added, her Latin accent clearer as her tone rose.

David cleared his throat. "Maria and I had better sit," he said. "Nice to see you all again—Lucy, Gretchen . . . Olivia." My name rolled off his tongue as if he were testing it out, the same way he'd said it the first time. Even without looking at him, I sensed his hesitation before he walked away.

"He remembered my name," Gretchen whisper-squealed.

"Because I just said it," Lucy pointed out.

Bethany leaned over the table toward Gretchen. "Details. Now. *Spill*."

"He's a friend of my fiancé," Lucy said.

Ava and Bethany both jerked their heads to her. "Who was that woman? His girlfriend?"

"Not sure," Lucy said. "I think he has lots of them . . ."

David took a seat directly in my line of sight. I made sure to keep my eyes on my friends.

"Hook a girl up," Gretchen said.

"Yeah, *this* girl," Ava said, pointing at herself as the others giggled.

Suddenly nauseated, I moved my napkin off my lap. "I'm going to use the restroom."

Lucy stood. "I'll go, too."

"Let's make it a threesome," Gretchen said, standing. She flicked her long, blonde ringlets over her shoulder as she shimmied out of her seat—surely for David's benefit. He had a perfect view of her rear, which was exactly what he'd be seeing if he were still looking in our direction.

As we made our way through the restaurant, Lucy drew us closer and lowered her voice. "I didn't want to say this in front of the others in case they try to stalk me at work," she said, "but David made an appointment for a consultation with me next week."

"Really?" I asked, the question flying out. David was seeping into every part of my life, and I didn't know if I was more thrilled or worried by it. Even though nothing had happened between us, our attraction felt too big to hide. Especially if he was going to be spending more time around my friends.

"You lucky *bitch*," Gretchen said. "You'll get to see him naked."

Lucy turned a shade of red I'd never seen on a person. "Being a stylist isn't like that, Gretchen. *God*."

I'd just entered the bathroom stall when my phone vibrated with a text from an unknown number.

Unknown only because I hadn't saved it in my phone earlier. Because keeping the number felt like a transgression in itself.

Was it also a sin that I recognized it anyway?

That I couldn't forget it?

That my heart leaped knowing the text was from David?

Back in the dining area, our waitress had littered the table with appetizers that looked as good as they smelled. I hid my phone in my lap and read David Dylan's text message a third time.

David: *Why the cold shoulder?*

I needed to delete it. Delete *him*. But I couldn't deny my flicker of excitement over the fact that not only was he ignoring his date to text me, but he'd also noticed *me* ignoring him—and had picked up on my discomfort when even my girlfriends hadn't. I sent my reply.

Me: *I'm not sure what you mean.*

"More wine, Liv?" Bethany asked, causing me to jump. "Oh. Yes. Thanks," I said just as my phone vibrated.

David: *Don't be coy. How are you getting home?*

Me: *Why?*

Gretchen was speaking, but I didn't need to listen. I'd already heard her story about becoming an accidental extra in Chris Hemsworth's latest film. I clutched the phone until David's response came through.

David: *You've been drinking.*

Me: *So?*

David: *I will come over there & ask in front of everyone if you don't tell me. How're you getting home?*

Me: *Thought I'd hitch a ride with legs over there.*

David: *Very cute. I'm coming over.*

Horrified at the possibility that he'd out us to my friends, I scurried to type a response, taking only a second to shoot a harried glance in his direction.

Me: *Lucy and I are getting a cab. Why does it matter?*

David: *You know it does.*

Some part of him cared. I didn't know why, but I couldn't deny it. I took another, larger sip and inhaled before answering.

Me: *You said earlier that you called me for a reason.*

David: *And you hung up on me, right before you told me not to call again . . .*

So, he wasn't going to tell me the reason. That was my punishment for hanging up. I shouldn't care what he did or didn't have to say anyway. Clearly, the Bordeaux was talking for me. I unfastened my clutch to put the phone away, but it pinged before I could.

David: . . . *but you never told me not to text.*

With a small commotion, I looked up.

Jeff the chef had emerged from the kitchen and was heading for our table. As we applauded, he broke into a grin. "Thank you," he said with a short bow. "How's everything, Gretchen?"

She tossed her long hair. "Delicious, Jeff."

"Great," he said, visibly reddening. "I can't stay, just wanted to say hello—and let you know I'm sending over a special dessert just for my favorite table." He blew Gretchen a kiss and offered the rest of us a quick wave.

As I watched him walk away, my eyes fell on David. Maria gestured as she spoke to him, but he didn't appear to be listening as he checked his phone.

Lucy leaned over. "Everything all right?"

I flipped my cell over in my lap to hide the screen. "What? Yes. Why?"

"Things seemed a little tense between you and Bill when I came to get you for dinner. And you're texting furiously. Are you fighting?"

"We argued earlier," I admitted.

"About?"

"House hunting again. It's stressful." I smiled at her. "You'll know soon enough."

"I can't see Andrew and me leaving our apartment anytime soon."

"I can't see *myself* leaving the city, either, but you'll see. Once the baby topic comes up—"

Her eyes widened as she clapped her hands together. "Are you guys finally trying?"

"Trying to what?" Ava asked, turning to us.

"No, nothing," I said quickly. The last thing I needed was Lucy on my case about this, too. Any hint of baby talk, and she'd team up with Bill against me. "Bill and I looked at some houses today. Nothing exciting."

Ava lost interest, but Gretchen looked up from her dish. "Hey, isn't tomorrow Leanore's birthday?"

I sighed. "Yes."

"Who's Leanore?" Bethany asked.

"My mother," I answered.

Lucy lowered her voice. "Are you going to call her?" she asked. "You should. I'm sure she'd like that."

I exchanged a glance with Gretchen. Every year I said I wouldn't call, but every year, I was guilted into it by someone. Usually Bill.

"Tell us more about our bridesmaid dresses, Luce," Gretchen said.

Lucy lit up and launched into fabrics, cuts, and colors, as if she'd just been waiting for someone to ask.

I mouthed a "*thank you*" at Gretchen for the subject change, and she nodded.

I tried to focus on the conversation around me. After all, this wedding would be the center of Lucy's world until it happened. But there was something about David. Since the ballet, I'd felt his eyes any time they were on me. That included now. I looked up and found his gaze narrowed in my direction.

After a moment, he picked up his phone again.

Seconds later, mine buzzed.

Our eyes met once more before I checked the screen.

David: *It's taking everything in me not to come over there. You are KILLING me in that gold dress, honeybee.*

Chapter Ten

Stirring from my wine-induced mini-coma, I stretched my legs under the covers. Bill's arm around my middle pulled me closer. He slid his hand up my front, his need pressing into my backside.

"I can't," I said softly when he nuzzled my neck and kissed my jaw. "I'm hungover."

Bill flopped over and sighed. "How was last night?"

"Nice," I said. "Spirits were high, and the food was good."

"And the head chef? Jeff, right?"

"Seems really sweet. Poor guy doesn't stand a chance against Gretchen, though."

Bill laughed. "How does she do it? She's hot and all, but damn. I wouldn't touch her."

I sat up and looked back at him with a frown. "Why not?"

"Who knows how many guys she's slept with? She's always seeing someone new. Gives me the creeps just thinking about it."

"Babe, she doesn't sleep with all the guys she goes out

with." I got out of bed and pulled on a t-shirt. "Even if she did, who cares?"

"I'm just saying, it'd be a deal-breaker for me."

Bill had a tendency to tease Gretchen, but it was all in good fun. What he was saying now, though? It didn't feel the same. "So if you'd found out I had a reputation, you never would have gone out with me?"

He remained quiet. Probably wise.

"You wouldn't say that if she was a man," I pointed out.

Irritated, I went to the kitchen to make coffee.

Eventually, Bill stumbled out in a t-shirt and boxers. "I just couldn't deal with knowing half of Chicago had seen my wife naked." He came over and kissed the corner of my mouth, his breath minty on my cheek. "I'm not going to find that out, am I?"

"Bill."

"I'm teasing." He took two mugs from a shelf and passed me one. "You're nothing like Gretchen."

I turned to face him. "See, what do you mean by that?"

"Babe. Seriously?" Picking up the coffee pot, he continued, "Sometimes she's dating more than one guy at a time. That's disgusting."

"She's our friend," I said as he poured two cups. "Don't call her disgusting."

"She's *your* friend. And let's be honest, she's a little slutty. One day it'll catch up with her."

I picked up a mug from the counter and warmed my hands with it. "I know for a fact there are guys at your firm who sleep with a new woman or two every weekend. I don't call them names."

"They're assholes," he said.

"*You* are acting like an asshole."

"Okay. You're right. I'm wrong." He raised a palm in

surrender. "The chef could be the one. I mean, look at me —I never thought I stood a chance with you, yet here I am."

He sipped his coffee.

I knew Bill well enough to hear the sincerity in his voice. He wasn't just saying that to end the fight, but I did smile in spite of myself. "Oh, please."

"It's true. I thought you were way out of my league. I got lucky." He squatted to pull a skillet from a cupboard. "How's an omelet sound for my hungover girl?"

I grinned. "Like maybe your asshole status is changing."

Horizontal on the sofa with my nose buried in *Vogue*, I almost didn't notice when something bounced off my calf. I lowered the magazine and retrieved my cell phone from the end of the couch.

"You know what you have to do," Bill said from the kitchen doorway, wiping his hands on his pajama pants. The smells of eggs, grilled peppers, and sautéed mushrooms gave way to Dawn dish soap.

My confusion morphed into panic when I remembered last night's texts with David. Suddenly, I couldn't recall if I'd deleted them in my tipsy state or even exactly what I'd said. "Where'd you get this?" I asked, gripping my phone.

"Your purse in the kitchen."

I blinked at him. "What do you mean, I know what I have to do?"

Bill rounded the couch, sat in a recliner by my feet, and took his latest thriller from the coffee table. "Leanore. Call her."

I deflated back against the couch and pulled a pillow over my face. "Why does everyone keep saying that?"

"You can't ignore your own mother on her birthday."

"I'm not ignoring her," I said. "Why don't *you* call her if it's so important? Get Lucy on the line, too. Make it a conference call."

"Liv," he said. "Come on. Just dial the numbers and wish her a happy birthday."

I pulled the pillow away and looked at my phone again. "And then what?"

"And then you can hang up. Once you tell her you love her. And that you miss her."

It was all true, but it had been for a long time. I missed who she'd been before. Before the paranoia, the excessive drinking, the divorce. Before she'd turned on my dad, on *me*—her own daughter—and left me with scars both inside and out that I wasn't about to reopen.

Talking with her—even talking *about* her—threatened to take me back to the last night we'd spent as a family.

But it made Bill happy to see us getting along, and I'd already threatened his sense of family once this weekend with our argument over the house.

I sighed as I picked up the phone and scrolled my contacts until I saw it.

Leanore.

"Hello?" she answered.

"Hi, Mom." There was a pause on the line. "Mom?"

"Olivia?"

"Unless you have some secret daughter I don't know about. Are you there?"

"Yes, yes," she said. "How are you?"

"I'm fine." I scratched under my nose. "I just, um, called to wish you a happy birthday."

"I didn't think I'd hear from you. It's been months."

"I know. Things have been crazy here." Bill cleared his throat, and I picked at something on the couch. "How've you been?"

"I'm well," she said. "I keep trying to get in touch with your father. Money is tight. I don't know what I'll do in a couple months. He won't take my calls."

"He doesn't owe you alimony anymore," I said. "As if I need to tell you."

"I don't understand why he can't just help me out, though. He has the money."

"You know why, Mom. He's not your ATM, and you've had a thriving career. Don't play the victim." When my temper began to rise, I took a breath and evened my tone. "Anyway, he's finally *just now* finalizing his divorce with Gina, so he has his hands full."

"That's what she gets for breaking up a marriage," Mom muttered, her usual response.

She didn't break up a marriage. You *did.*

I kept it to myself. There was no point arguing with her. She wanted to believe my father had cheated with Gina more than she wanted to live in the reality that he'd never crossed the line. In the months leading up to their divorce, it was my mother's increasingly frequent and extreme accusations that had driven him away—and into Gina's arms. If not physically at first, then emotionally. But who could blame my father when years of my mother's drinking and paranoia had been wearing him down?

"How's the book coming?" I asked, hoping to change the subject.

"All right."

"Care to tell me about it?"

She sighed. "It's not there yet."

"You're keeping busy, though?"

"What do you mean by that?" she asked.

"Nothing. Just making sure you aren't . . . bored."

"Stop insinuating," she said.

"I'm not, Mom." Well, maybe I was a little. She could seem coherent and still be drinking. "Actually, you sound well."

"How's Bill?" she asked with a lighter tone.

"He's working a lot, but he's good." I glanced at my husband, but he was engrossed with his phone. "He says 'hello.'"

"Good boy. He works hard so he can take care of you, you know. Don't take that for granted. I did, and I can tell you, it's not easy being alone. Not easy at all."

If my mother was alone, it was a prison of her own making. Bill would never leave me. He'd always continue to offer me love, a home, a family. For giving me the security that had been stolen from me at thirteen, I owed him a great deal.

I should never have left the house during an argument, and I especially shouldn't have flirted with another man. That was something my mother would've done, and had done, to make my dad jealous.

I'd been making out-of-character decisions ever since David had entered the picture, and I couldn't really ignore that red flag anymore.

I nudged Bill's arm with my foot, and he put down his phone. I gave my husband a small smile, grateful he hadn't turned our argument yesterday into anything bigger than it needed to be. That he'd been waiting up when I'd come home, and had welcomed me when he could've made me feel like shit for walking out on him.

His steady emotional support held strong. Even now, from a few feet away, he comforted me.

No matter how trying these phone calls were, he encouraged me to make them, and truth be told, had I not made the call, tomorrow I would've stressed over it. I didn't want my mother to feel alone on her birthday.

"*Thank you*," I mouthed to him.

He cocked his head. "What for?"

"I should get going," my mom said. "I've had a long weekend. Thank you for calling, and give Bill my love."

"I will. Happy birthday."

"That was nice," Bill said when I'd hit *End*.

"I tried, but you know how she can be."

He nodded slowly. "I know how you both can be."

"What's that supposed to mean?"

"It means that . . ." He shifted in the seat. "This way that you are, Liv? You learned it from her. When it comes to you and your dad, she's cold, even if she doesn't mean it."

Cold? Did he not see how her ridiculous passion and lack of self-awareness had set fire to our family? How she'd lost everything as a result but couldn't accept an ounce of blame?

"When my dad and I left, it just gave her an excuse to be unhappy. And something to crucify us for. It's always been one extreme or the other—narcissistic indifference or irrational madness. She's never been good at expressing herself."

"Neither have you."

I crossed my legs under me, chewing the inside of my cheek. "So . . . does that mean you think I'm cold?"

"Sometimes, yeah," he said, flipping through the pages of his book but keeping his eyes on me.

"Oh." It wasn't an entirely unfair assessment, but it was nonetheless painful to hear out loud. I never meant to be cold, just not hot enough to burn those around me.

Including Bill.

If he truly believed I acted that way, then why describe

my icy phone call just now as *nice* instead of calling bullshit on me? Instead of forcing me to ask my mom how she *really* was, or tell her how *I* really was? Or make me confront the reasons for him and for myself that I couldn't go deeper?

Because my ability to enact logic over emotion suited him, even if it made me cold.

And that was why Bill suited me.

He never would've married someone emotional and fiery like my mother. He'd never be that person, either, never pick up and disappear the way Greg had done to Gretchen, or drive me away as my mom had done to us.

And I'd be a complete fool to risk the stable life we'd built for the chaos and destruction my parents had subjected me to.

But was starting a family the one thing that Bill couldn't give up? A concession I'd have to make to keep this life? As my mother had said, he took good care of me. Whenever I called, he answered. When I told him in the morning that I needed an ingredient to make dinner, he never forgot to pick it up on his way home. Small things like that made for a big deal in a partnership.

"Could you tell if she was drinking?" Bill asked.

"I don't think she was."

He put an arm behind his head and glanced at the ceiling. "I know I've offered before, but we can send her some money. Now that I've got more coming in—"

"Dad says it's 'enabling.' He only sent money as long as it was court-ordered, and the combo of free time and income made her indulgences worse."

Her addictions, more like. I knew I should verbalize her disease, but nobody else ever did. Not my father, not Mack nor Davena, not even Bill. Nobody called her an alcoholic, so I didn't, either.

"She's in her fifties," he said. "Leanore's not going to change."

"She *could* change," I said, "but not until she acknowledges there's a problem."

"I just hate to see you two fight."

"We don't fight anymore," I said. "That's the underlying issue. If I say even one wrong thing, it can cause the next World War between us, or between her and my dad. So I don't say anything at all."

"What I mean is . . . when the time comes, I want our children to know their grandparents," Bill said.

I didn't. My toxic mother should stay away from impressionable children. But voicing that sounded harsh, and it could invite questions I knew Bill didn't want to ask, and ones I didn't want to answer. And I knew if I ever told Bill the whole truth about the night my mom had put me in the emergency room, there was a chance he'd take her side. Nobody could understand sitting on a hospital bed at dawn, answering invasive questions about my home life while I'd balled my bloody pajama top in my lap—a concert tee with Shania Twain's face on it.

But it wasn't fair to blame Bill for not getting it when I'd kept some of the worst details from him. It hadn't necessarily been intentional on my part, but although Bill was a good listener, he wasn't one to dig for more, either. He knew my father and I had left one night after an argument, and that was as much as I was willing to volunteer. As for the scar on my side that had been left behind? Bill never asked about it, and I was fine with that.

I looked over at him as he flipped through his book, trying to find where he'd left off. Did he think I was worse than her? Colder?

I'd lost count of how many times I'd opened my mouth to explain what it was like. How it'd felt to live through the divorce knowing that Mom cared more about losing my dad than me.

How she maybe even loved the idea of us more than the reality, and that she was happiest in her misery because she could blame it on us.

If I tried to get Bill to understand, and he didn't— would that mean he was right? That *I* was to blame for the irreparable rift between mother and daughter?

I woke up from a nap in a daze, confused by the setting sun and the warmth of a heavy blanket draped over me.

Bill had tucked me in. Thawed me. Yet I'd fallen asleep thinking about David's suggestive texts. The balls it'd taken to send them, to comment on another man's wife's dress, to give her a pet name.

Had he thought of glittering gold and honeybees when he'd laid his head on his pillow last night?

Did he ever spend a Sunday evening with a woman, or was that too intimate?

That wasn't my business. I turned my face into the couch pillow.

I closed my eyes, giving in to a second round of sleep, when Bill spoke from the hallway. "Yeah?"

"Hmm?" I asked.

"You called for me."

Had I? On some level, I knew what I needed. Not silly fantasies made of lust but the steady love I already had.

I reached for Bill. He climbed in with me, tented the blanket, and kissed my bare shoulder.

"Do you still think I'm cold?" I whispered, looking up at him.

"No." He rubbed a smooth cheek against me. I lazily

pulled him on top of me and ran the soles of my feet over his long calves. The inside of his mouth was hot and soft, and when he drew away, I almost pulled him back.

Instead, I told him to get a condom.

We made love under that too-hot blanket, sweating and groaning into each other. After a second time, we lay panting until my phone began to chime.

"That's my birth control reminder." I wiggled out from under Bill, but he caught my forearm. I turned to meet eyes that asked me to stay. To skip today's pill, and tomorrow's, too. The moment stretched as we stared at each other in the almost-dark punctuated by melodious chimes. But it didn't matter how desperately Bill wanted it or pleaded with me—I wasn't stopping birth control today. Or tomorrow, either.

Slowly, I slid my arm through his hand and left to take the pill.

Chapter Eleven

From: David Dylan
Sent: Mon, May 7 08:23 AM CDT
To: Olivia Germaine
Subject: The reason I called

Olivia,
I'm headed over to my latest project today. I'll pick you up
on the way for our lunch appointment to discuss my bachelor status.

P.S. Got your Meet & Greet invitation. I'll be there.

DAVID DYLAN
SENIOR ARCHITECT
PIERSON/GREER

I re-read David's e-mail with a frown. We didn't have an appointment—and he knew it. Hadn't it crossed his mind that I might have lunch plans already? It didn't matter. Nothing was as important as securing the elusive David Dylan as a Bachelor and proving to my boss that I was the right woman for the promotion.

But what would it cost me to spend an hour under his spell, subjected to his charm, at the mercy of our attraction?

With him, I seemed to forget what was at stake. Not just my marriage, but a future I'd fought hard for out of a need to escape my past. It hadn't been easy to learn how to love carefully and choose wisely—I was like anyone else who wanted to give in to impulses, wants, desires. But I had to be stronger than that to get the life I wanted. One that wasn't painful, even if it was never euphoric, either.

I hit respond, changed the subject line, typed out my response, and hit *Send* before I could second-guess myself.

If there was any chance of steering clear of David during this process, I had to try.

From: Olivia Germaine
Sent: Mon, May 7 08:31 AM CDT
To: David Dylan
Subject: We don't have a lunch appointment

Unfortunately, I already have a meeting scheduled, but I'd be happy to send Serena in my place to conduct the interview.

Olivia Germaine
Associate Editor
Chicago Metropolitan Magazine
ChicagoMMag.com

From: David Dylan
Sent: Mon, May 7 08:34 AM CDT
To: Olivia Germaine
Subject: If you hadn't hung up on me and told me not to call back, you'd know about our appointment

That doesn't work for me. I trust you to do this interview. Only you. 11:30.

DAVID DYLAN
SENIOR ARCHITECT
PIERSON/GREER

The nerve, I thought as I mentally canceled my non-existent lunch appointment.

At eleven-thirty on the dot, Jenny buzzed me from the front desk. I smoothed a hand over my hair and was about to swipe on pink lip gloss when I stopped myself. I couldn't risk my promotion by turning down an interview with David, but I didn't have to look good doing it. At least I wouldn't send the wrong message in my conservative outfit —a short-sleeved, white button down and navy, high-waisted pencil skirt. For insurance, I fastened the button at my throat, one more than I ever did.

That should do it.

Clutching my briefcase to my chest, I found Serena and Beman talking giddily with David.

"I wasn't aware Mr. Dylan would be gracing our offices today." Beman nodded at me approvingly. "We're so

137

thrilled you've agreed to be part of the piece this year, David."

David rubbed the back of his neck. "This isn't the type of publicity I usually do."

"I expect you'll receive an *emphatic* response." Beman brushed his hand along the sleeve of David's suit jacket. "This is Italian, isn't it? I know my wool."

David cleared his throat. "I . . ."

Though his rare discomfort kind of made me want to laugh, I threw him a bone. "We should get going," I said. "I'll be conducting David's interview at The Revelin."

David arched an eyebrow. This time, I'd done my homework. Well, some of it. After his e-mail, I'd looked up his firm's current projects. David was the lead architect on a hotel coming to the Riverfront, but that was as much as I knew.

"I've followed your work since that piece in the *Tribune* years ago," Beman said. "I'd love to come along and see the space?"

"Miss Germaine and I have set aside this time for our interview," David said. "With my hectic schedule, it's the only time I could spare."

I smiled at Beman. "You understand."

"Completely," he said, glancing at David. "Consider Liv at your disposal."

David frowned as his jaw ticked, but the hint of his impending scowl quickly vanished as he turned to me and set his hands on his hips. "You ready?"

I indicated the door. "After you, Mr. Dylan."

"No." He shook his head and chuckled, swinging the door open with ease. "After *you*."

In the hallway, once alone, my shoulders depressed. David's charisma expanded in large spaces yet in small ones, his towering frame and easy smile offered more comfort than intimidation. In the same ways his bluntness and prying wracked my nerves, his presence somehow calmed them.

"That guy tells *anyone* you're at their disposal again," David said, "I'll throw him through the wall."

I tilted my head up, searching his face for teasing but there was none. "What?"

"I said, I'll put your boss through a wall if I hear him speak to you that way again." After a deep breath, he smiled. "How are you?"

Overheated, that was what. A flush worked its way up my chest as David's intent settled in. Had I ever heard someone stand up for me that way? For anyone?

Flustered—and, if I was honest, *flattered*—I glanced at the ground to hide my smile. I had to stay strong. This was *business*. "I'm fine, thanks," I said, crossing my arms when he looked at my elbow.

"How's the arm?"

"Healing."

He tapped his foot and peered down at me while the numbers above the elevator ticked up.

When I realized he was waiting for me to reciprocate, I rolled my eyes playfully. "And how are *you*?"

"Better," he said with a beatific smile that took a hammer straight to my resolve.

Downstairs, David led me to a classic black Porsche 911 so shiny and spotless, it must've taken a deal with the devil to keep it that way. Especially in this city.

"This is your car?" I asked when he opened the passenger door.

"Get in."

I crouched, slid onto the smooth leather seat, and ran a hand along the dash. "It's beautiful," I said as he got behind the wheel. "*And* it's a Turbo."

"You a car girl?"

"My dad always had a different sports car when I was growing up. Currently, he has a '68 Shelby I'm trying to take off his hands."

"Mustang," David said.

"The faster the better."

"Even the buttoned-up ones have to get a rush somehow, huh?" he asked with a wink.

I touched my collar. How ridiculous I'd been to think an extra button could protect me from his charms.

"I take it your dad doesn't want to part with the car?" he asked as we pulled into midday traffic.

"No, he would, actually," I said. "It's Bill. He says it's impractical for the city."

We slowed for a red light. "What about the *suburbs*?"

I curled my hands into loose balls, keeping my eyes out the windshield. "Then I'm getting my car. If we move there, I'm going to need something, that's for sure."

"If?" he asked.

I couldn't look at him for fear I'd never be able to picture myself anywhere in the world except in this car with him. Especially not that dust-free nursery-to-be.

"Hmm," David said with a sidelong glance.

"What?"

"Your energy changed talking about the car. That's who I saw at the ballet," he said. "Not white wine, suburbs, and pencil skirts, but someone trying to break through. *The-faster-the-better* girl in a sparkling gold dress, tipsy on Bordeaux . . ."

If he thought that's who I was, he was wrong. I was the person I made myself into. Life couldn't be all glitter, speed, and indulgence. There had to be compromise, sensibility, sustainable pace—and office appropriate attire. "What's wrong with my pencil skirt?" I asked.

He glanced at my bare knees. As his eyes roved up my thighs to my hips, the fabric changed from the shield I'd intended into skin-tight, revealing, and hugging my every curve. "Not a thing, Miss Germaine. I like it as much as your dresses, the green and the white ones—but the gold? That's my favorite."

He had a favorite. It was mine, too. I tried not to wiggle in my seat. "Has anyone ever told you you're very forward?"

"Yes." He accelerated when the light turned. "It's what got me where I am. Hungry?"

I blinked at the enigma that was David. "Excuse me?"

"Lunch," he said. "Will you indulge me by stopping to eat first?"

"Indulge *you*?" I asked. "I'm starved. I'm ready to chow down."

His eyebrows shot up. "Chow . . . down?"

"Guess you aren't used to a date who actually eats," I said and snickered. "What about your 'hectic schedule,' though?"

"Funny," he said. "It just opened up. And this isn't a date, by the way. When you're on a date with me—believe me, you'll know it."

When? He was teasing. He had to be. Did he think the ring on my finger was for show? "I believe that," I said.

"Do you?"

"Anyone with eyes could see Maria was *definitely* on a date Saturday night. Did you two have a nice time?"

"Moderate," he said bluntly. "I went to support Arnaud and the firm, but I was—let's say, distracted. I'd rather've been at your table."

"No doubt, considering it was a table of five women."

"I meant that I'd have preferred your company."

I scoffed. "*My* company? Maria was the most beautiful woman in the room."

He glanced over at me. I feigned interest in something outside.

"Do I sense a hint of . . . jealousy?" he asked.

Jealousy was not my thing. Bill and I didn't play that game. He'd never cheat. Nor would I, because that would turn me into the person my mother had accused my father of being.

She'd met his client, Gina, accidentally. Months before the night that changed everything, my mom had gone by Dad's office unannounced and found him in a meeting with a beautiful woman. That simple thing that had kicked off her final descent into madness. My dad *had* eventually ended up with Gina, but only once my mom had tipped from the jealous wife she'd always been into a person I didn't recognize in those following weeks. She'd started drinking more, maligning my father to me whenever he was at work, and twice that I knew of, she'd physically attacked him when he'd gotten home.

I stood on safe ground now with Bill. Entertaining anything with someone like David was a spiral I couldn't afford to get anywhere near—because madness ran in my blood. One wrong step and I could get sucked into chaos I'd been trying to confine since thirteen years old.

"Maria's a friend. I'm not a playboy, Olivia," David continued. "But obviously, I *do* date."

I turned back to him. "You can call me Liv, you know. Everyone else does."

"Don't change the subject."

The hair on the back of my neck prickled. That usually worked on Bill. "All right," I said. "So you date beautiful, exotic women. I don't see any reason why you wouldn't."

"It doesn't need to be that way," he said just over the

hum of the Porsche's powerful engine. "In fact, I *want* to be exclusive with the right woman. Very much. Is that something you wish to discuss further?"

My chest tightened. I let myself appreciate his profile while he drove. His strong nose—there was no better adjective for it—ended in an acute tip. Though smoothly shaven, I could see a shadow forming. He blinked long lashes and furrowed black eyebrows as he glided in and out of traffic. The crow's feet around his eyes deepened. Defined muscles strained against a crisp shirt when he shifted gears. My hand twitched, desiring to reach over and feel his biceps.

His dating life was something I *desperately* wished to discuss, and not because of the article. I didn't want to just know what he considered his perfect woman. I admitted to myself that I wanted to *be* her, even if I couldn't have him. How could I tell him that the first night at the theater, I'd wondered what it would be like to disappear into a dark corner with him? Or that I'd wondered what thoughts lulled him to sleep? I couldn't. Nor how I worried that the closer he drew me in, the further I stood from Bill.

Or that I'd begun to question my marriage or if the reasons I'd chosen it were still enough.

David looked over at me, waiting for my answer.

"No," I said quietly. "Let's not discuss it."

We rode in silence the rest of the way.

Once we'd parked, David strode ahead to the restaurant to hold the door open for me.

I walked in first, but the hostess looked right over my head with a megawatt smile. "Good afternoon, Mr. Dylan. Your usual table?"

I glanced back to find his eyes on me. He raised his chin. "Unless my lunch companion has a preference?"

I held up the notepad I'd brought to take notes for our interview. "I'm an observer today. *The usual* is exactly what I want to see. Pretend I'm not even here."

He snorted. "Not likely."

"Great! Right this way, David." The hostess giggled. "Oops. I mean Mr. Dylan."

I had to admire her effort, but her sleek ponytail, low-cut top, and smiling red lips didn't seem to catch his attention.

Unless she'd already been hooked, flayed, and thrown back to sea? The thought both fanned the unwelcome ember of jealousy Maria had incited earlier, and—shame-fully—made me grateful I wasn't stupid or single enough to fall into bed with someone like David.

David lowered his voice as we crossed the restaurant. "This place is close to the site. We're here a lot."

As we settled into opposite sides of a booth, a short, flaxen-haired man approached. "Dylan," he said in a strong, French accent.

I recognized him as the leering man David had intro-duced to the table on Saturday night.

"Arnaud, you remember Olivia Germaine," David said. "She writes for *Chicago M*."

"Of course." Arnaud held out his hand and bowed his head. "Hello again, *mademoiselle*."

"*Madame*, actually," I corrected, reluctantly allowing him to kiss the back of my hand.

Arnaud lifted his bent head and looked between the two of us. "I apologize. *Madame*."

"And that goes for you, too," I said to David. "No more calling me *miss*. It's *Mrs*. Germaine."

The corner of his mouth ticked as he suppressed a

smile, but he didn't argue. "Are you going back to the office?" David asked Arnaud.

"Yes."

"I need you to stop and look at the light fixtures we discussed. Today. We'll make a final decision when I get back later." David returned his attention to me, effectively dismissing him.

"Enjoy your lunch," Arnaud answered before he left us.

"Germaine," David mused. "That's not your husband's name, is it?"

"How'd you know?"

"I did my homework," he said, a gleam in his eye.

"It's not. But Germaine or Wilson—it doesn't change a thing. I'm still married." I smoothed a hand over my hair. "I'm making it official soon anyway."

"Five years later?" He smiled into his menu. "I'd say it's about time."

He saw right through my fib. Well, just for that, maybe I *would* finally start the paperwork and even send out an office-wide e-mail to start addressing me as Mrs. Wilson. She sounded like a better fit for the suburbs anyway.

"You're obviously a regular here," I said. "What's good?"

"I know just the thing." He took my menu and set it on the edge of the table. I was about to object, but the excitement in his eyes stopped me.

While he ordered for us, I took a large gulp of water, hoping it would extinguish the heat David's nearness inspired. Ice water coated my insides. Suddenly, my white, form-fitting blouse didn't seem so conservative. Nor did my skirt, as I remembered how David had scanned my bare knees and followed my curves with his eyes.

I swallowed, my scalp warming. I had to remember

why we were here—business. "So, David. Tell me about yourself. What do you do in your spare time?"

"I keep pretty busy with work."

"But you must blow off steam somehow?"

"I sail," he said. "And swim whenever I get the chance."

Wet. Shirtless. I shook my head. Was there a swimmer's body under that perfect suit?

He leaned his elbows on the table. "How about you," he paused, his eyes concentrated on me, "*O-liv-ia?*"

"This interview isn't about me."

"I didn't realize the interview had begun."

"We're on the record," I said, reaching into my purse for a pen. "Are any topics off limits? Work, travel . . ." I kept my eyes down to hide my reddening cheeks as I broached the aspect of his life that—infuriatingly—most interested me. "Love?"

"I'll make you a deal," he said, his eyes narrowed as I opened my notepad on the table. "You can ask me any question you want. No restrictions. All in the name of research."

I bit my lip. Where my interview process ended and my personal interest in him began, I had no idea. This meant I wouldn't have to make that distinction. "What's the catch?" I asked.

"You have to answer the question, too."

Ah. For David to offer that deal, he must've seen how uncomfortable his questions made me.

I realized I was playing with my earring when he glanced at it. He reached out and took my wrist, tugged my hand away, and placed it on the table. "I don't want to make you nervous." His palm warmed the back of my hand. "I'm just curious about you. So, I told you a couple of my hobbies. What're yours?"

I could so easily flip my hand and take David's, link our fingers together, smooth my palm over the calluses I was sure he had from his hobbies and profession.

Those were all reasons to pull away. I slid my hand from under his and picked up my pen to make notes.

Maybe David could see I didn't open up easily, but what he didn't know was that I'd worked hard to build these walls around my heart, and nobody, not even him, could bring them down over one lunch. "Also work," I answered.

"I didn't say work was my hobby, although I love my job. If work is yours, why? Do you ever write for the magazine?"

"When I need to," I said. "I prefer editing."

He arched an eyebrow. "Now we're getting somewhere."

I almost laughed. "Are we? Why?"

"Most people I know want to be writers. It's romantic, esteemed. Writers get the glory—but editors . . . very rarely do they get the credit they deserve."

I glanced at the table. David had unknowingly just described much more than my career. That was my *life*. My mother, a combustible artist, an award-winning novelist, loved the spotlight and knew how to put on a show, even when things crumbled behind the scenes.

That would never be me.

I held concepts and storylines and sentences together. Yet, I'd been unable to keep my family from falling apart.

"Or maybe there's more to it than that," David suggested, staring at my mouth. He didn't hide his longing. What was it he craved? Did he want to . . . kiss me?

He licked his lips.

No.

This surpassed *want*. He yearned. What for?

A peck on the cheek? To slide his tongue along the seam of my lips?

Maybe it wasn't that innocent. Maybe he imagined my nude lips wrapped around his finger. Or my *plump, dark,* Ruby Red mouth, my Malbec-coated tongue, sucking until lipstick smeared all over his . . .

I vaulted back in the booth, knocked breathless by my uncharacteristically sordid thoughts. I wasn't the type to get caught up in a fantasy, even in the dark. Much less in the middle of the day.

I forced myself back to our conversation—equally dangerous, but less likely to spur one of us to jump across the table and devour the other.

Something told me that the more I withheld from David, the harder he'd pry, so I volunteered something harmless. "Editing is methodical," I explained.

He nodded, but his eyes remained on my mouth.

"Like a puzzle. There are rules, and—do I have lipstick on my teeth?"

His eyes darted up to mine. "No. Sorry. I heard every word. Editing soothes you. Writing scares you."

"That's not what I s—"

"What do you do for *fun*, Olivia?"

I sighed, slightly frustrated, mostly resigned. "I also volunteer at my local animal shelter most weekends."

He crossed his arms on the table. "Do you have a pet?"

"No, I just love animals." I bit my lip as I gave in to a smile. "I want a dog, but it's not the right time."

"Maybe in the suburbs," he said evenly, not quite serious, but not teasing, either.

I nodded slowly. "Maybe. How about you?"

He glanced into his water glass, then picked it up. "Our family dog, Canyon, is sick. It's been tough on everyone."

So David was close enough with his family to share

concern over their pet and possibly consider it his own. "I'm sorry."

I wanted to ask more, but getting deeper into topics irrelevant to the article meant getting to know him better for no reason. And answering more questions about myself, too.

The waiter set down two stacked burgers with leafy side salads. My stomach grumbled, and I wasted no time diving in. I'd almost finished my salad when I glanced up.

David grinned. "You eat salad like it's your last meal."

"My dad always made me eat my salad before I got to the good stuff, so I'm used to inhaling it."

"You know your dad isn't here, right?"

"It sounds stupid when I say it out loud. But it's a good habit, so why break it?"

"Italians often serve salad after the main courses," he said.

"Doesn't work for me," I said, chewing. I shook my head. "After a burger, I usually just want a nap."

He laughed. "Interesting."

"What is?"

"Just soaking up everything I can before you cut me off."

I paused and casually stabbed the last bite of lettuce with my fork, suddenly conscious of my eating habits. My notepad still had only three words.

Hobbies: sailing, swimming,

"You've worked at Pierson/Greer eight years, right?" I asked.

"Ah, so you at least looked me up this time."

I took a bite of my hamburger, and my eyes rolled to the back of my head with a mouthful of juicy patty, grilled onions and mushrooms, creamy avocado, and tangy sauce. "Wow."

"That's a look of pure satisfaction." Before I could stop him, he reached over and swiped a smear of sauce from the corner of my lips with his thumb. "Sweet," he murmured.

My cheeks warmed at his overt display, and I picked a paper napkin from a dispenser to wipe my mouth. "Is Arnaud married?" I asked to keep us on topic. "Single?"

David licked his thumb. "Why? Are you considering him for the article also?"

I almost choked. Creepy lingering stares didn't sell magazines. "God, no."

He laughed. "Arnaud's single. Eternally."

"Must be a hazard of the job," I said, chancing a glance at David from under my lashes. He'd said something similar on the balcony about not having time for women. If I could get him to open up without technically *asking*, then I wouldn't have to reciprocate, right?

"It is," he said. "We work constantly. Developing a meaningful relationship takes time we don't have."

"I get that," I said. "The firm's always sending Bill out of town since we're in the no-kids club."

"Right." David glanced away. "Women say they can handle my schedule, but they always want more."

I tilted my head. "We should leave that out of the article. If you're not ready to give more—"

"I am." His eyes returned to mine with renewed heat. "Like I said in the car, I'm not just ready to give more. I have everything to give—to the right woman."

To a lucky *woman.*

The unbidden thought disturbed me. *I* was lucky. I'd found everything I'd wanted in a partner in Bill. He was what I'd asked for. Calm. Safe. Easy to get along with. Thoughtful. Loving. And David was everything I pushed away. Passion. Heat. Unknown. Risk.

"Is that why you agreed to do the issue?" I asked. "To find something . . . meaningful? Someone to give your all?"

He examined his plate and looked up. "No. That's not really why I decided to play along . . . there was a much larger factor."

His expectant look dared me to ask what that was. Would he go through all this just to spend time with me? After his forwardness at Lucy's party and since, it wouldn't be far-fetched for him to admit that.

But if so, it was better left unsaid.

I continued chowing down, eschewing any chance at keeping it cool. It was too hard not to make a spectacle while plate-licking-good sauce dripped down my hands, and I chased slippery avocado into my mouth. "Next, I'd ask about college," I said. "You went to Yale for under-grad, then Architectural Association in London."

He nodded. "And you?"

"That wasn't a question—I already knew." I smirked. "So I don't have to reciprocate."

"Notre Dame," he said.

I stopped chewing and swallowed. "When you take an interest in something, you don't really hold back, do you?"

"Now you're catching on." His eyes gleamed. "I know where, but I don't know why. What took you there?"

"Legacy," I said. "I grew up in Dallas but my father went to Notre Dame."

"Mine, too. What are the chances?" His dimples deep-ened with a large smile. "Wonder if they know each other. And your mom?"

"A novelist," I said. "Or she was. She hasn't put a book out in years. I'd assume her publisher dropped her, but if they had, my dad and I would've heard about it non-stop."

He inclined his head to catch my eye. "Divorced?"

I nodded. "Right before I entered high school."

"That must have been hard."

Hard didn't begin to describe. My father couldn't leave Dallas because of work, but he'd relocated us to a different part of the city immediately, practically overnight. I'd started high school with no friends, no mom, and no understanding of my social status. I'd had no one to show me how to pick out clothes as my body changed or apply makeup to my angry, teenage skin. All the while undergoing a six-month-long custody battle where lawyers probed at me, child protective services asked questions I didn't know how to answer, and people tried to make me choose between my parents.

I shrugged as casually as I could, wiping away the threatening memories as I dabbed my mouth with my napkin. "Is high school easy for anyone?"

David cleared his throat. "I suppose not."

What was I thinking? He was not my audience. I couldn't imagine someone like David Dylan ever experiencing an excruciating lunch period of not knowing where to sit or who to avoid. Of finally sitting down and being asked by a group of strangers if the rumor was true that my own parent had tried to murder me.

And then, upon learning that wasn't true, watching as the excitement in their faces had quickly turned to boredom.

"High school was a breeze for you, wasn't it?" I asked.

"I have only fond memories," he said. "But that doesn't mean I can't be a good listener."

"A good listener?" I asked.

"What was it like for you? Not easy. I can see it on your face."

Damn it. He picked up on too much. I wasn't used to that. I had to be *vigilant* about schooling my expression around him. "I have fond memories, too," I said. "My best friend convinced her mom to let her and her older brother transfer to my high school during my sophomore year. Their parents are divorced, so they understood. The three of us are still very close."

David tapped his chin. "Since Lucy told me you two met at Notre Dame, you must be talking about Gretchen."

Nothing got by him. Then again, Gretchen was hard to forget. I wondered if he'd noticed her at dinner, too. I still hated the thought of them hitting it off, but I had no claim over David, and he would've been a good match for her. "I can introduce you if you want," I said.

"I've met her." His gaze intensified. "If you could go anywhere in the world, where would you choose?"

"My turn again? I don't know," I said. "I'm not writing this article about myself, anyway, and so far you've only told me things I could've found online."

As if he hadn't heard the second half of my statement, he half-smiled. "You *do* know where you'd go," he said. "Where?"

"I don't have time to think about that." I shifted in the leather booth. "Bill doesn't like big vacations."

"That's a shame. He's missing out on surfing perfect breaks in Bali, gorging on oysters in Montauk, late-night, winter-time hot-tubbing with a view of the Swiss Alps . . ." He sighed happily. "Nothing to dislike about *my* vacations."

Wet. Shirtless. Surfboard. Aphrodisiacs. Snowy mountains through the steam . . .

What girl could resist any of that with a god like David? But that was clearly a fantasy. No way he'd done all that. What about work? Obligations? Money?

Were there places I wanted to see? Of course. Bill and I really hadn't taken an international trip in years. There was no use in daydreaming about it now, though.

"Whatever place you're hiding in your head, you'll get

there," David said. "You seem like a girl who knows what she wants."

"I'm hardly a girl," I bristled.

"How old are you, anyway?"

"Well, Mr. Dylan." I moved my elbows to the table. "I reckon that's not a very polite question."

"I see. Is politeness something you look for in a gentleman?"

I twisted my lips. "Is that not a *defining characteristic* of the gentleman?"

"Touché. Is politeness something you look for in a *man*?"

My smile wavered. He was a man if I ever saw one. Unruffled by anything, chivalrous, inquisitive. He'd barely taken his eyes off me the entire meal, not even when the red-lipped hostess had stopped by to check on us.

"Come on. I'm here to find out what *you're* looking for in a *woman*," I reminded him, folding my hands. "Not the other way around."

"I could tell you, down to the color of her eyes, my perfect woman," he said, shifting to get out a leather billfold. "But that would end the interview here, and we're just getting started. Let's head over to the hotel."

"I can expense lunch—Beman's delighted we're doing this," I said, reaching into my handbag.

His expression sobered as he picked up the check. "Lunch is on me. This time together is ours, and only ours. When you're with me, no other man will ever pay my bill."

My heart skipped with his declaration. By *no other man*, I suspected he didn't mean Beman. And he didn't mean money literally, either, but time.

My time with David belonged only to David.

He had a possessive side, and over someone who didn't even remotely belong to him.

It should've opened my eyes to the fact that even a simple lunch was dangerous territory for us. David's company today had been far too natural, his questions too spot-on, his observations welcome when with anyone else, I would've shied away.

It was just one more thing to feel confused about.

Chapter Twelve

David's hotel overlooked the Chicago River. He and I walked from the restaurant, winding our way along the water in easy silence.

Fluffy, dense clouds spotted the sky, passing over the high sun. The river gleamed with the reflection of light, as if covered in gold sequins.

You are KILLING me in that gold dress, honeybee.

David's inappropriate text about my dress shivered through me. I'd been likened to an owl before by my father, for wide, curious eyes he'd said I'd had since childhood. But I'd never had a pet name like *honeybee*. Innocent—yet sexy, only because it had come from David.

"That's it," David said, nodding ahead. I tilted my gaze back and took in the imposing building. Gray slate made up the lobby's exterior, while the guest rooms from that point up were silver, mirrored glass. The building defied physics by curving outward along one side, dipping in, and then bowing out again slightly in the shape of the letter "B".

"What do you think?" he asked.

"Wow," I murmured. "It's something else."

"Is that good?"

I turned to face him. There was no humor in his expression. "Do you really need me to tell you it's good?" I asked.

"I really need that, yes."

I looked back, squinting against the sun. "I love how the glass reflects the blue of the sky and the water, but also the sun. Against the stone slabs—both smooth and sharp, it's almost—fluid? It's perfect for the waterfront, yet it stands out . . ." I blinked rapidly, no idea what I was saying. I didn't really have the right vocabulary for this. "But you're the architect. You should be the one telling me."

He shook his head quickly. "I love seeing it through your eyes. I put a lot into this, but I can't control how people interpret it. What you feel looking at it could never be wrong." He stuck his hands into his pockets and started toward the entrance while I stared after him. "Coming?"

I could easily listen to him go on about his work as if it were art, and it clearly was.

I had to take long strides to catch up to him.

Large palm trees sprung from the ground, greeting us as they lined the walkway. "These are unexpected," I said.

"This will all be grass." He motioned toward the empty lots by the entrance. His face lit up. "And the lobby opens up. These glass doors slide open during the warmer months."

I walked over and touched the stone at one corner, smooth to the eye but coarse and uneven under my palm. Clean gray edges and long rectangular windows that reflected blue sky structured the front of the hotel, ocean waves crashing and foaming on black sand beaches.

He slid open one of the floor-to-ceiling doors and motioned me through. "Welcome to The Revelin."

"Dave," a man called from across the hollowed-out space.

"I can't get a second," David said with a smile. "Excuse me."

While they spoke, I wandered the room, envisioning what it would become. It wasn't much to see because of the construction, but windows filled the future lobby with sunlight.

I looked back at David. Three people surrounded him now, each one looking to him for something. His presence at my office had been strong, but it grew here in his element, even in all the empty space.

He stopped talking suddenly and searched the area until he spotted me. That new, yet somehow familiar, tether pulled between us. Just like when we'd met eyes at the theater. He held my gaze, a language only we spoke that said more than words could. It had to. Whatever draw existed between us shouldn't be made real by anything said aloud.

David came directly to me, leaving behind questioning faces. "Are you okay?" he asked as he approached.

Was I? His attention was like a drug, catapulting me to terrifying heights with each hit. What would happen when he took it away? I'd fall—and smack against the concrete of reality. Even if I had to be the one forced to break the connection. Because it *would* be broken at some point.

David exhaled a breath and touched my upper arm. "I understand," he said, squeezing my shoulder. Heat seared through my blouse, stinging the flesh directly beneath it. His broad shoulders shielded anyone who might be watching our restrained contact. I wanted nothing more than to step into him. Feel that same heat pooling in my tummy against my cheek, my breasts, under my hands.

My gut smarted—even this was too close for us. Any

nearer, and I didn't trust myself not to forget the consequences and fall into him.

The creases in his face deepened. "I don't want to push you," he said, dropping his arm. "You need to make your own decisions."

His insinuation jarred me back to the moment. "Decisions?" I repeated, frowning. "I made my decisions years ago."

"Nothing is permanent, Olivia. I know what's happening here is sudden, but believe it or not, I'm biting my tongue. If you weren't married, you and I would be on a different path. At Lucy's party, I would've—"

"Don't," I rushed out. "It doesn't matter." My chest constricted as I tried and failed to catch a deep breath. What was he saying—or not saying? Bill and I had history. I'd barely *met* David. "There are no decisions. No options. No confessions. If we want to have any type of friendship, I need you to understand—"

"I do," he said, shoving his hands back into his pockets. "I understand."

"No, you don't. That text the other night—what if Bill had seen it? And now you're going to be working with Lucy, too?"

"Is that a problem?"

"I haven't told her about the article yet."

He cocked his head. "Why not?"

His infuriatingly kind yet astute eyes bored into me, mining for answers whether I wanted to give them or not. I turned away. "I don't know."

"Yes, you do, Olivia. You haven't told her because just being in the same room with me feels like you're doing something wrong." He stepped forward. "And you're going to tell me that doesn't mean something?"

It *shouldn't*. I was married—and David? I had a feeling

he'd meant something to half of Chicago's female population at one point or another. I balled my fists and faced him. "I'm going to tell you that it doesn't *matter* what it means. There's no scenario in which I sacrifice a perfect marriage for a playboy I met five minutes ago."

I went to go around him, but he took my arm, pulling me close. "A perfect marriage?" He chuckled something dark. "Now I know you're living in a fantasy."

I whipped my gaze to meet his, a spark igniting between us. "You don't know anything about my life."

"Wrong. A perfect marriage doesn't exist. My parents are the happiest couple I know, and even they have flaws. If you think yours is perfect, it's because you've crafted it that way. Molded it. But just because you ignore the cracks doesn't mean they don't exist. This foundation you're standing on? I had to repair it because the previous owner ignored the cracks too long and did extensive damage."

My heart raced as he unfurled the truth before my eyes. It wasn't as if that was some huge revelation, though. "I'm not some project of yours. This is my life. A life I put together because it's the life I want. I *chose* this."

"Well, I'm sorry, but I'm not going to stand here and play a fucking role in that act like everyone else," he said. "You've surrounded yourself with people who let you get away with it, including your husband. It sounds to me like he lets you walk all over him. That's not me, Olivia."

I nearly vibrated. Bill had chosen this, too. I did *not* walk all over him. But the way Bill and I were—I knew instinctively that David would never put up with it. "And it never will be."

"If you're determined to live a lie, then no, it won't," he said. "What's happening between us is real. You can run away, but that won't change anything."

I jerked my arm, but he held it just firmly enough to keep me from fleeing. "Let me go."

"We're not finished here," he said. "Walk across the room. Get on the elevator. We're going up to the roof to finish our interview."

I sucked in a breath as my knees weakened with his commands. It wasn't only indignation reverberating through me, but also arousal for the way he spoke to me. The way *nobody* spoke to me. My brain fought my body's urges to obey. To do anything he said, to please him, to relinquish the control I'd held so tightly for so long.

God, I'd fought *damn* hard to gain and keep control in every aspect of my life—how could I possibly want to give it all up to David in this moment? And how did he know I needed that?

He released my arm, looking me over. "Go."

He expected me to do exactly as I was told. Dared me to find out what would happen if I refused.

I turned and walked through the scaffolding and over to the hoist, my breath coming fast, excited.

He met me there and handed me a conspicuous red hardhat.

I wrinkled my nose at it and then looked up at him in full pout mode. My hair didn't need another reason to act out.

But with his stern expression, and the thrilling demands he'd just made of me echoing through my mind, I placed it on my head.

I stepped in the cage, testing the sturdiness of it. He followed a second later, and it jolted to life, carrying us up.

David leaned down and spoke near my ear. "And if you call me a playboy one more time, Olivia—I'm going to put you over my knee."

Desire exploded in my stomach, my heart pounding.

He would . . . he would *spank* me? I was certain I'd never been more turned on than I was in that moment. But why? I'd never fantasized about being spanked.

"You wouldn't," I breathed, barely recognizing my breathy voice.

"Try me."

When the car stopped, David sauntered onto the rooftop with complete aplomb, as if he hadn't just turned my world upside down and lit a fire in me without so much as a touch.

My feet followed him, my mind too stunned to protest. I tried to focus on what he was saying.

"This outdoor space will be accessible to the guests in the penthouse suite," he explained. A breeze passed over us, and I stepped into sunshine for warmth. "This gutted area, next to the deck, will be a private infinity pool. It has a glass bottom so you can see into it from the suite."

I followed the line to the edge. A small part of the pool would jut out from the building, hanging over the side.

"It's cantilevered so you can swim out and over the city. Listen," he warned, "as you can see, there's no barrier, so keep back. I just wanted you to see the view."

I rotated to take in all of the Chicago skyline, lit by the brilliant sun, then edged closer to the side, exhilarated to be high above everything—and completely alone with David. The heat of his palm remained on my shoulder, my skin still buzzing from his touch, my mind reeling at the thought of that same hand warming my backside.

What was I thinking? What was I *doing*?

I didn't want to force the thoughts away or lose this dangerous feeling.

I craned my neck and stepped forward.

What would it take to feel him again, to get that rush

of electricity? I rolled on the balls of my feet. *Lean just a little more . . .*

He gently tugged me back. Chills broke out over my skin, his touch so stimulating, it should have some kind of knob so I could turn it down.

"It's . . ." I looked out at the water, trying to find the words.

"Humbling," he finished.

There wasn't anyone else in our world, not one person who could see us on our glass mountain. The breeze kicked up, blowing my hair in my face. I removed the hardhat and tucked it under my arm to smooth some strands away.

As David took in the view, I couldn't not look up at him. Out here, away from prying eyes, I could stare. I got my fill. I gave in, despite the fact that I'd just told him to cool it.

Another whip of wind blew more strands into my lip gloss. The air crackled with a charge that quickened my breath.

Finally, David lowered his eyes to mine and wet his lips so quickly, I almost missed it. My yearning to know how his mouth would feel on my skin *had* to be written on my face. Any woman who looked as I must have right then knew exactly what she was doing.

David's impassive expression did nothing to slow my heartbeat. He was going to kiss me. I had to speak up. Stop him. Stop *myself*. My breath shallowed in anticipation. I leaned in, complicit. Guilty. Wanting. I didn't care what the consequences were, I needed his lips to land on mine. I needed him to quiet the kaleidoscope of butterflies taking over my stomach.

The wind lashed violently, whistling around us. David flinched and turned his head, squinting somewhere beyond us.

The helmet slipped from my grip and bounced on the ground.

He swooped and grasped it effortlessly, handing it to me. "Don't take that off again," he said, avoiding my eyes.

As the moment faded, my sense returned—this time, tinged with irritation that I'd not only submitted to David's commands but had been about to give in in an irreversible way. And that David *hadn't*.

"From now on, we conduct these interviews at my office," I said.

"That won't be necessary."

"No?" I asked. "Why not?"

"You don't have to worry about us being alone. I'd never kiss a married woman."

His abruptness momentarily stole my response. "Then you will never kiss *me*."

A slow grin spread across his face. "I wouldn't be so sure."

I curled my hand into a fist. "We won't *ever* be alone again. If you can't respect that, then I'll pull you from the article. Even if it costs me the promotion."

I walked away and left him staring after me.

Chapter Thirteen

By Chicago's standards—or, at least, compared to my seven-hundred square foot one-bedroom in Lincoln Park—Mack and Davena owned a small mansion. In their townhome in the Gold Coast Historic District, I sat on a plush, ivory, cabriole sofa that brought the eighteenth-century-fashion room into the present.

I held a mug of tea, leaning against shiny pillows with gold tassels, as Davena stood over me. She studied the *Just Listed* postcard I'd taken from the Oak Park house Bill and I had seen over the weekend.

"It's lovely," she decided with a firm nod. "I agree with your realtor. I think the neighborhood is great for a young couple."

"Bill really likes it." I sipped my spiced chai. I tried to visit Davena often—especially when my thoughts weighed heavy. As my godparents, she and Mack knew me better than most. And that was lucky, because Davena always gave great advice.

"I'm on the fence," I admitted.

"Why's that?"

"I guess it just doesn't feel like the right place. Across the street, there's this *terrible* home—"

Her eyebrows shot up. "As in dangerous?"

"No, no. I mean run-down, overgrown, probably a hazard. But . . . the bones are amazing. It has lots of potential. And character. I shouldn't like it, but I do." I indicated the postcard. "This house, though—it didn't inspire anything for me. And maybe that's a good thing? To feel emotionally detached about a decision like this? Bill isn't, though. He has his heart set on it."

She sighed loudly. "Well, sometimes you have to compromise a bit."

I cupped my hands around the steaming mug. "But I'm already compromising."

"How?"

I pursed my lips. "I'm not ready to leave the city. I'm happy here."

"But you won't be far."

"It's not the same to me."

"It wouldn't be to me, either," she said. "Why are you leaving then?"

"Bill's the opposite. He wants something quieter." I scratched under my nose. "And . . . he's ready for, you know . . . the 'B' word."

"Ah. Babies." She handed back the postcard and looked down at me. "You say *he's* ready, which indicates you're not."

"I don't know how to feel," I said. "I don't see myself as a mother, but Bill says that will come. I'm just not able to picture it, so I can't give him the answer he wants. Or *any* answer, really. Did you ever regret not having children?"

"We did have one," she said. "Many years ago—but he didn't make it a day."

I frowned. "I had no idea, Davena. All these years, you've never mentioned him."

"You were a baby when it happened," she said, waving her hand. "God's plan. I just didn't have the heart to try again, and Mack was supportive. Next thing I knew, I was just too old. But no, I don't regret it—kids aren't for everyone." She smiled to herself. "Mack would've made quite a father, though."

She left the room but returned a minute later in just a bra and drawstring pants with a brush in her hand. She teased her short, blonde hair in jerky, upward motions. "You know, not everywhere is going to feel like home right away. It takes time. It's about who you make the home with. With Bill, it doesn't matter where you live. Does it?"

Her brow arched with a question that sounded rhetorical and was surely meant to make me think. I agreed. It didn't matter where we lived, Bill and I *should* be home for each other.

As Davena spoke, I couldn't peel my eyes from the large bandage on her ribcage and the purple bruise spreading from both ends of it.

She stopped brushing and dropped her hand to her side to catch her breath. After a moment, she sat down next to me. "The doctor's not optimistic, Liv." Her sunken eyes twinkled anyway. "I've made peace with that, though. And I'm not in much pain. All right?"

For her to admit there was *any* pain, it had to be serious. I balanced my mug on my thigh and reached for her hand. "We should talk about it."

"We should talk about you," she said.

"Davena—"

"Please, dear. Take my mind off death and tell me about life. What's new?"

I couldn't refuse a request like that. "Bill and I are

going away this weekend with Lucy and her fiancé. Bill's been working overtime, so it'll be nice to get a break."

"Wonderful idea. Show that Bill of yours how much you appreciate his hard work." She lowered her voice. "Get yourself over to La Perla before you go. Look for Alejandro. He's gorgeous, but he knows shit about lingerie." She patted my hand, then waved hers. "So when you're done looking at him, ask for Joanne. Tell her to put it on my account."

I laughed. "I can't remember the last time I spent money on good lingerie."

"No? I still do all the time." She leaned forward to where I'd placed my handbag on the coffee table. The spec-sheet our realtor had given me along with the post-card stuck out from the bag. "May I?"

I nodded. Davena unfolded the paper, turning it over to see more pictures. "It's a nice, easy house. What exactly is it you don't care for?"

I glanced over the interior photos. "I just didn't get a gut reaction. You know, when something feels right?"

She cocked her head. "Is that usually how you operate? Off your gut? You've always seemed more practical than that."

I nodded slowly. "My father is practical . . ."

"And Leanore is as irrational as they come," Davena completed my thought.

"There isn't room for two of my mother in any family."

"I agree," Davena said. "But why the sudden need to trust your instinct over your sense? This isn't about finding the right house, Liv. If it were, you'd be able to step back and see that this"—she handed me the flyer—"is perfectly fine. So what else is going on?"

I fidgeted with one corner of the page. "Once I make

this decision, then Bill and I will go down a path I can't come back from."

"You can always come back," Davena said gently. "If there's one thing I've learned, it's that nothing is permanent. There's always time to start over, especially at your age."

"But if I'm already thinking of starting over, then I don't think that's a good sign."

"You can't stay in limbo, Liv." She took my hand. "I drive Mack crazy the way I bounce from thing to thing. I constantly make mistakes—sometimes they pay off, but I never regret them. I do the best I can with the information I have. But you only have one shot at life, Olivia, and take it from me, you don't want to miss anything. If you want something, say it out loud."

I looked at her frail but manicured hand on mine. If *my* life were ending, would I even think to do my nails?

For Bill, the question wasn't *if*. It was *when*. He'd offered me the only thing I'd wanted—security. Had he recognized the risk in me, or had I made him feel safe, too? Could I take that from him without becoming someone I resented as much as my mother?

I'd entered my marriage sure I'd be ready for all of this one day. But *one day* still seemed so far away. Buying the house meant I was all in on our future. I'd be trading the city and my freedom to be a wife and mother.

"And if what I want—or don't want—would hurt others . . .?" I heard myself ask Davena. "Break promises? Destroy lives?"

"That's something only you can answer," she said.

Her eyes lingered on mine a moment while her words hung in the air. Perhaps sensing that I wouldn't—couldn't —answer just then, she looked away. "Listen, sweetie. Can

I keep this spec-sheet? I know Mack would love to put in his two cents."

"Of course. Bill has one up on the refrigerator," I said, setting my tea on a coaster as I stood. "I'd better get home."

She walked me to the door, kissed me on the cheek, and hesitated. "If you'd asked me years ago if a person's own happiness was worth destroying many others', I might've paused. But now, knowing my time here is limited . . . you can't hide from your desires. You can suppress them, ignore them, maybe even kill them off. But they'll stay buried and rotting inside you." She drew back to look me in the eye. "What kind of person will that make you over time?"

My throat closed. I'd seen firsthand what rotting emotions could do to a person. To a marriage. To the lives of the people you loved.

Even when Davena had revealed her diagnosis to me, her expression hadn't been so grave.

Everything I'd asked for, wished for, worked for, stood within reach. To say that any of this had fallen in my lap would be a lie. I'd chosen Bill. I'd willingly started down the path I was on.

To walk away from it all for the unknown? To turn my back on a perfect house for one that might have a faulty foundation with deepening cracks, that could be moments from crumbling—and expect an architect with nothing invested and even less to lose to swoop in and fix it?

I'd be a fool to pursue any of that. But after so many years of trying to keep every hair in place, and the sudden, growing feeling that I might be trapped . . . maybe foolishness was the only way out.

Chapter Fourteen

I walked through the doorway of Lucy's small but organized office—and froze, one foot in the room. My best friend, my *engaged* friend, kneeled in front of a man in a tuxedo, her hand inside his pant leg.

A man who, known for his bachelorhood and playboy ways, was likely all too familiar with his current view.

Even with his back to me, I recognized the broad shoulders, jet-black hair, and towering height before me.

"I'm sorry," I said, retreating. "Your receptionist said—"

Lucy peeked out from behind his leg. "Come in, come in," she said around a pin stuck between her teeth. "David, you remember—"

"Olivia," he said and turned his head over his shoulder to meet my gaze.

How had he known? The man had a sixth sense for me. I had one for him, too, evidenced by the way I'd felt him at the restaurant opening a couple weeks earlier before I'd even laid eyes on him.

My surprise must've shown on my face.

"With a voice like that," he said, angling to give me his profile, "I'd know her anywhere."

I touched my neck. I'd met with another bachelor that afternoon who'd said my "rasp" reminded him of Lauren Bacall.

With a measured step into the room, I set my purse and some work I'd brought for the weekend on a chair. Normally, I would've kicked off my heels and curled up with *Vogue* while Lucy finished. But the pair of sky-high YSL pumps on my feet suddenly felt wasted on anyone who wasn't the god before me, so I left them on.

Lucy removed the pin to stick it in David's pant leg, then gasped. "I just had the best idea," she said, glancing up at David—and up and up. "Olivia's in the running for a competitive promotion at work. She's looking for bachelors for *Chicago M* magazine's 'Most Eligible' feature. David, since you're such a popular bachelor, maybe . . ."

David arched an eyebrow at me.

"Actually, David already agreed to do it," I said. "It turns out, Diane had reached out to him."

"Of course she did." Lucy beamed. "David must be the most eligible bachelor in all of Chicago. You'll be great, David," she said, and added, "and now that I'm your personal stylist, best dressed to boot."

"Thank you, Lucy," he said, his ridiculously deep voice rumbling through the small space.

"I'm sorry, Liv," Lucy said. "I know we're supposed to leave in fifteen minutes, but David had a sartorial emergency."

"Black-tie gala at the Museum of Contemporary Art tonight," he explained, "and my Prada tux is at my New York apartment. I didn't mean to keep you."

"Not at all," Lucy said. "Liv and I have a double date this weekend up at Andrew's parents' cabin on the lake.

Andrew and Bill—Liv's husband—are picking us up on the way out of town." Lucy stood, brushing off her dress. "I'll be right back. Make yourself comfortable, Liv."

She rushed out, leaving David and me in complete silence.

David rotated to face me. I stayed across the room, as far as I could get, resisting the infuriating urge to be near him. To go to him. If he commanded me again the way he'd sent me to the lift at the construction site—I worried I'd be unable to resist.

"I'm surprised to see you," he said finally.

"Last time we spoke, you forbade us from being alone." I crossed my arms. "I didn't know you'd be here."

"That's too bad." His eyes scanned over me. "I'd kind of hoped you'd worn that outfit for me."

I inhaled under his perusal, willing myself not to react. A snakeskin belt cinched the waist of my fitted black dress, giving the illusion of curves. The neckline scooped, revealing a small glimpse of cleavage. I was wearing higher-than-usual pumps, but they matched the belt—unavoidable. With the four-inch boost, I figured my lips would come right up to his neck, or maybe just past, to his chin . . .

"If you expect me to behave, don't wear things like that," he said and opened his arms to display a classic black and white tuxedo. "What do you think?" he asked. "Does it suit me?"

My fingers curled into fists. My cheeks burned. He was so goddamn beautiful. Why did he have to be *so* beautiful? I could throw caution and sense aside and run and leap into his arms. Cover his face with kisses. Linger on the soft spots and *relish* the coarse ones. Press my willing self against his hard body, locking my snakeskins around his lower back so we were perfectly aligned . . .

I blinked, forcing myself from the fantasy. "It—it needs tailoring," I said, bridling the heat rising in me.

He moved in front of a floor-length mirror. "Agreed."

My eyes darted to a rolling rack with four crisp ensembles. "Are these all yours?"

"My event starts in an hour. Lucy had these on hand and pulled them all to see what would work."

Lucy's heels clicked in the hallway, muting once she hit the carpeted office. "They're leftover rentals from a Chicago Bears event," she said behind me. "David's got a similar build to a couple of the players. Not a perfect solution, but it works in a pinch."

Lucy went to the rolling rack and removed a different tux. She practically pushed David into a curtained off area. "Try this one," she said. "If it doesn't work, I'll have to fix the hem of the one you're wearing real quick." She gave him a dress shirt. "And the shirt you're wearing is too tight. This should fit better."

I perched at the edge of Lucy's desk, fingering my earlobe as she bustled around me. Behind the curtain just feet away, David shed one suit for another. Those long fingers undoing his buttons, hard muscles too big for a dress shirt that fit a *football* player.

I closed my eyes and heaved a deep sigh. *Get it under control.*

"What do you feel like?" Lucy asked.

I frowned at her. "Huh?"

"For dinner?" She lowered her voice. "There's a great pizza spot Andrew and I usually stop at on the way to the cabin."

"Um." I rubbed my eyebrow. "Bill won't want to splurge on eating out."

"Oh, I'd hardly call it a splurge," she said.

"Me neither," I agreed, but I knew my husband. Bill

had learned thriftiness from his parents, and he remained careful with every dollar, even though we'd never hurt for money. Especially now that he was making far more than he had in the public sector.

"I'll convince him," Lucy said with a firm nod.

David stepped out, closing up his dress shirt, each button swallowing a little more of his tanned chest.

"Oh, David," Lucy said as he shrugged on the blazer. "You look *dashing*."

David straightened his shoulders in the mirror and tugged on the sleeves. His hair was like black marble, styled into a sophisticated, shiny ripple, less tousled than normal.

My throat dried. I swallowed. Our back-and-forth from lunch filtered through my head. Standing tall in the urbane tux, he looked every bit the refined gentleman.

And gentleman becomes him.

When Lucy was occupied pinning again, I glanced at David's black American Express on the desk beside me. The invite-only card had monthly fees in the thousands.

Exactly how much do architects make?

The desk vibrated under my thighs. David's phone lit up, and the name *Brittany* bannered across the screen. He didn't make any effort to move or see who was calling, so I didn't mention it. *Brittany* didn't exactly sound like a pressing matter if you asked me.

"I brought snacks." A cheery voice entered the room before Lucy's assistant did. Kimmie backed into the office and she turned to show off a haphazard tray of items she'd clearly found around the office breakroom. "Goldfish, apples, Go-Gurt, croissants—from this morning but I think they're still fresh . . ." Kimmie nodded as she named each thing on the tray. With a goofy smile plastered on her face, she set it on the coffee table and turned to David. She cleared her throat, trying to catch his eye in the reflection.

"Um, is this all right, Mr. Dylan? Would you prefer something else? Coffee?"

"I can't move," he said, nodding his head down toward Lucy.

"Oh, of course—what can I bring?" Kimmie nodded enthusiastically, picking up the tray.

"No, that's all right," he said when she started toward him. "I'll grab a Go-Gurt later."

I stifled a giggle, wondering if women were always this eager around him.

"Oh." She set it down again. "Well, if you need anything—"

"I'll take an apple," I said.

Kimmie motioned toward the tray on her way out the door. "All yours."

David grinned, but silence fell over the room in her wake.

"So, Liv." Lucy glanced at me and resumed pinning. "Do you think you'll get the promotion? Are you nervous?"

"I'm optimistic," I said.

"It's my favorite time of year," Lucy said. "Liv gets to work with all these hot guys while I live vicariously through her." She blushed as she smiled. "Don't tell Andrew."

"Women, too," I clarified.

David stared at his reflection, his smile gone.

"I don't care about the women," Lucy declared. "Who else are you interviewing?"

"Actually," I said, "I just got back from meeting with Brian Ayers."

David's gaze shifted to mine. "Brian?"

"Yes." I smiled. "Thank you for giving me his name. He's *perfect* for the piece."

"Perfect?" David's eyes narrowed on me. "I offered you

an introduction in place of my spot. I didn't give you his contact inform—"

"Hold still, David," Lucy said. "I might accidentally stab you!"

"He's a freelance photographer," I told Lucy, "and one of the most charming men I've ever met. Really interesting guy—beguiling, actually. Don't tell, but he fed me wine and cheese."

"While you're working?" Lucy asked.

"You went to his apartment?" David asked.

I met his eyes in the reflection. "Yep."

"How do you know him?" Lucy asked David.

"We've been friends a while." I thought I detected a hint of a growl, but I couldn't be sure.

"So, what do you think, David?" Lucy asked, looking up. "Would this Brian guy make a good Bachelor?"

David's nostrils flared, but Lucy didn't notice as she worked intently on the hem of his right pant leg.

"He's . . . he's a good guy," David said with obvious reluctance. "I suppose *some* women might find him attractive."

Lucy's eyes flitted to me. "Is he, Liv?"

Brian, a doppelgänger for Paul Walker, had greeted me with a huge smile, a hug, and compliments before showing me around his studio loft. He'd worn a nice suit but hadn't bothered to even brush his chin-length blond hair. And when he'd crossed an ankle over one knee during our interview, I'd spied colorful, patterned socks.

"He looks like a distinguished beach bum if that makes sense," I said. "Like, I could see him hitting the waves before a board meeting. But he doesn't have board meetings, because he's a photographer. I don't really know how to pin him down, which is why he'll be great for the article. He'll appeal to different demographics."

"Distinguished beach bum." David snorted. "Maybe that should be his headline."

"He sounds great," Lucy said. "I just remembered—David, while I have you trapped here, can we go over a few things? Since we haven't really had a chance to discuss your wardrobe needs at length, would you mind answering some questions?" Lucy pointed behind me. "Liv, grab the sheet from my desk and take notes, please?"

"You're putting me to work?" I asked, picking up a clipboard.

"We're almost done, promise." Her eyes pleaded with me not to be upset.

If she only knew. I could sit and watch this all day.

"So, aside from work and the occasional event—"

"Frequent," David interrupted Lucy. "I have events weekly."

"Right." Lucy nodded. "Frequent events. Aside from that, what else do you need? You mentioned you're a swimmer," she said.

"A sailor," I said and bit my bottom lip when David's gaze shifted to me.

"I do both," he said. "I swim most days to keep in shape."

Swimmer's body. I knew it.

"My free time is limited," he continued. "But I also do some construction on the weekends."

My mouth twitched. Every muscle sculpted by the water. Defined and roughened by hard labor.

He was trying to break me. Between gentleman, swimmer, and construction worker, he was hitting triggers I hadn't even known I'd had.

"Construction for what?" Lucy asked.

"Right now, Arnaud and I are flipping a house in

Evanston—but I don't need an outfit for that." He winked at her. "I just wear an old t-shirt and jeans."

A house flashed across my vision—the magnificent teardown disturbing the perfect neighborhood in which Bill saw us living. Would David have called the house appalling as our relator had?

No. He wouldn't. He'd even told me as much.

You have to get your hands dirty to unearth the good parts. That's work I love to do.

I swallowed down the flush of excitement working its way up my neck and stared hard at the clipboard so David wouldn't notice. Or, more importantly, so *Lucy* wouldn't.

"Do you need, um, new t-shirts?" I asked, scanning the form in front of me. That question wasn't on it, but I couldn't think of anything other than trying to hide my reaction to David. "Or swim trunks? For—for swimming?"

"I'm all set, thanks." A smirk twisted his mouth. "You can put me down for new undergarments, though. Will you make a note of that?"

I raised a scolding brow at him. He thought just because we weren't alone as I'd mandated, we could play?

Game on.

"Boxers? Briefs?" I asked.

"I'm not picky. Why don't you mark down what *you* prefer?" he said.

Lucy glanced up as he continued.

"How about you, Miss Germaine? Anything *you* need?"

"*Mrs.* Germaine—and I'm good," I said, losing the battle against my blushing skin. "Bill has great taste in that department."

Lucy raised her eyebrows at me, and I lowered my gaze, pretending to make notes.

"Ah," David said, his tone lightening. "You know what, there actually *is* something I could use. Shoes. Size fourteen. And a half." His sincere expression didn't hide the gleam in his eyes. "They're hard to find, so don't forget to write that down."

Fourteen-and-a-half? That was . . . unheard of. Sometimes even Bill, a twelve, proved hard to shop for. And if David's shoe size was any indicator of the rest of him . . .

It took me a second to realize I'd dropped my pen.

I could've sworn Lucy sneaked a peek just north of where she was crouched.

"Well." Lucy cleared her throat and stood. "This tux is better, but I still need to let out the pant hem a bit. Your legs are so long! Take these off while I go see if our seam-stress is still here."

She left the room. David turned from the mirror and walked toward me, swiping an apple from the tray on his way. "Do you really think it's wise to go drinking wine in strangers' apartments?"

"I thought you knew Brian."

He stopped a foot from me, tossing and catching the apple in the air. "He's a stranger to you."

"Is he a bad guy?"

"No, but that's not the point." David ran his free hand over his face and exhaled loudly. "And in *that* dress?"

I looked good today, and I knew it, but Brian had only remarked on how well my high cheekbones would photograph.

David was the one who, with a single once-over, made me feel as if I'd be less exposed wearing nothing.

"It's just business," I said.

When he stepped forward and inclined, I stiffened. "Do you really find him attractive?" he asked near my ear, pushing the apple into my hand.

My breath caught, but I managed to compose myself. I shook my head slowly and made eye contact. "I suppose some women might think so," I echoed his words. "But, no. Brian Ayers isn't my type."

David only grunted and picked up his phone from the desk.

When he eased back, only a half a foot from me now, a hint of men's hair product perfumed the air.

Holding the clipboard over my breasts like a shield, I turned the smooth, firm apple over in my hand. "How's Maria?"

"We can call her and ask if you'd like." David arched a scolding eyebrow. "Listen, Olivia. I'll tell you anything you want to know," he said, his words measured. "But after the way you told me to back off on the roof, you're going to have to ask if you expect me to open up."

He'd heard my plea for restraint earlier in the week. I needed to heed my own request. But being bathed in his presence, his hint of cologne, his beauty so *here*, so unavoidable. Our playful banter had me wishing for just a little more time with him.

I looked into the apple, searching for an answer it couldn't give me. I even shook it slightly, hoping for a Magic-Eight-Ball miracle.

David sighed and returned to the changing area, drawing the curtains closed.

The image of Maria's perfectly browned skin and slitted green eyes had haunted me since the night I'd seen her at the restaurant. Did I really need more details to torture myself with?

"So?" he called from the other side of the fabric.

"Okay." I took a bite of the apple and chewed slowly. "You said she was a friend. Is she your *girl*friend?"

"No."

"Do you have sex?"

He chuckled a moment and fell silent. "Yes."

My heart dropped as my insides simultaneously tightened. Of course I'd known the answer, but instead of picturing her underneath him, I thought of myself looking up at him from the bed. I thought of him over me—*fucking*.

Through the tiny sliver where the curtains met, his tan skin flashed as he changed, and my blood coursed a little faster.

"We have an unspoken arrangement. Maria accompanies me to some events." David paused. "We sleep together. But we're not exclusive."

The apple crunched as I took more crisp and juicy bites. "Not exclusive?" I asked after swallowing.

He reentered the room in what I assumed were the suit slacks he'd worn here, his upper half still in the tuxedo.

He crossed his arms, positioning himself in front of me. "No. We're allowed to see other people."

"I thought you didn't have time for dating around."

"I don't," David said, lifting his chin fractionally. "I'm too busy to seek women out, but that doesn't mean I don't find them."

Or they found him, more likely. "Brittany?" I asked.

He nodded. If he was surprised I knew of her, he didn't show it. "My date for the gala tonight."

"Who is she?"

"Nobody, Olivia. Ask me to cancel on her and see what my answer is."

I swallowed. A dare—not a guarantee that he'd actually cancel. And why should he?

If I *did* ask, and he complied, then what? It wasn't as if I could take her place.

I was headed to a secluded cabin with my husband and our best friends for a weekend of relaxation, time on the lake, and card games by the fireplace.

What, was I going to stay behind to be David's arm

candy? Have him escort me to the museum, order me Merlot, sneak me into a dark corner, kiss me, gather up my dress to my waist?

My chest rose and fell faster. Why me, when he could take anyone? David probably had a little black book so thick that it better resembled a dictionary. "How many women are you seeing?"

"At the moment, technically, none. It's very casual," he said. "But I *can* sleep with who I want, and I do."

I didn't know why his honesty startled me. I'd known all along that he was a player—casual encounters and all.

I suddenly felt out of my league, which was becoming an all too familiar feeling around him.

I glanced at his phone as it buzzed.

One thing to be grateful for? He couldn't notch me on his figurative bedpost like the others.

"Anything else?" he asked.

I forced a smile, a front for the sinking feeling of picturing him with not just Maria but other women. "I think I've heard enough."

"What's wrong?"

"Nothing." I set down the clipboard and went to stand. "I should check on Lucy."

"I read some of your articles online."

I paused, looking up at him.

His shoulders loosened. "You write very well, Olivia."

My heart somersaulted, but I shook my head. "I contribute when I can, but I told you, I'm an editor. My mother's the writer in my family."

"Don't sell yourself short. You're talented."

"Thanks," I said, embarrassed that it came out sounding like a question.

My heels sank into the carpet. Had I been leaving? I'd told David we could never be alone again, and yet, he warmed me in a way that made me wonder how I hadn't realized I'd been so cold.

I didn't *want* to go. But this had never been about desire. Wanting David was easy. To be near him, to hear whatever bold, wicked thing would come out of his mouth next . . .

Davena had warned me I couldn't hide from my desires. And here I was, back in a room alone with David.

If you want something, say it out loud.

I couldn't think of anything I wanted more in that moment than to be kissed in a dark corner at some anonymous event by David Dylan.

Drawing a breath, I forced the fantasy away. I raised the apple rind and tossed it across the room, sinking a perfect shot in the trashcan. "Three-pointer," I said.

He looked from the wastebasket to me. "You watch basketball?"

"Bill does," I said. "You?"

"I'm a Bears fan myself."

"Football? I could see that."

"Oh?" he asked.

"Sure. I can picture you as a quarterback, working the field, leaving a trail of cheerleaders in your wake. I mean, for God's sake, you fit into their clothing. The next step would be a uniform . . ." I bit my lip to try to hide my smile. "Did you play in high school?"

"I did, though I would've preferred to focus on the swim team."

"Quarterback? Linebacker?" I leaned back against Lucy's desk again, running my hand along the edge. "Tight end?"

"QB."

"Thought so. I had a crush on our high school quarterback." I cocked my head. My eyes wandered down. "He looked a little like you, but not as tall."

David's hand twitched, and he tightened his arms over his chest. "What are you doing?" he asked.

I shrugged one shoulder, staring him down. "What?"

"You're flirting with me, just like on the roof the other day, even though you asked me to back off."

I couldn't deny it. My need for him was beginning to seep out of the cage where I'd locked it. Davena had warned me that would happen. One moment, I was in control. The next, I didn't know what might come out of my mouth. Was this how my mother had felt, unraveling in the weeks before my father and I had left? Fantasies bordering too close to reality?

David's nearness set me on fire no matter how I tried to douse the embers of desire.

No matter the fact that I wore another man's ring.

"Olivia, I'll put on a show in front of your friends, at your work, whenever we're in public. But I'm growing tired of pretending when we're alone. Don't tempt me," he warned.

His tone meant to scold me, but my body thrilled with his words.

This was pretending? What happened when he stopped?

Lucy burst through the door. "Sorry," she exclaimed. "I looked everywhere, but the seamstress is gone."

David stepped back, but I couldn't take my eyes off him. "What now?" I asked.

"I can tailor the pants," Lucy said, "just not as well as she could've. I'll get the suit ninety percent there before you have to leave, David. Are you okay with that?"

He shrugged. "I'm man enough to walk into a party looking ninety percent good."

As if David could ever look anything less than a hundred-percent handsome.

My phone *dinged*. David glanced at my handbag before I went to it, took out my phone, and read a text from Bill.

Bill: *We're pulling up out front. Come down when you guys are ready.*

"Your event is soon. Give me your pants." Lucy hurried into the curtained area and grabbed the pinned slacks. "While I work on sewing this, finish getting ready. Liv can help."

The moment Lucy disappeared again, my stomach knotted. As I returned my phone to my purse, it started to ring. I caught a glimpse of myself in the mirror as I silenced Bill's call but turned away quickly.

I should've been gathering my things to meet my husband. Instead, I was going to stay to help dress a man who seemed to be herding me into his arms every day since we'd met eyes across a crowded room, popping up in my life at each turn, becoming less of a stranger each moment we spent together.

My eyes drifted over him as it hit me. "You were wearing a tux at the ballet."

He paused only a moment, then picked up a dark leather box from Lucy's desk and removed a pair of cuff-links. "It's being cleaned."

"Is it?" I asked. "Or did you know I'd be here today?"

"How could I have known?" He made a fist around the delicate silver pieces and walked toward me. "You're mistaken if you think I need to scheme to get what I want, Olivia. I agreed to do the article to spend time with you, and to help you with your promotion—but if necessary, I would've found another way to see you again." He stopped inches from me. "When you walked into Lucy's engagement party in that tight white dress, I knew with complete certainty I wouldn't be leaving without you on my arm. I wouldn't let you get away like I had at the ballet."

My head tilted back to take him in. When I'd walked *in* to the party? So those chestnut browns had been on me before I'd even known David was there. Observing me. Learning. Not just watching but *seeing*.

"Yes, I noticed you instantly," he said, reading my expression. "I followed you into the kitchen to find out your name, which I did, and to ask you on a date." His jaw firmed. "Which I did not."

I touched my chest when my heart fluttered. "And you didn't leave the party with me."

"I had no idea you were married. It never even occurred to me to look at your hand," he glanced at my ring, currently pressed over the same spot the wine stain had been, "because when I saw you, I felt like . . . like I'd found something I'd been looking for. And life wouldn't be so *fucking* unfair that it was already taken."

"Don't say that," I said, hearing the rasp in my voice.

"I warned you—I'm dangerously close to dropping the act," David said. "It's taking everything I have not to put you over my shoulder and drag you to my event so I can warn the whole world that you're *mine*."

He walked away toward the mirror, leaving me trying to catch my breath and resist from melting into a puddle of need for him.

Jesus. He was wrong. He wasn't pretending shit. There *was* no pretending. Not when we were alone.

I said the only thing I could think of that might knock some sense into each of us. "My husband is downstairs."

"I don't give a fuck," he said, back in front of the

mirror, fiddling with his sleeve, growing visibly irritated when he couldn't get the cufflink in.

I walked over and took his wrist, my throat thickening. "This tuxedo, these cufflinks—they don't belong to you," I said. "They're on loan. You can't just walk out of here with them and never bring them back."

"I can if I want," he said levelly. "Lucy has my credit card."

I pursed my lips. My fingers brushed the inside of his wrist as I slipped the cufflink through its hole. "So, you want something, you buy it. That's how it works, Mr. Black Card?"

He flexed his hand, and I flinched as his fingertips nearly grazed the fabric over the scar on my stomach. "I want something, I find a way to get it," he said.

If David could touch my scar, he was too close. Heat radiated from him, or maybe our chemistry warmed the space between us. *We're too close.* "And if it belongs to someone else?"

"I doubt he'd miss it."

"He would," I said, keeping my eyes on David's size fourteen-and-a-half shoes. "A lot."

A deep breath filled my nostrils with his spicy after-shave. David's stare followed me as I moved to the left cuff, then took a step back and admired him. Aside from wearing the wrong pants and the bowtie hanging loosely around his neck, he was ready for his gala.

With a determined furrow in his brow, he started to fix the tie.

"Let me." I slipped between the mirror and him. The spicy scent mixed with fresh soap, intensifying as I leaned in. I quickly molded the fabric into a neat bow. With my mom no longer in the house as a kid, I'd helped my dad get ready for many black-tie events in Dallas.

As I pulled the bow taut, my fingers stilled and lingered. I could no longer avoid David's penetrating gaze. I watched the rise and fall of his chest until my eyes traveled up his exposed neck. His Adam's apple jumped as he swallowed. Even his hair obeyed, every strand in place, starkly black against his olive skin. His mouth slackened, creases fading. Finally, our eyes locked.

In one slow, measured movement, he wrapped an arm around my waist and pulled me to him. His other hand rose and raked through my hair, tilting my mouth upward.

My eyes fluttered shut.

His lips touched mine, and everything else fell away. Warmth pulsed through me as he tested the new territory with a purposeful but tender kiss. My mouth parted, and he answered by opening it farther with his lips. An ache blossomed between my legs. My head swam with the hot breath and heady taste of another man after so many years.

He cupped my face and backed me against the mirror as the kiss became needier. His hands moved down my neck and over my collarbone. They covered my shoulders, pressing me into the glass. That throb grew painful, eager for relief.

I took his cheeks in my hands, his skin smooth over a sharp jaw, and moaned on his tongue.

He tore away suddenly and stepped back. "Fuck."

My heart pounded as I gasped for air, but my throat constricted. Heat vanished, the mirror cooling my back in an instant. I couldn't move. I could only watch David, waiting for his direction.

He turned his back to me, shoving his hands through his perfect hair. "*Fuck*," he yelled so loudly, I jumped.

He pounded a fist against the wall, whipped open the door, and stalked out.

I covered my tingling mouth. The kiss had happened both fast and slow, the swell of a wave pulling me down into tranquility before it crashed over my head.

God. Oh, God.

I hadn't meant to do it. I'd gone right up to the line, walked along it, and so had David on the other side. I'd never meant to cross it.

I hadn't meant it. What had I done? And what did I do now?

Not even footsteps in the hall could move me. My heart fluttered with each solid step of dress shoes against tile. David wouldn't leave me this way. He'd walk back through the door.

And then what?

I'd slipped just now, but letting it happen again couldn't be called anything other than intentional.

Falling into his arms, letting myself be devoured . . .

Bill walked in instead, stopping short as his eyes landed on me.

Everything in me ceased to function. Bill could see it on my face. Everything. The betrayal of David lips on mine, the guilt that I'd pulled him closer, the shame that I wished he'd return just now.

"Did you get my text?" Bill asked. "Car's all loaded up, and we're ready to hit the road. Where's Luce?"

I couldn't respond, afraid I'd choke on the words. What could I possibly say? Any word out of my mouth would be a lie if I didn't confess. Now.

"I'm here." Lucy popped up behind Bill, a pair of slacks draped over her arm. "Where's David?"

They both looked at me.

I could read the slight irritation on Bill's face that he'd had to come upstairs and we still weren't ready. He'd have grumbled to Andrew about my not answering his call, his road trip playlist plugged in, The Cure on the car speakers.

My husband. A man I knew inside and out. We had a life. A routine. We had a weekend away with our best friends planned and waiting for us.

And I was—what? Going to admit I'd kissed a stranger, even though it would *never* happen again?

Upend Lucy's weekend, her working relationship with David, and pull the plug on my feature and the promotion?

I swallowed.

"He . . . David had an emergency," I said. "He . . . had to go."

"Wait, *what*? He *left*?" Lucy's mouth dropped. "But he's wearing the wrong pants!"

And I had kissed the wrong man. I had made the wrong choice. But when? Just now, or years ago?

Was I living the wrong life?

Chapter Fifteen

Andrew's family cabin glowed in the dark as we wound through the woods. After an hour in the car, and twenty minutes at a grocery store that'd felt like hours, I couldn't wait to get out and make a beeline for the shower. I'd been sitting in my own shame, the memory of David's kiss taunting me one second and tempting me the next. His unrelenting clasp on my shoulders and surprisingly tender lips claiming mine. The memory was made of details I should've been desperate to forget.

As Bill and Andrew unloaded their fishing equipment, I went directly to our room, dropped my suitcase and heels by the bed, and locked myself in the bathroom.

I couldn't face myself in the mirror. Evidence of my transgression wouldn't be visible, but I'd see it in my eyes.

I flipped on the shower, cranking the handle to get the water as hot as possible.

"Livs?" Bill called from the bedroom.

"I'll be out soon," I said, stripping down.

"We're going to make food." He tried the door handle. "What do you want?"

Food was the last thing on my mind. I needed to cleanse, not consume. "I don't care," I said, piling my dress and undergarments on the tile floor.

"Want a sandwich?" The handle jiggled. "Let me in, Liv."

I braced myself against the sink and shut my eyes. I couldn't even face myself, let alone Bill. I needed solitude. But now, I was the kind of person who had to try to act normal so my husband wouldn't get suspicious.

I unlocked the door and cracked it. "I'll just have the chicken noodle soup I got at the market," I said.

I started to shut the door, but he caught it. "Hey. Hey, wait." He pulled my naked body against his clothed one.

My muscles tensed, but he just kissed my forehead and tucked some of my hair behind my ear. "You've been silent all night. Are you feeling okay?"

"I think I might be coming down with something."

He pressed his knuckles to my forehead. "What's the matter?"

"I'm sure it's nothing. I just need a good night's sleep."

"And you're going to get one now that we're under the stars, away from all the noise. Doesn't get much more peaceful than a cabin in the woods."

For me, the best lullaby was the telltale sounds of a city not quite asleep. But Bill longed for tranquility only nature could provide.

He leaned in for a kiss. I drew back, glancing away. "I don't want to get you sick."

"Good point."

I swiped the back of my hand over my mouth and curled my lips into what I hoped was a smile. "I'll be out in a few minutes."

He turned and left.

Alone, I stepped under the showerhead, dumped too

much body wash in my hand, and smoothed it over my skin where the water burned.

I closed my eyes and saw David's lusty ones reeling me in before his body cast me aside. Why had he reacted so violently, as if he'd been the one to commit the crime?

He'd nearly put his fist through the wall, but moments earlier, his solid arm had surrounded my middle, his rough hand raking through my hair, strong heartbeat thudding against my body. I squeezed my shoulders the way he had, but my grip was pitiful in comparison. I pretended my hands were his, sliding them to my breasts, my taut nipples.

Please stop.

I opened my eyes, shook my head, and twisted the dial closer to red, forcing myself in the water's punishing path. The ache from earlier gnawed at me, dragging my hands downward. My chest heaved as I gave in to the memory, to the feel of David's gentle, firm, rough, soothing lips against mine.

My palm pushed against the mound between my legs, slippery from the soap. I circled my opening, massaging as my arousal mounted.

I had never been so turned on by just a kiss. Maybe by *anything.*

David did this. Two fingers slipped inside. *Firm, muscular hands. Pinning me against the mirror.* He'd yank up my dress, his fingers pumping in and out and over my clit. *Unforgiving hold. I was his in that moment. He'd claimed me in seconds.*

I shot my other fist against the wall across from me and lost myself to thoughts of him. Lifting one leg to the opposite wall, I continued to pump and rub with my other hand. I gasped for air as David threw me on the desk, opened me with his fingers, and shoved inside me.

I pushed my foot into the tile as waves crested,

throwing me into a fierce, blinding orgasm that seemed to go on for minutes.

Once my heartbeat slowed, I lowered my foot. My red and raw skin quivered. I hadn't come in here to give in to the fantasy but to scrub myself of David. Yet, he seemed to become even more embedded. And I was filthier than ever.

I exited the shower, toweled off quickly, and took my birth control before throwing on a robe. At the thought of going out to the dining room, my throat ached. Pressure built behind my eyes. Maybe any illness was in my head, but in that moment, I couldn't do more than lower myself onto the edge of the bed, massage my temples, and breathe deeply through my panic. I eased back against the mattress and closed my eyes.

When I opened them again, the room had gone dark, my body warm between the flannel sheets.

David's lips touched my neck. His hand slid over my hip, curving against my backside. "We let you sleep," Bill murmured.

My heart vaulted against my chest. "Bill?"

"Who else would it be?" He chuckled. "You were tossing and turning. Must've been dreaming."

"I . . . I was."

"Are you feeling better?" he asked, his voice lifting. "It's so romantic out here, alone in the woods . . ."

"Lucy and Andrew are in the next room," I pointed out, my throat threatening to close again. I was enough of a traitor to kiss and fantasize and get myself off to David's beautiful face, strong grasp, his fierce need for me. I couldn't let Bill inside my body within hours of that. "And I'm definitely coming down with something. What if you catch it and can't go out on the boat tomorrow?"

Bill sighed and wrapped his arm around me, hugging me close. "You smell nice from your shower."

I was a horrible person. I swallowed dryly as I whispered, "Thanks, babe."

"You're right, though. Don't want to get sick."

I exhaled my immense relief as he rolled onto his back, away from me.

I'd betrayed Bill. Another man's hands, another man's lips, another man's scent had been on me.

One thing had been tugging at my conscience all night, a transgression I hadn't been able to bring myself to acknowledge until now—in the complete dark, wide awake, and alone with my guilt.

David had stopped the kiss. I hadn't.

I'd been too wrapped up in him to see the mistake I was making. How long would I have let it go on? Long enough that Bill would've walked in on us?

I hid my face in my pillow and prayed I'd never see David ever again. Things were dangerously easy with him, and I'd proven myself as weak as any of his girls.

But I had the memory, and it was unshakable. I began to drift amongst thoughts of wandering arms and curling toes, gripping fingers, yearning lips and eyes, smooth skin, rough palms, tuxedos, cufflinks . . .

The following night, seated at a round oak dining table, Andrew placed his last set of cards on the dining table. "Rummy."

The three of us groaned and threw down our hands. "I'm done," Bill said, leaning back in his chair. "That's three in a row. Let's play something else. Something Andrew sucks at."

"How about Texas Hold 'Em?" I suggested.

"You'd like that, wouldn't you?" Andrew asked, narrowing his eyes at me.

"Good idea, babe," Bill said, tugging on my sweatshirt. "I think I saw a poker set around here somewhere."

"Veto," Lucy said. "Andrew was cranky for a week after the last time we played."

"Don't like losing to a girl?" I asked, shuffling the deck.

"I don't like losing a hundred bucks, period. Two hundred if you count Lucy."

"But I used it to buy the most beautiful leather boots," I said wistfully.

Bill chuckled and leaned over to plant a kiss on my cheek. I snuggled in the crook of his arm.

"Anyone want more salmon before I put it away?" Lucy asked. "It shouldn't sit out any longer."

"I'm full," Bill said. "We got lucky with that Coho, man. The guys next to us said they usually cap around five or six pounds."

"Yeah?" Andrew said. "Let's see if we can pull it off again tomorrow."

"If you do, throw the fish back," I said, pushing away from the table. "We have plenty of food."

"I'll throw *you* back," Bill joked as I took my empty beer into the kitchen.

Rinsing out the bottle, I looked out the small window over the sink into the dark forest. David's strong hands clasped around my shoulders the same unrelenting way they had in Lucy's office. He turned me around, and his hips fastened me to the counter, his erection begging against my stomach. His hold on me confident, unyielding, but his lips reverent as they touched mine. I bit my lip as his tongue slid against it. The fantasy washed over me, made of new details, unlike my furious memory in the shower.

"Enough fishing talk until I'm out of earshot or extremely drunk," Lucy declared, her voice tearing through my thoughts.

"Then the same goes for wedding talk," Bill said.

I set my empty bottle in the recycling bin and frowned over the breakfast bar. "*Bill*," I scolded.

He glanced at me. "You girls can talk cake and center-pieces till you're blue in the face while Andrew and I are on the boat."

Lucy made a noise. "I don't talk about the wedding that much."

"How many bridal mags did you bring up here?" Bill asked.

"Well, nine. But it's because I'm so behind, and I need Liv's help. For one, I can't stand white shoes. I need an alternative."

"*Tsk, tsk*," Bill said, shaking his head. "Tomorrow."

"Ignore him," I said, wiping my hands on a dishtowel before heading for the fridge. "He's just being mean."

"But one more thing real quick," Lucy said, twisting in her seat to address me. "The tailor called this morning. Your bridesmaid dress will be ready for your first fitting a week from Monday."

Bill's eyebrows shot up. "Bridesmaid dress? How much was that?"

I carried four beers to the table. "We can talk about that later," I said with warning in my tone, not wanting to make Lucy uncomfortable.

"It's just that you didn't mention it," Bill said, accepting the bottle. "I'll have to review the budget for the month."

"Then do that," I snapped.

Lucy exchanged a glance with Andrew as she passed him a beer.

Andrew cleared his throat. "I was actually going to ask—"

Lucy touched his arm. "Maybe it's not the best time, sweetie."

"What is it, Andrew?" I prompted, stopping behind Bill's chair.

"Well . . ." Andrew gestured his beer at Bill. "My brothers make up most of my bridal party as you know, but I thought I'd see if you'd be part of it, too."

"Oh," Bill said. "Sure. Of course, man."

"That's so nice," I said, suppressing a laugh. Bill hated weddings. That, on top of the additional cost and time Andrew had just imposed on Bill—I knew I'd be hearing about this later. "Thanks for asking," I added.

"Yeah," Bill echoed. "Thanks."

With the chime of my phone alarm, I leaned over to kiss Bill's cheek, my irritation with him dissipating with Andrew and Lucy's kindness. "I'll be right back," I said before heading to the bedroom.

I rummaged through my suitcase for my birth control. When I didn't find the pack there or in my handbag, my heart began to race. I pulled out two neat clothing piles from my luggage and checked all the pockets, then unzipped Bill's duffel bag in a hurry and dumped his stuff on top of mine. Squatting on the floor, I rubbed my temples. I'd taken the pill last night after my shower, hadn't I?

"Bill," I said into the cabin. When he didn't respond, I yelled for him.

"Coming," he said.

I tried to think. I'd *definitely* taken a pill the night before and tossed the pack back into my suitcase. It had to be there, but it wasn't.

I needed that little pill to keep my life in order. And

though I hated to think it, Bill felt the opposite. He wanted that fail-safe gone, and just like with the house, I had a feeling he wouldn't be opposed to nudging me along when I resisted.

This time, I used my angry voice when I called Bill's name, and he came quickly.

"Yeah?" he asked, scanning the mess on the floor.

"Where's my birth control?" My foot tapped against the floor, but I couldn't stop it.

"What?"

"My birth control. Where is it? Did you do something with it?"

He raised his chin and looked down his nose at me. "What would I do with it?"

"I don't know, but it's not in my bag where it should be, and I've looked everywhere. Did you take it? Did you hide it?"

"Hide it . . .?" he asked. "You can't be serious."

It sounded crazy, but was it really? Bill had admitted, the day we'd gone to the suburbs, that he thought deep down, I wanted him to push me.

To start a relationship. To move in together. To get married.

If he didn't move us forward, I'd stay right where I was. But that was what I wanted—to stay here until I knew for sure what the next step should be.

"I'm serious, Bill. If you took my birth control, I need to know."

"Do you hear yourself?" he asked, reeling back. "I'm not a monster."

"No, I know that, but—"

He strode past me and jerked open the top drawer of my nightstand. "I put it in here," he said, pulling out the pack. Instead of handing it to me, he tossed it at my feet.

"You left it there on the floor last night, and I didn't want you to step on it."

Oh.

Shit. What had come over me just now? Bill wanted me to choose pregnancy, but of course I knew he'd never trick me into it.

With an exhalation, I shook my head. "I'm sor—"

"You know what else?" he asked, moving by me and reaching into his suitcase. He unzipped a side pocket and pulled out a string of condoms, thrusting them toward me. "I packed these. Lots of them. I didn't want to take any chances you might feel uncomfortable making love while we were out here. Which we haven't done. Even though it's the perfect setting."

I'd gone too far just now. Bill wasn't the bad guy here. I was the one changing the terms we'd agreed upon, asking him to wait for something he'd been honest about wanting from the start. I ran a hand through my hair, shutting my eyes briefly. "You're right. I guess I'm just stressed. You've been bringing up the baby thing so much—"

"Don't blame this on me." He walked by me on his way out, adding, "That's something your mom would do."

Blood drained from my face as my throat closed. *Oh my God.* He was right. My mother's paranoid, frantic episodes would come on fast and fizzle, ending with her tears and apologies. They'd grown worse over time, less sensical, more outlandish—especially in the months before she'd snapped.

I'd let my guilt over my kiss with David turn me into someone I didn't recognize. Did that mean I could suddenly snap, too? It was a question never far from my mind, but I'd been able to control the possibility for so long by making the right choices. Until now.

I hadn't been acting like myself for a while. Not since the ballet.

Not since *David*.

That night, I'd unknowingly stood on a precipice. I hadn't realized until this moment that I'd taken a step over the edge. And since then, I'd begun to spiral down.

Chapter Sixteen

David Dylan had been staring at me all day—from the cover of an *Architectural Digest* magazine Jenny had left on the desk for Lisa and me. In an urbane suit, arms crossed as he leaned in the doorway of a beautiful, midcentury home, while wearing an expression somewhere between *smirk* and *smile*, it was no surprise he'd landed the cover of *Architectural Digest*. He stood like a king in front of his latest masterpiece.

All day I'd avoided his stare, but as day turned to night, and the office emptied, my resolve to stay away weakened. With Bill back in New York on business for the week, and mostly giving me the silent treatment after Saturday night's accusation, I'd been working late each night.

I scanned the three-page article. David's firm, Pierson/Greer, was within walking distance from my office. I'd already known he was a pioneer in modern design, but apparently, he was one of the most in-demand architects in Chicago, too.

I closed the magazine and moved to my laptop to type his name in a search engine.

D-a-v-i-d D-y-

David Dylan. There he was. The first link went to *Architectural Digest,* and the next few, I'd already visited for research on the feature. Farther down the page, things shifted away from David.

"GQS will acquire Multi-Parcel Express, CEO Gerard Dylan announces"

Gerard Dylan. David's *father* was the CEO of worldwide shipping company Global Quick & Speedy? A search on Gerard provided endless articles, both business and personal. A profile of his home life presented four perfect smiles: Gerard and his wife, Judy, a daughter, Jessa, and son, David. There was no mistaking David's sister, who had the same obsidian hair that complemented clear brown eyes and long black lashes.

David was magnificently photogenic with a piercing gaze and sturdy features. I sifted through images of him, mostly working or at events. His tall frame and broad shoulders dwarfed anyone who posed with him. A profile shot with his sister, laughing and dressed in head-to-toe black, could've been from an advertisement.

A few rows down, red-carpet David's arm rested around Maria's waist. Her green eyes narrowed at the camera as if gloating. Two more photos with her. And another with a leggy redhead.

Was anyone immune to his spell? Could he turn *any* married woman against herself, make her question the life she'd been so certain was right? I hated that these women got to live in David's attention out in the open—and take it home with them at night.

Get wrapped up in his embrace.

Senses stolen by his kiss . . .

I shouldn't know how that felt, but I did. I'd tasted it only a few moments, but I wanted more. But perhaps even *more*, I vehemently wished these women would never experience it again. That the kiss had meant something to him, and I hadn't just been another in a long line.

But what right did I have to even think like that?

Bill couldn't have known how right he was comparing my behavior to my mother's.

Jealousy. Madness. Irrationality. Obsession.

In the weeks before she'd lost control, she'd picked fights with my dad and me over stupid things like not turning out a light after leaving a room, or over not-so-small things, like how she suddenly hated Dallas and wanted to move. She'd confided in me that she'd begun following my father and had seen him get out of a cab with the same woman she'd found in his office—his client, Gina, I'd later learn. But at the time, hiding my mom's secret stalking had kept me up at night.

Now, here I was, unable to stop scrolling down the page, except when I saw David with a different woman. Who was the blonde? An ex, a friend, a fuck buddy?

Why was I doing this? It'd gone beyond research and morphed into—

"Bad news?"

I gasped, nearly jumping out of my chair when David appeared in the doorway as if I'd conjured him. I slammed my laptop closed. "What?"

He took a few measured steps into the office. "You look upset."

Any hope I had of calming my heart rate went out the door as it raced at the sight of the most beautiful man I'd ever seen, come to life from the cover of a magazine. Here in my office. At night.

Since our kiss almost a week earlier, I'd had one pervading thought—*don't think of the kiss.*

It never happened.

Never speak, or think, of it again.

Yet the harder I tried to forget it, the more I remembered.

His breath caressing my lips, a man so dashing in a tuxedo that he could sweep any girl away within seconds . . .

"What are you doing here?" I asked.

"I was driving home from my office and saw your light on."

At the end of the workday, in a tailored suit jacket, his slacks wrinkle-free, dress shirt open at the collar, David was both put together and casual. "That's not a reason," I said.

He cleared his throat and checked his watch. "There's no one at the security desk downstairs," he said. "I walked right into the building and up here. Didn't even need a keycard."

"And?"

"It's unsafe. You should file a complaint." He glanced at the *Architectural Digest*, opened to his spread, then at one of two framed pictures that'd been added to the corner of the desk since his last visit. David picked one up. "Who's this?"

"Lisa. The other woman up for my promotion."

"Why do you have her photo on your desk?"

"We share this office," I said. "When Lisa saw the picture of Lucy and me, she brought in one of hers."

"To mark her territory." He picked up a picture from this weekend. Bill and me at the cabin with Lucy and Andrew. "And it looks like you retaliated. That was quick."

Lisa had been taking over the desk, as if she'd thought my photo had been a challenge. Her planner sat in the top drawer. Her stationery on the desk had multiplied. But that wasn't why I'd displayed the picture taken over the dinner Andrew and Bill had caught us. Before my fight with Bill had ruined the weekend, we'd laughed, snuggled, and shared memories with our friends. I needed to keep that close.

David set down the frame. "Thank you for the help with the tuxedo."

I flattened a hand on my desk and forced away the tempting memory. "How was the event?"

"That's not why I'm here." His jaw set, his expression unreadable. "I came to find out if you need anything else from me for the article."

I moved my hands to my lap with his clipped request. "Well—we need to do a photo shoot for the spread. I may need some details to fill in the article—"

"Are you writing it?" he asked.

"Yes."

"You said you prefer to edit."

"I do." I shifted in my seat. "But I write, too, as you know, and since you insisted on *only* working with me, you're *my* bachelor. So I thought . . ."

Our eyes met, my claim over him hanging between us.

"You said you trusted me and only me to handle it," I reminded him. "So that's what I'm doing."

"Things change," he said abruptly. "I'd like to arrange for any remaining obligations of mine to go through someone else."

"Like a liaison?" I asked.

"And do you need to be present for the photo shoot?"

In the short time I'd known David, determination had

hardened his voice many times, but this was something else. Finality. Resolution.

Maybe even . . . good-bye?

"I should be present, yes, but I can have Lisa—"

"It's best that we end our personal and professional relationships here," he said.

My heart dropped. Except that I should've been grateful. I'd prayed for this, and my pleas had been answered.

David and I had crossed several lines. Not just personal ones, but professional, too. On Lucy's balcony weeks ago, panic had risen in my chest at the thought of never seeing David again. It happened again now—and it had nothing to do with the fact that this could threaten my promotion.

I cleared my throat and slid a rogue paperclip across the desk, depositing it into its compartment in the top drawer. "The Meet and Greet is this weekend," I muttered.

"I'll be there. I'm not backing out. I've made a commitment, and I intend to see it through. But I *will* work with—was it Lisa?—going forward."

It was the dismissive tone I'd heard David use with others like my boss and even his associate Arnaud. But never with me.

And it hurt.

This was why I'd been honing my self-preservation skills since thirteen years old. This was why I acted on logic, not emotion.

Anything else ended in pain.

"I understand." It was a struggle to get the words out, but I hid my disappointment behind a mask. "I'll make the arrangements."

He looked to me, waiting.

"Was there something else?" I asked.

Frustration flashed across his features. "Yes, there is. I

told you I'd never kiss a married woman, Olivia. I *believed* that about myself."

I didn't want to care, but a sliver of relief worked through me that *he* did. His iciness was more deeply rooted than he'd let on. I'd take his anger over his apathy, even though I was doing my best to come off indifferent as well. "How is that my fault?" I asked. "You've been pursuing me since the moment we met."

"But not because I was interested in having an affair. I'm not."

"What then?" I asked, curling my fingers against the surface of the desk. "You came onto me at the ballet, and then at Lucy's apartment, then almost kissed me on the rooftop. Then you *did* kiss me. You can't stand there and blame this on me."

He snorted. "It's not your fault, Olivia. I told you I wouldn't cross that line, and I did. I take full responsibility, but the truth is . . ." His expression turned pained. "I've *never* been unable to trust myself. And I can't with you."

I knew the feeling, and yet, I couldn't dismiss the evidence against David. Not just what I'd heard, but what I'd seen moments ago on my computer screen. There was no way in *hell* he'd not been presented with an opportunity like this before. "You asked me if I've ever had an affair, and I told you I haven't," I said. "Have you?"

"Never. My attraction to you goes against all of my beliefs." He ran a hand through his hair, shaking his head. "My parents, who are my world, have been happily married for thirty-seven years. I'd kill anyone who tried to come between them."

I sat back in my seat, surprised by his candidness. He struggled with our connection, too. Despite his persistence, loyalty meant something to him. *That* was why he'd stormed out of Lucy's office. But his idolization of his parents' marriage made him even more attractive. Maybe he wasn't pursuing me because he wanted to. Maybe he wasn't playing with fire. Maybe, like me, the burn found him wherever he went, consuming and growing stronger, compelling him toward me.

"Then why are you here?" I asked. "Why did you come to my office the first time—why threaten to stop pretending when we're alone if it's not because you want to fuck me?"

His Adam's apple bobbed as he swallowed and glanced away. "Do you really want me to answer that?"

Once he did, once he said it aloud, that would be it. If David truly wasn't after me for an affair, for one night of giving in, then did that mean he wanted . . . more?

More could only mean one thing.

Breaking up my marriage.

Taking a hammer to the life I'd sculpted.

And it was clear to both of us—that wasn't an option.

"Fine," I said. "Serena will be in touch about anything else. I'll see you at the event."

He rubbed his eyebrow, staying where he was. "Let me drive you home."

"*What?*" I frowned. "You *just* said we couldn't see each other again."

"It's not again. It's after dark. The Loop is quiet this time of night. And without a security guard—"

"No," I said firmly.

"Then I'll at least walk you to the train. Get you a cab. Whatever. It's your safety."

"Look, I get it," I said with a sigh. "This is your thing."

His brow furrowed. "What's my thing?"

"You're a gentleman. You're just not *mine*."

With us, it was all or nothing—and it couldn't be all. If he even walked me downstairs, we'd be doing something wrong. Just *being* here with him was a transgression.

I didn't have to explain that to him. David hesitated a moment, then turned and walked out.

I should've been thankful. I should've been relieved. I thought of Bill, and knew this was the right thing. I thought of David, and the idea of not seeing him again after this weekend hurt in the spot my heart should be.

I got up from my desk and went to the door. In another life, I would've called David back. If I were a different woman, I wouldn't let someone like him get away. Was it him, though, or was it that he sparked things in me I'd been able to control for the last sixteen years?

I closed the office door and leaned my back against it, physically steeling myself from going after him.

I'd committed a greater crime than kissing another man. I'd let him believe my marriage could be penetrated. That he could waltz in and take me from Bill. That I was missing something in my life that he could give me.

I'd let *myself* believe that.

No—I'd already known I'd never have those disruptive and often sought-after wild emotions with Bill, but I'd made an agreement with myself when I'd made a commitment to him. A stable, predictable life was better than a volatile one. Passion always came with pain.

The clock above the door ticked down, but I couldn't bring myself to move. If I opened my laptop again, I'd be faced with David and his girls. If I went home, I'd be alone with my David-fueled thoughts.

But then, the elevator *dinged*. My heart soared as shoes hit the ground.

David.

He'd come back. Or had he never left?

Was he also doing everything he could to convince himself staying apart was the right thing?

Or was it simply that he couldn't resist getting me home safely, even though I wasn't his to protect?

My heart pounded faster as his footsteps neared and then stopped outside my office. My willpower was only so strong. He was the one who'd said this couldn't go on. Why was he back to make us each suffer more?

I turned slowly, hesitated with my hand on the doorknob, then opened the door.

And met the angry, burning gaze of Mark Alvarez.

Chapter Seventeen

My mind struggled to catch up, my limbs frozen in place. I'd opened my office door expecting to find David Dylan and was now staring down a man who'd recently threatened my life.

Fuck.

What the fuck.

Where had he come from? How? Why?

With my attempt at a step back, Mark Alvarez lunged to grab my blouse. "You didn't deliver my message," he said, anger flashing in his brown eyes.

"I did. I swear, I did." My heart slammed against my ribcage. Out of nowhere, sweat trickled down my temple. "But Bill doesn't work with the DA's office anymore," I rushed out, pleading. "He can't just get someone out of jail."

"It's Bill's fault my brother's in there, and he'll find a way to—"

Fear surged in me. I kneed Mark in the balls. He released me with a curse. With no time to be shocked over my instinct to hurt him, I darted to the right.

I was almost past him when a fist in my hair yanked me back. "I don't think you understand," Mark said, dragging me deeper into the office. He pulled a knife from his waist. "Bill fucked with my family, and now I fuck with his. Eye for an eye."

My heartbeat *whooshed* in my ears, and the room began to spin. The short blade, silver and jagged, looked nothing like a kitchen knife, but my mind went blank like I was thirteen again.

Mark shoved me, and with my eyes on the knife, I backed away until I hit a wall.

"This is your second warning." Mark advanced until he was nearly on top of me, breathing hotly in my face. He put the blade to my throat. "And we'll keep coming back. Lou should've got out with me. We did the same crime. Your husband fucked up."

My head began to throb where I pushed it against the wall, trying to keep my throat from the blade. "I'll tell Bill, I promise." I wasn't sure what Bill could do, but I needed to say anything to escape the knife. "Don't hurt me."

"Hurt you? Nah. I'm going to make you feel good." He stuck the blade between his teeth and ripped open my blouse with both hands. Buttons scattered on the carpet as I screamed.

He smacked me across my cheek, and my face flew to one side. "Shut the fuck up or I'll gag you."

I went silent. I'd never been hit. It shocked me into immobility, but I had to move. *Run. Get out.* This wasn't a warning. It was a message. It was life-altering, world-shattering—something I'd never recover from. I stretched my jaw as it throbbed with pain and willed myself to fight back, but as my vision blurred with tears, the knife sharpened in my view.

The thought of blood instantly nauseated me. I could

already see it smeared on my pajamas, pain searing through my side, the shouting, my father's voice soothing me between roars to call 9-1-1, the sirens, my mother's sobs . . .

Mark put the tip of the knife to the spot he'd hit me, stinging my cheek with the cold blade. He dragged it down my face, my neck and chest, between my breasts. When I flinched, a slow smile spread across his face. "I want there to be *no* question," he whispered, pressing his body flush to mine, "that Bill Wilson understands what we're capable of—"

Mark flew backward and landed on his back with a *smack* so loud, it knocked the wind out of *me*. Standing over him, David Dylan looked like a superhero in a pressed suit.

"Run," David commanded me. "*Now.*"

He grabbed Mark by his shirt, levied him off the ground, and hit him square across the face, putting him back on the ground.

I yanked my blouse closed as my entire body shook. Where was the knife? David was definitely bigger than my attacker, but Mark fought dirty and had an axe to grind.

Blood trickled from Mark's nose as he writhed. "Who the f—"

"*Go*, Olivia," David said, anger shaking his voice. He lifted Mark by his shirt collar just enough to hit him again. Mark groaned but reached under himself, searching for something in his waistband.

"He has a knife," I cried.

Still bent over my attacker, David whipped his head up to me, his hair and suit disheveled. "I said get the fuck out of here, Olivia. Go—"

Mark rammed his boot into David's stomach, sending him onto his back. Mark scrambled to his hands and knees, shot up, and ran.

On his feet in the next second, David put a hand out. "Stay here, Olivia. I fucking mean it," he said and bolted out.

I searched the office for the knife, but it wasn't there. Mark still had it. As much as that fact made me want to hide, I had the stronger urge to help David, who'd put his life on the line by coming back here.

I fisted my top closed with one hand and hurried through the doorway. Two shadows darted through the dark office's cubicles and crashed through the lobby's glass doors.

With a gunshot, I yelped. *David.* I sprinted forward, my eyes frantically roaming the dark. When I reached the dimly lit lobby, I found Mark on his back with David straddling him. Each man had his hands locked around the other's neck.

David wasn't shot. He wasn't bleeding. Relief didn't come, though.

The gun sat a few feet away on the glossy porcelain tile. I snatched it off the ground. Small but undoubtedly powerful against my trembling palm. *Jesus.* Growing up, my father had kept a gun in the house, but I'd never held it.

And I'd certainly never aimed one. I did now, raising it at both men.

Was I really going to shoot someone?

I couldn't. My heart hammered too hard. My hands too unsteady. And they were moving too much.

"Stop," I pleaded. "I'll shoot."

David's back straightened, and he released Mark's neck. When Mark looked over at me, David pummeled his fist into his face over and over until Mark groaned and started to go limp.

David got to his feet, came toward me, and took the

gun. "I told you to run," he rushed out, sticking it in his waistband. He whipped off his suit jacket.

"I wasn't going to leave you."

A charged pulse beat between us until David wrapped the blazer around my shoulders and turned around. Gun in hand, he raised it. "Get back," he said to me over his shoulder, then spoke to Mark. "You. On your feet."

The self-possessed David I knew had returned, his posture straight, at ease with the gun, as though he'd done this before.

"Who the fucking shit are you?" Mark asked, struggling to his feet.

"The cops are on their way," David said. "But take a step in her direction, and I'll blow your head off."

"Fuck you," Mark said, wiping blood and saliva from his chin. "You don't think more of us will come after her? After *you*?"

"Let them try," David said.

It occurred to me that David had just willingly stepped into the middle of a bad situation. He'd risked his life and possibly put a target on his back. For me? I pulled David's blazer closed around my ruined blouse, mildly soothed by hints of his cologne.

But my ease was short-lived. Vibrating with rage, David took two massive steps toward Mark, backing him into a corner. I gasped as he shoved the gun into Mark's neck.

"Anyone goes near her again," David said slowly, "I'll shove this down your throat and blow your guts out your ass. You, and everyone you care about. You fucking hear me, you piece of shit?"

My throat dried. David's conviction almost convinced *me* he was capable of that. But he couldn't be. Could he?

He was a businessman, not law enforcement, nor criminal or superhero.

"Let me go," Mark said. "If I get arrested, others will come."

"Then maybe I should just kill you now to send a message."

"Do it," Mark said. "See what happens."

Even in the dimly lit space, I could see the hatred radiating off David. He cocked the gun with a click and pushed it under Mark's chin, forcing his eyes up.

"David," I said as calmly as I could manage. "Stop."

Distant *dings* signaled that the elevator was on its way up.

"David," I repeated. I wouldn't let him kill a man, even to defend me. Especially not with the chance the cops could walk in on it. "Someone's here. Please, David."

After a moment, his shoulders eased, and he took a step back. With his free hand, he grabbed Mark, flipped him, and shoved his cheek against the wall. David stuck the gun in the waist of Mark's jeans and leaned his forearm across his back to hold him there.

The elevator opened and three policemen flooded out, guns drawn, followed by a heavyset, forty-something man in an ill-fitting suit. "Well, well. Mark Alvarez," the man said gruffly. "Lou's going to love that you're coming for a visit."

Taking in the scene, the officers kept their guns raised but laughed at the joke.

As my adrenaline ebbed, my split cheek prickled. I touched it, and my fingertips came back bloody. My head thundered as my heart skipped a beat. *Blood* . . .

"He's armed," David said somewhere in the distance as I tried to expel the metallic smell from my nostrils.

My head swam. Metal *clinked* as a policeman cuffed Mark.

Suddenly, David was in front of me, his broad shoulders blocking me from the policemen. "He hit you," he said, lightly cupping my cheek to turn my face. "Did he—did he hurt you anywhere else?"

The pain didn't bother me. I hated the smell, sight, and sticky feel of blood on my skin. I just needed to breathe through this. I couldn't answer, or I'd gag. I just shook my head.

"You're too pale." David's brows knit. "What's the matter?"

I shook my head as the urge to vomit rose in me.

"You might be in shock," David said gently. "Or is it something else?"

The rumpled-suit man came and planted himself nearly between us. "Detective Cooper," he said to me. "You all right?"

The detective wasn't forty-something like I'd thought. Up close, under the lights, he looked too young to be balding. Maybe even close to David's age. His calm demeanor reminded me that this could've gone much worse. I drew up my shoulders with a deep inhalation. All things considered, I was . . .

"Fine. I'm fine." I glanced at David. "You called the police?"

"I saw that asshole in the lobby downstairs." David nodded at Mark as they led him away. "He was boarding the elevator. I only saw his face a second, but something felt off. I thought I recognized him."

"How?" I asked. "You've never seen him."

"You told me his name over the phone. I, uh, may have looked into him."

Of course he had, I thought, exhaling a breath. He was always keeping an eye on me.

"Sorry I didn't get here sooner," David added, "but I took the stairs."

My mouth fell open. "That's fourteen flights."

"I couldn't wait for the elevator to come back down and then up." David turned to the detective. "Cooper's a friend. I called him immediately."

"Before you even knew for sure it was Mark?" I asked.

"I never ignore my gut."

"Never?" I asked.

"Never." David wet his lips, holding my gaze. "Even when it gets me in deep shit."

"How do you know Mark Alvarez?" Detective Cooper asked, looking from David to me, getting out a notepad. "Why was he here? Did he threaten you, and if so, how exactly? Word for word."

It'd all happened so fast. My clutch tightened on David's blazer, keeping it closed. "I . . ."

"Not now, Coop," David said. "Can we do this later?"

"I need a witness account to detain him, Dylan," Cooper said, then sighed when David raised his brows. "But I suppose it can wait until tomorrow." He turned to me, his expression smoothing. "I'm sorry, I didn't get your name."

I extended my hand. "Olivia."

Instead of shaking, he handed me a card.

Detective Cooper, Chief of Detectives

Chicago Police Department, Organized Crime Division.

I repeated it to myself, trying to think of why it sounded familiar.

"Can I give you a ride somewhere, Olivia?" he asked.

As I started to accept, David cut me off. "I'll take care of it."

"I'm asking *her*," Cooper nearly growled.

"Come on, Coop. You know me."

Coop gave David a very ungracious look. "I don't care," he said. "This is about her, not you."

Both men turned to me.

"It's best that we end our personal and professional relationships here."

David's words from earlier came back in a rush, stinging all over again. I had no desire to leave the bubble of his protection, but he'd made it clear he didn't want me around, and getting closer to him wasn't a good idea on *any* level.

Especially if he intended to cut me out of his life once tonight was over.

"I appreciate the offer, David," I said carefully, "but I think I'll go with Detective Cooper."

"Olivia, wait." David took my elbow and withdrew when he seemed to think better of it. "I'm not letting you out of my sight until I know you're home safe. Even if that means I get in Coop's car with you."

"I'm not taking you home, Dylan," Cooper warned.

David inhaled through his nose and kept his eyes on me. "Do you trust me?"

"Do you trust yourself?" I said back, echoing his earlier words.

He didn't. Not around me. He'd made that clear, and the right thing to do here was keep the promise to each other that we wouldn't make this any harder than it already was.

David's expression eased. "Yes, I do," he said. "I'm not leaving your side until I know you're a hundred-percent safe. Even if that means sleeping outside your door tonight."

My cheeks warmed at the bold declaration, and at the

irritatingly thrilling thought of David guarding me all night. He would absolutely do it, too.

I sighed. "I don't want to put you out, Detective. I'll go with David."

"Are you sure?" Cooper rubbed his jaw. "It's no problem at all."

David nodded dismissively. "You heard her."

"All right." Cooper's shoulders slumped back into their default position. "If you need anything else, you call me," he insisted. He slapped David lightly on the shoulder. "I'll be in touch tomorrow, Fish."

Cooper walked over to where David and Mark had tussled and squatted with the remaining officer, who was putting Mark's knife into a plastic bag.

"Come," David said, nodding for me to follow him to my office. As we approached, I stopped in the doorway. At some point, we'd overturned a chair. And my little white blouse buttons dotted the carpet.

My throat thickened. If David hadn't come back . . .

I shook the thought away. I couldn't go down that path, especially not with David's curious eyes on me, looking as if he could read my mind clearly. I had to be strong.

I stooped to pick up a couple buttons, but either the motion or the act of witnessing what could've been made my stomach churn. When I stood, I met David's broad, hard chest inches away.

He pulled me into his arms. I knew I should protest, but I didn't have the energy to resist the only thing that felt right in that moment—his warmth, his strength, his stability. In his all-encompassing embrace, safety surrounded me, even when danger had nipped at my heels.

"Let go," he murmured. "You can't pretend this didn't happen or that it's not a big deal." His muscular arms wrapped around me so firmly, I could barely move. "Try to relax."

I thought I already *had* relaxed, but now, my shoulders loosened, and my cheek rested against his hard chest.

"Oh." I pulled away reluctantly. "I don't want to get blood on you."

He ghosted his thumb over my cheek, but I still flinched. David shut his eyes, sighed heavily, and opened them again. He was so close, the brackish musk of fresh sweat lingered.

"I should have *fucking* shot him," he said with complete conviction.

"If you had, you could be in the back of that police car."

"Self-defense," David said.

"It's not a guarantee," I said. "I've seen that defense collapse in some of Bill's cases. Usually, there's gray area."

"I'm taking you to the hospital," he said, ignoring me. Or ignoring the mention of my husband? "No," I insisted. "No, I'm fine."

"*Fine?*" he repeated. "You're shaking."

I hadn't realized, but while in his arms, I'd begun to tremble. "I'm really fine," I said, trying to even my tone. "Just a little frightened."

He pulled me close again, running his hand slowly over my back. After a beat, he gathered the hair from my neck, sweeping it into a loose ponytail. He pulled lightly to get me to look up. With his other hand, he lifted my chin higher to inspect the cut. My head was almost vertical, and I focused on the ceiling.

"It's not deep enough for stitches," he said, licking his thumb and wiping away some blood. "But it's probably a good idea to stop by Northwestern."

"No," I said. Panic entered my voice. If David made

up his mind to take me to the hospital, I wouldn't be able to convince him otherwise, and I didn't do hospitals. Sterile, cold rooms, doctors and nurses pricking me with needles, stitching me up. "I don't need to go. Please," I begged him. "I've had a rough night. I just want to go to sleep."

"Okay, shh," he said, rubbing my arms. "I just think it would be wise to check your head. What if you hit it—"

"*No.*"

He smiled for the first time all night. "You're a little stubborn, aren't you?" he asked.

I glared at him.

"All right, no hospital," he conceded. "But you can't be alone tonight. If Mark's threats held even an ounce of truth, I'm not taking any chances."

I glanced at the ground. If I was honest, I didn't want to be alone. What if there were others looking for revenge against Bill? If Mark could find and corner me at my workplace, they could easily get to me in my apartment.

But if David was suggesting what I thought he was, that was equally as dangerous in a different way.

Slowly, I raised my eyes to him. "What do you propose?"

"Come home with me tonight."

I bit my lip then released it quickly. To spend the night with someone like David—any woman would be a fool to turn him down.

"You know I can't do that," I said.

"You can when your safety is on the line."

"What about everything you said earlier? You can't even communicate with me without a liaison."

"Forget it." He smiled a little and held out his hand for mine. "Come on. We can start being finished with each other tomorrow."

I crossed my arms. "No. Either we start now or . . ."

"Or what? We don't start at all?" He arched an eyebrow. "I'm sorry if I hurt your feelings, but I'm not sorry I said it. I needed to be firm. I needed it to stick."

"So?" I asked. "This isn't firm. This isn't making it stick. Look, it's fine. I get it. It's done. Just let me get a cab home."

"I just said—*Jesus*, Olivia." His tone harshened, suddenly deep with bass. "I'm not letting you out of my sight. We can discuss all of this tomorrow, but tonight is not up for debate." He stepped closer to me, waiting until I looked up and met his eyes. "I swear to you, Olivia, you'll be safe tonight. Not just from predators, but from . . . from me as well. I can control myself."

I suppressed a shudder. David implied that he was as dangerous as Mark, that he was such a threat to me, he had to restrain himself—and it didn't scare me one bit. It excited me that he had to make us both a promise he'd refrain from ravaging me once he had me alone.

I believed he'd behave, so I nodded my agreement. "I'll get my things."

Chapter Eighteen

The elevator of the Gryphon Hotel stopped at the top. The *penthouse*. As it turned out, David lived in a hotel that also had residences. And it wasn't just any hotel, but the same one where, at David's suggestion, we'd be hosting tomorrow night's Meet and Greet for the magazine. No wonder he'd been so knowledgeable about the rooftop bar above us—and Amber, Gryphon's event coordinator.

David's shoulders sagged as he stepped out into a simple, elegant foyer with a single door.

I folded my arms into myself and followed, still in his blazer, which I'd put over a North Shore Turkey Trot t-shirt David had found in the gym bag in his car.

"Make yourself comfortable." He tossed his keys onto a circular marble table in the entryway and disappeared down a hallway.

A brightly lit, pristine living room with floor-to-ceiling windows displayed Lake Michigan on one side. Where the dark shore ended, Chicago's skyline started, interrupted by the apartment's smooth white columns.

I removed my shoes and walked over cool, ebonized

mahogany wood panels to a plush ivory carpet. Three steps down deposited me into a sunken living room with a pine-green, mid-century fabric couch. Somehow I doubted the black leather and walnut Eames lounge chair and ottoman, which ran north of five grand, was a knockoff.

A monochromatic stone wall housed a cozy fireplace, the focal point of the room. A glass coffee table, with a base fashioned from the same wood as the floor, held three small, colorful, abstract sculptures and a stack of design books. Their worn corners offset clean black-and-white spines, just like the carpet springing between my toes warmed the jagged stone fireplace and high ceilings. With the white-paned windows curving to show both vast lake and downtown buildings, the space felt both big and cozy.

"Well?" David called from somewhere in the apartment.

I scanned the dark horizon from the eighty-fourth floor. The carefully curated yet lived-in room could've easily been cold. In some ways, it was. It needed a little more of a woman's touch. "It's not quite what I expected," I said, picking up a remote from the mantel. With the push of a button, the fireplace flickered on.

"Not bachelor pad enough for you?" he asked from the other room.

"As an architect, don't you want to build your own house?"

"Without question. But I'm waiting for input."

"From?" I asked. When he didn't answer, I smiled to myself. David was secretly romantic. Not so secretly around me, it turned out. But if I'd only known him by his reputation, I wouldn't have guessed it.

"Finally, a smile," he said, reappearing with a balled towel in his hand. He walked to me at the fireplace and touched my chin to get me to lift it.

"This might sting a little." He gently pressed the towel to my cheek, and cold prickled my skin, my cut tingling. His gaze met mine a brief second, then shifted to the towel. "All right?"

This close, I could see the five o'clock shadow forming on his jaw. The dark, coarse bristles that had burned my lips when we'd kissed. We were nearly close enough to repeat the forbidden scene. He'd assured me his best behavior tonight, but he'd made me that same promise before.

And broken it.

I nodded. "Thank you."

"You must be exhausted."

I inhaled sharply as he adjusted the ice. "I never even asked if you were okay." I didn't see a scratch on him. The only indication of his scuffle were wrinkles in his dress shirt, a faint smudge of my blood on the crisp white fabric, and strands of his normally styled hair falling over his forehead. "Did he hurt you?" I asked.

"I'm perfectly fine."

"Like a superhero," I said without thinking, then bit my lip, as if that would retract the comment.

"Hardly." He scoffed. "Although, I'll admit—it isn't easy to chase and subdue someone in dress shoes."

I thought maybe I laughed, but it was only to cover up the fact that I felt as if I'd been sucker punched. *Chase and subdue.* That was what David had been metaphorically doing since the moment he'd met me. He'd found me at the bar during the ballet. Followed me to the balcony at Lucy's. Come to my office to do the article.

But it wasn't the metaphorical chase that made me lose my breath.

It was the vision of David acting out those verbs on me. Lust reared in me at the thought of David cornering me, tossing me over his shoulder, having his way with me despite all the reasons not to.

"Keep the towel there," he said, jolting me from the fantasy. I took the ice. He disappeared again and returned with two pills, a glass of water, and a tube of Neosporin. I handed over the towel and gratefully took the painkillers.

"Let's get you out of those clothes and into bed," he said, and my head snapped up at what sounded like an invitation.

He tilted his head. "I have a guest room you can stay in, Olivia."

"Of course," I said with a shaky laugh. "I knew that."

I followed him out of the living area as he showed me to a room furnished with nothing more than a queen-sized bed, two nightstands, and a dresser.

It was becoming obvious that despite David's talent for design, he spent far more of it on his clients than on himself. Why?

He pointed across the room. "Bathroom," he said, and added on his way out the door, "You can sleep in that t-shirt, but I'll get you some bottoms."

I removed his blazer and placed it over a chair. In the bathroom, I splashed cold water onto my face and examined the damage. David was right. The cut was minimal, and most of the blood had washed away. But I could already see the beginnings of a bruise forming around it. I dabbed antibiotic ointment on it, then tugged my fingers through my hair, but there was nothing I could do to improve the shadows under my eyes. I looked better suited for a night at the trailer park than as a guest in David's spotless home.

"I'm a mess," I said when he appeared in the mirror behind me.

"Yes, you are." He sighed. "Somehow you still look exquisite."

I rolled my eyes. "Okay. *Sure.*"

"Will either of these work?" He handed me folded black sweatpants and a pair of plaid boxers. "They'll be a little big, of course. But it's better than nothing at all." His mouth popped open. "Well . . . not *better*. I'm perfectly fine with nothing if you are."

I raised a scolding eyebrow at him and resisted from following that tempting path. Pulling taut the t-shirt he'd given me, I read in a teasing tone, "Turkey Trot?"

"If I'm in town for Thanksgiving, my dad and I usually run the 5K to support the local police department while my sister and mom prep dinner."

God. That was sweet. And unsurprising, since he'd already hinted he was close with his family.

That was not the David I needed to know right now. I couldn't forget that after tonight, he and I would no longer have a relationship of any sort.

I took the bottoms. "This is great. Thank you."

He nodded once and closed the door on his way out of the bathroom. I changed out of my slacks slowly as soreness descended, then whiffed his clothing—fresh laundry and David. Though it was a little warm for sweats, they seemed like the safer option for this sleepover.

When I came out, he was setting a glass of water on the nightstand.

"How's this for exquisite?" I joked in sweatpants rolled three times and a t-shirt that hung to the tops of my thighs.

"How come you roll your eyes when you say that?" he asked.

"Because it's a ridiculous thing to say when I'm in oversized pajamas, no makeup, with a bruise forming on my cheek." I walked to the bed and pulled back the comforter.

"Then again, I can't really blame you. I don't doubt *many* girls buy whatever you tell them."

"You do look exquisite."

I stopped, glanced down at my outfit, then back at him before bursting into laughter.

He tilted his head and smiled in a way that could get even the Virgin Mary into trouble. My laugh vanished as he looked me up and down. His eyes morphed from curious to hungry, as if he might leap across the room and devour me. I felt less desirable than ever, but the way my body warmed under his perusal, I might as well have been naked.

"One day," he said slowly, "I'm going to tell you, in detail too explicit for the moment, *exactly* how exquisite you look right now. I promise you that."

I clenched my jaw and swallowed. His eyes lingered too long, and that empty heaviness returned between my thighs. I doubted I could even dream up the explicit details he threatened.

"Well," he said, totally unruffled, "you're all set. I'll be back to check on you in a few hours. I want to make sure you don't have a concussion."

"I didn't hit my head," I assured him.

"Indulge me. I didn't see the assault with my own eyes, so I'll do as I see fit."

"Does someone as determined as you ever do as you *don't* see fit?"

A roguish grin was his only response.

I climbed into the bed and got under the covers.

"Goodnight," he said, switching off the lights on his way out.

Every time I began to drift, a cold blade touched my exposed chest. A pair of hands shoved my back against a wall. My scalp screamed as someone yanked my hair.

I would've sworn I hadn't slept, except that somewhere in the middle of the night, David's comforting voice broke through the dark.

"Olivia."

I blinked my eyes open.

"I'm just checking on you." Faint light slivered through the room from the doorway. "Need anything?"

"Yes," I said suddenly, sitting up. "Why'd you come back?"

"When?" he asked.

"You had no reason to believe I was in real danger. Mark could've been anyone, going to any floor in the building."

He paused. "If there was even a chance you were in trouble," he said slowly, "I wasn't going to risk it."

"Is that the truth?" His set jaw and determined gaze as he'd ended our relationship seemed so far away now. "You weren't coming back for . . . for another reason?"

"No. There's no in-between for us, Olivia. I can't come back for you. And I can't stay. Or we'll both get hurt."

I swallowed hard and nodded. I understood. But I was also tired of fighting, and I wasn't going to get any rest tonight. Not when I didn't feel safe. Without meaning to, I whispered, "Stay."

"What?"

Silence stretched between us long enough for me to take it back. To question why I'd said it. To tell him never mind.

Of course, he couldn't stay, and it wasn't fair to ask that of him. But my safety had been threatened tonight, and I felt exposed—in more ways than one. David had hurt me tonight by trying to end our relationship. He could do more damage than even Mark Alvarez. Ironically, he was the riskiest, most dangerous thing in my life, and yet I needed him now to feel safe.

"Stay," I repeated.

I couldn't see him in the dark, but I felt his struggle. I'd learned tonight that he *wanted* to do the right thing. It was who he was. But did he want me more? Was it fair to hope he did?

Footsteps crossed the room. The mattress dipped as he got onto the opposite side of the bed, far enough that I would really have to reach to touch him. I wouldn't, though. Just having him there allowed me to give in. Exhaustion descended. I closed my eyes knowing I was safe tonight, even from him.

Chapter Nineteen

I woke slowly from a deep sleep, my eyes opening to a room gray with broken dawn. Across the bed, David slept facing me, lying on top of the comforter in a white t-shirt and heather-gray sweatpants. At rest with tousled hair, he almost looked relaxed, except that his arms were crossed over his chest. He was so far away that he was almost falling off the bed.

Was it out of respect that he kept his distance? Or had our new arrangement gone into effect at the stroke of midnight?

I could reach out and touch him, pull him close. Snuggle into his chest. Desire welled in me, less urgent than in the past, but deeper. I couldn't help but think of what he might do if the circumstances were different. Lean over and finish the kiss he'd started in my office, letting his hands wander over my t-shirt. Reach between my thighs and feel my want, my need . . .

He shifted and opened his eyes. "Morning."

I cleared my throat. "Morning."

"How do you feel?"

"Good," I said and meant it. "I slept really well once you stayed with me."

He nodded and stretched his long limbs before leaning over me to see the clock. "Five to seven."

"I'm going to be late," I said.

"Call in sick." He turned back with a smile far too tempting for my tenuous, early-morning willpower. "You can stay here today if you want."

"That's a terrible idea." I sat up, grimacing as my sore muscles protested. "Setting aside the fact that we agreed to end this, the big party is tonight."

David sucked in an inhale, and I caught his cringe. "You're a little black and blue," he said, also getting up and scooting across the bed. He took my chin in his hand again —something I enjoyed far too much. "The cut looks all right, but your cheek is bruised." He shook his head and swept the hair from my face. "Poor girl."

We looked at each other, his hand lingering. The memory of our kiss swept over me again, more vivid with his vicinity. I pushed the dangerous thought from my mind but a sound escaped my lips.

"And what about the wounds I can't see?" he asked. "We should talk about what happened. What Alvarez almost—"

"Stop." I set my jaw. Why bring that up? I'd managed to temporarily forget the terror of Mark's hands on me, on what could've happened if David hadn't returned. Surface scrapes and bruises were easy—once they healed, it was done. But knowing I'd come close to being . . . I couldn't even bring myself to think of the violation.

I glanced at the comforter between us. "I'm fine."

"You have to talk about it."

"I will." I raised my eyes and ended the conversation, even if it was with a lie. "With Bill."

"Right." David glanced away, then lifted himself off the bed. "Let me at least save you a trip home. I can have an outfit sent up from one of the boutiques downstairs," he said and plucked at his shirt collar. "I've got great taste."

As a new day began, last night's shock wore off and left no excuses to hide behind. To stay and spend more time with this intriguing, sexy man—who wouldn't want that? To let him dress me as he would his girlfriend and send me off to work?

It definitely broke the rules of our non-existent relationship.

I pulled the covers off and climbed out of bed.

"Jesus, Olivia," David said, raking his eyes over me.

I glanced down to find my legs bare, and his long t-shirt grazing just below my underwear. "Shit," I said, tugging down the hem. "I must've taken off my pants in the middle of the night."

"I'm trying to behave," he said, "but you're making it nearly impossible."

I smiled, waving him off, though I understood. He exaggerated shielding his eyes as he left the room.

After a hot shower, I came out of the bathroom to find a shopping bag on the bed. God, that was quick. Normally, I would've left it where it was, but with my blouse destroyed, I couldn't exactly show up to work in a t-shirt and slacks. I unfolded a simple, forest green dress conservative enough for the office. I knew why David had chosen the green. It matched my eyes, and it was also Bill's favorite color on me.

I attempted to make myself presentable by twisting my damp hair into a loose chignon and breaking into the makeup essentials I carried in my purse. I lingered over the bruise, dabbing the area with cover-up, but eventually gave up trying to look good to go meet David in the kitchen.

He still wore a faded t-shirt and gray sweatpants that hung dangerously low. I glimpsed skin when he pulled two mugs from a cupboard.

"Thank you for the dress," I said, looking around his place more time. "How much do I owe you?"

"Just a quick breakfast," he said, quickly scanning my outfit. "What do you eat in the mornings? Want coffee? OJ? Both?"

I sighed, half-longing to spend my morning ogling him over a coffee mug. "I need to get going."

"You should eat first. I'm not a great cook, but I can whip something up."

Not wanting to be rude, I nodded to a bowl of fruit behind him. "How about a banana?"

He swung around and grabbed one to offer it to me. "What else?"

I narrowed my eyes and smiled at him. "You're kind of persistent, aren't you?" I said, mocking how he'd called me "a little stubborn" the night before.

He grunted. "When I want something, yes."

"What do you want, David?"

He flexed his hands in his pockets, inadvertently tugging his sweatpants lower. "Just to feed you, Olivia."

Was David this attentive to all his overnight visitors? He must've run up quite a tab on breakfast foods. With the irritating thought, I turned away. "The banana will suffice."

"At least let me get you a cab, too," he said, walking me to the door.

"You're in your pajamas," I pointed out. "What's it like living in a hotel anyway? Don't all the people disturb you?"

He gave a short laugh as we passed into the entryway, where he hit the elevator call button. "That's not usually the first thing people ask when they find out I live in a hotel. But no. Last night we used a private entrance and elevator. So unless I come through the front, I'm generally spared from people-ing."

I turned to face him. "You're still coming to tonight's Meet and Greet, right?" I asked. "Beman will kill me if you don't show. The press will be there to debut the list, starting with a red carpet out front of the hotel as people arrive."

"I'll be there," he said. "But all I have to do is ride the elevator one floor up to the rooftop. Looks like I'll miss the red carpet."

"But you're the most sought-after man in the feature —" I stopped myself. Clearing my throat, I tried shifting from teenage fangirl to a more professional approach. "We need you for the press you'll bring. You're walking the red carpet—even if I have to come up here and drag you there myself."

David paused a beat, then reached up to lift my chin. I assumed he meant to inspect my injury again, but instead, he leaned in, his mouth nearly at my ear. "I can almost assure you that plan would backfire," he said levelly. "Next time I get you willingly alone in my apartment, even the gentleman in me will step aside."

My eyes hit the marble floor as my warming cheeks gave way to a furious blush. Any joking left his demeanor. Was he serious? Did he think I could respond to something like that?

"Good grief, you're red," he said, drawing back. I peeked up to see his lips spread into a devastating smile. "And go easy on that poor banana."

I loosened my death grip around the fruit just as the elevator *dinged*.

Saved by the bell.

"I'll see you tonight," I said.

"Tonight." He nodded once and slipped his phone from his pocket when it rang. "Shit," he said and answered the call. His molten-brown eyes stayed on me as I boarded the elevator and leaned against the back rail, soaking in every last second with him.

He nodded once and said into the phone, "Got it."

I could've stared at him all day. It shouldn't have been anything remarkable, a man on a phone call in his pajamas, but his beauty, even like this, took my breath away.

The doors started to close, stealing him from me inch by inch.

Until he shot his hand between them, stopping the elevator. He hung up his call and met my eyes.

"Cooper wants us at the station as soon as possible."

Chapter Twenty

In a small windowed room at the police station, David moved a stack of paperwork from a chair to a desk with an engraved placard that read *Detective Cooper*.

David gestured at the seat. "Sit. Coop should be here any minute."

I sat. The chair wobbled. Without a word, David fixed it with a magazine under one leg. On the drive over, he'd also been quiet. Next, he straightened the stack of papers he'd moved and flipped open the top file folder.

"Should you be looking at that?" I asked.

"Nope," Detective Cooper answered, entering the office and closing the door behind him. "Hands off, Fish."

I followed the detective with my eyes as he sat at his computer. "Fish?"

"Always in the damn water," Cooper muttered. "Swimming, surfing, sailing—"

"They're called hobbies," David said. "You should try getting one."

"Do I look like a thirteen-year-old girl?" Cooper shook

his computer mouse, and the screen lit up. "I got enough bullshit to deal with on an hourly basis."

At Cooper's bookshelf, David picked up a worn paperback with a rifle target and blood splatter on the cover. "Like read crime fiction?"

"What?" Cooper shrugged. "I enjoy them."

"No, you don't." David glanced over his shoulder at the detective. "You read them so you can rip the story to shreds for its inaccuracies. Gives your black heart an excuse to get angry."

"How do you two know each other again?" I asked.

"High school," they answered in unison.

So they *were* around the same age. Truth be told, I was more interested in hearing what David was like as a teen than recounting the distressing events of the night before.

"Can we get started?" I asked. "I'm hosting a big event tonight, so I don't have a lot of time."

"Got it." Cooper sat back in his seat and looked to David. "I'll take Olivia's statement first. You can go."

David turned, his expression crestfallen. "I'm not going anywhere."

"That's not up to you. It's Olivia's call." Cooper opened a notepad on his desk, wet the tip of his index finger, and flipped the page. "Some of my guys are headed over to the crime scene now—"

"The crime scene?" I asked. "You mean my office?"

"Yep. They'll brief your boss on last night's events."

For the first time, I wondered if Bill should be here. I needed to call and fill him in. And how would he react to hearing I'd spent the night with another man?

He wouldn't. It wasn't the kind of honesty that served any purpose. And we weren't the kind of couple that needed to share every damn thing.

A statement was fairly straightforward anyway.

David cleared books from a chair in one corner and picked it up by its seatback.

"That's not sturdy," Cooper warned.

David placed the seat next to mine, still gripping the wooden back. "I'd like us to give our statements together."

I wanted David there. Just his presence comforted me. Just his association with Cooper made this a safe space. "Stay."

His hardened features eased and his hand twitched, as if he'd been about to reach for me. Instead, he took the seat so each of us faced the desk.

Cooper heaved a sigh and opened a drawer. "Alvarez number two is now in custody for violating his parole," he explained, rummaging through the drawer. "He not only had a gun on him, but cocaine as well. Dumbass. Since he's a felon, he's going to get it even worse." Cooper looked from me to David. "Between us, he'll probably take a plea bargain."

"What about retaliation?" David asked.

"Unlikely at this point." Cooper shook his head. "When Lou and Mark went away, their gang fragmented. I've heard rumblings they think Mark gave the cops info to reduce his charges. It's not true, but that doesn't matter. The Alvarez family is out, and that's why Mark is so worked up. He's got no one left."

"So you don't think they'll come after us?" I asked.

"They got no reason to stir up trouble with our department for two guys who'll be locked up for a while. But first, let's make sure Mark stays put."

The detective held up a tape recorder, hit a button, and spoke into it. "Witnesses Olivia Germaine and Lucas Dylan, incident involving Mark B. Alvarez on May seventeenth," he said into the recorder.

May seventeenth? I'd completely forgotten it was almost

my thirtieth birthday. I supposed that everyone else had, too, since nobody had mentioned it.

"All right, Miss Germaine," he began.

"Olivia, please," I said.

"Olivia. Can you give me a general recount of what happened?"

"I was working late when I heard the elevator. I got up to see who it was. When I opened my office door, Mark was standing there."

"So your office door was shut?"

"Yes," I said. "Is that important?"

"It must be a loud elevator."

"Coop," David said, his brows lowering.

"Just trying to get the facts as straight as possible. That's why it would've been better to do this last night, while her memory was fresh."

I cleared my throat. "Yes, from my desk, I probably wouldn't have heard it. But, now that I think about it, I was actually standing against the door."

Listening. Waiting. Hoping against all sense you'd come back . . .

I raised my gaze to David's.

He seemed to read everything in mine.

"What happened in the time it took for Mark to walk from the elevator to your office?" Cooper asked, then lowered his voice to the recorder. "By my estimation, it's about twenty-five to thirty yards."

"I—I just stood there," I said. "I guess I should've called security, but it never crossed my mind I was in danger."

"Who'd you think would arrive at the office that late?" he asked. "A co-worker?"

"I thought it was David," I said frankly.

Cooper's eyes shifted between us. He turned off the recorder. "You two dating?"

"Olivia's married," David said.

"Fuck." Cooper leaned back in his seat and rubbed his hands over his face. "You're going to make this complicated, aren't you, Dylan?"

"It's not like that," I said. "David's part of a feature I'm spearheading for the magazine, so he and I have been working together."

Cooper's frown gave away his skepticism, but he pressed *Record*. "Victim is referencing Lucas David Dylan, who goes by David. Go on, Olivia. Why would you think he'd come to the office at that time of night?"

"The magazine is featuring him as one of our most eligible bachelors of the year."

Cooper rolled his eyes *hard*, and David flipped him off.

"David's extremely busy and difficult to pin down—" Pin down, straddle, lower my face to his and stay just outside his reach as he tried to capture my lips with his . . .

I lost my breath at the fantasy—and my words.

"She asked me to come by when I had a few spare moments to go over things," David said, picking up where I'd trailed off.

"And that's what you did?" Cooper asked.

"Yes," we answered in unison.

Cooper looked between us.

I didn't want to lie and possibly muddle the details of the case against Mark, but I couldn't exactly explain that we'd been arguing over the fact that a man I'd just met wanted me to choose him over my husband of years.

"Sounds like you knew who Mark Alvarez was," Cooper said.

"He's threatened her before," David said.

Cooper raised his eyebrows as he took notes. "Did you file a report?"

"My husband didn't think it was necessary."

David's chair creaked as he shifted.

"Tell me about that encounter."

"I was walking home one evening—"

"When?"

I paused to calculate. "A few weeks ago. He stopped me outside my apartment building, looking for my husband. Bill was the prosecutor against Mark's brother, Lou."

Cooper nodded. "Got it. Bill Germaine? I'm not familiar."

"Wilson."

"Oh. Right." Cooper looked up. "I know Bill."

That was why the organized crime unit on Cooper's card had stuck out to me the night before. Bill's case had relied heavily on gang violence specialists. It was likely that he'd worked closely with CPD during the trial.

Whatever I said here today, and David, too, could potentially get back to Bill. "Can I, um, get some water?" I asked.

Cooper tossed his notepad down but left the recorder going as he rounded the desk and went to the door. "Sally," he yelled across the office. "Water."

As Cooper returned to his desk, David said, "He assaulted her that first night."

"Mark?" Cooper asked, rubbing an eyebrow.

I nodded. "He tried—"

"He put his hands on her and left marks," David said, his chair creaking as he sat forward and then back, unable to get comfortable.

"Mark said he wanted Bill to get his brother out of prison," I explained.

"Lou's serving a life sentence. Why—and how—would Mark think Bill could do that?"

"Mark said he and Lou committed the same crime but that Bill 'fucked up' and Lou got a worse sentence."

Cooper's pen flew across his notepad. "Sounds like Bill did exactly what he was supposed to."

"He takes his work seriously," I said. "He worked really hard on that case."

"Yeah. Good guy far as I know." Cooper glanced at David, whose uncharacteristic silence did nothing to dampen his presence. "What else?"

"After that, I didn't hear from Mark again," I said. "Until now."

"We'll come back to that night. What happened next at the office?" Cooper asked, eyes on his notes. "When did he put his hands on you? Be specific."

I steeled myself to recount everything, but the words wouldn't come. Why not? I'd been spared. David had prevented anything bad that might've happened.

When he visibly tensed beside me, I wondered if I should make him the leave room. He seemed to be struggling with his own internal monologue. "Are you sure you want to stay for this?"

"I'm not going anywhere," he said. "Take your time."

I just had to relay the facts. That was all. With another breath, I said, "Mark wasn't there to warn Bill. This time, he wanted to send a message. He ripped open my blouse. When I screamed, he hit me across the face."

With a knock at Cooper's door, David shot up from his chair. Mumbling to himself, he strode to the back of the room and whipped open the door. A short, elderly woman with a pitcher and three plastic cups stared back at him.

"Thank you, Sally," Coop called.

David took everything from her, shoved Cooper's files

aside, and nearly slammed the pitcher on the desk. After pouring a glass, David handed it to me.

Cooper watched all this with narrowed eyes, then turned to me. "Do you think Mark's intent was to scare you or to sexually assault you?"

"What the fuck does it matter?" David barked, back to pacing. "What kind of question is that?"

"Details," Cooper said simply. "They matter. Intent matters."

"I should've shot the motherfucker. *Fuck* him," David said as he grabbed the back of his chair and slammed it down. With a *thunderous* crack, two of the legs broke off, and the rest toppled onto the ground.

Cooper jumped up, his office chair rolling back into the wall of books. "What the hell—?"

"Sorry." David tossed the broken legs into the trash and sat against a windowsill, massaging the bridge of his nose. "I'm sorry," he repeated. "I'll pay for the chair. Continue."

Cooper sat back down while grumbling a string of curses. "Another outburst, and I'll kick you out, Dylan," Cooper said. "This is about her, not you."

My heart pounded as David's words reverberated through the room. It'd definitely been a mistake to do this with him here. "You should leave."

"No. Not unless you need me to." David pinched the inside corners of his eyes. "Go on."

I turned my attention back to Cooper. "David stopped the attack before it could go any further."

Cooper blinked a few times at his friend. "Olivia said you were there for a meeting, but that you'd left. Why were you still in the building?"

I took an extra-long sip of water to hide my face.

"I'd left," David said. "But as I said last night, when I

saw Mark in the lobby, I thought I recognized him and turned back."

Cooper eased back in his rolling chair. "I see."

David's simmering anger was almost as hard to watch as reliving the attack. "It's okay," I reassured him. "Everything turned out fine."

"Fine? It's not fine to me." His jaw sharpened. Veins corded his forearms as he fisted his hands. "You could have been seriously hurt or—or worse. And if anything had happened to you, I . . ."

The room stilled. Confusion marred Cooper's face at David's extreme reaction. We barely knew each other. There was no denying our attraction, but I wasn't his to protect. I wasn't his responsibility. And this wasn't his fault. So why was David acting as if none of that was true?

As if I belonged to him?

Chapter Twenty-One

Outside the Chicago Police Department, I squinted up at blue sky, waiting for David since Cooper had asked for a moment alone with him.

When my handbag vibrated, I took out my phone. The screen flashed with Bill's name. I checked over my shoulder to make sure I was alone before answering.

"I've been trying to reach you," Bill said, urgency in his voice.

News traveled fast. Not too surprising—the legal community here wasn't as big as one might think. I took a deep breath. "You heard?"

"Yeah. Why didn't you let me know when you found out? You haven't picked up anyone's calls."

"Cooper had me put my phone on silent," I said. "And what do you mean when I 'found out'?"

He sighed, sounding . . . irritated? "Look, I know you've been raised to keep things like this inside. I've learned to deal with that. But this is huge, Liv—you can't shut me out."

Twin threads of relief and surprise worked their way

through me. My first encounter with Mark had worried Bill, but in truth, part of me had questioned how much of it was concern for my well-being . . . and how much was him seeing an opportunity to get me to leave the city.

"I'm sorry I worried you," I said. "But I'm okay. How'd you find out?"

"Mack."

"Mack?" I asked. "Mack Donovan?"

"Well, yeah," Bill said as if it were obvious. "He called me when he couldn't reach you."

I frowned. "How'd *he* find out?"

"What are you talking about? She's his wife," Bill said. "And who's Cooper?"

His wife? "Davena?" I asked. "What does she have to do with this?"

With Bill's answering silence, the hair on the back of my neck rose. Was there news about Davena? That could be anything from remission to . . .

"Is—is she okay?" I asked, panic threading my words. "Is she back in the hospital?"

"Olivia," Bill said gently. "She passed last night. She's gone."

Gone? I froze. Or, I thought I had. I somehow found my ass landing hard on the metal seat of a bench. "What . . . how?"

"I don't think Mack or Davena wanted us to know how advanced the cancer was."

"Last time I saw her, she said the doctors weren't optimistic. She was trying to tell me . . . and I never got to say . . ."

Could it be? All that life, light, love—*gone?* Without so much as a good-bye?

What about Mack? He had to be utterly shattered.

I gripped the arm of the bench as my chest collapsed.

Davena had warned me I'd only have one shot at life. She must've known it was the end.

I waited for tears as I stared at the mottled, gray sidewalk under my feet. Despite watching her grow frailer, it'd never occurred to me that . . . that she'd actually *die*.

How could this happen? How could someone leave, just like that? How could she let that happen, when we needed her here? How, how, *how*—

I wanted Bill. To hug him, to have him tell me it would be okay, to come home so we could cry together. And I wanted to be alone. To hide my emptiness from him. Because I *couldn't* cry. I didn't even have the urge. Was I too cold and hardened? How could I feel everything and nothing?

I opened my mouth to tell him all of it. How much it hurt to lose someone who'd been a mother to me when my own couldn't. How I hated that we hadn't been there when she'd passed, or that I'd missed the true meaning in her words last week. Then maybe, when he got home tonight, I'd even share the truth behind the scar on my side, all the ugly details.

The weight of everything I held inside was suddenly greater than the pain I avoided by keeping Bill at a distance.

"Olivia?" Bill asked. "You still there?"

People passed on the sidewalk. Potted trees at the curb smelled of damp soil. Beneath me, the bench was strong and supportive.

I needed someone else to carry this grief. And maybe Bill just . . . couldn't. Maybe that was why I shielded him from the things that haunted me most. He'd try to rationalize it all away, slipping and sliding over the parts he didn't get so he could solve this and move on. I didn't want that. But I shouldn't have to do it on my own. It wasn't fair.

Davena had asked me to try to open up. Before it was too late.

I put my head between my knees. Sometimes I could hardly keep from crying out because of all the things I held inside. Bill might think I was cold, but fear, pain, beauty, love—I felt it all. It was too much to keep inside, but I didn't know how to speak it. I couldn't tell Bill I was scared to love him the way he deserved. If I told my mom all the ways she'd hurt me, she'd just respond with all the fabricated ways my father was to blame. There wasn't room for two victims in our relationship. And my dad had dealt with enough of that from her for a lifetime. He expected the emotional strength he'd instilled in me.

I steeled myself, sat up, and looked over my shoulder toward the station. I met David's concerned gaze as he stood near the doors. He was giving me distance. To speak to my husband. Who was waiting for me to respond.

"I'm at the police station," I said.

"*What?*" Bill asked. "Are you all right?"

"Mark Alvarez came to my office last night. I thought you were calling about that." David didn't take his eyes off me for a second. "Mark was more aggressive this time, but the cops arrived just in time."

"Holy shit, Olivia. Did he hurt you?"

"I'm fine," I said. "I'll tell you the whole story later, but I just gave a statement, and he's in custody."

"I knew that bastard would break his parole," Bill said. "You said earlier you're with Cooper? The detective?"

"He said he knows you."

"I'll give him a call now," Bill said. "But you really shouldn't talk to the police without me present."

"It all happened so fast, and Cooper called us in first thing—"

"Us?"

I took a breath. If I didn't tell Bill about David, Cooper would. "One of the bachelors from the article was in the office," I said. "He's the one who called the police."

"Jesus."

"He was just filling in some details for the piece," I explained. "We could've probably done it over the phone, but—"

"Thank God you didn't and that he was there," Bill said. "Is he with you now? Thank him for me, all right?"

An uncomfortable knot formed in my stomach. It didn't even occur to Bill that someone else could threaten our relationship. I'd made him feel safe in our marriage, as he'd done for me. That was not just the vows we'd taken, but also the silent contract we had—don't rock the boat. I nodded. "I will."

"So Mark's in custody, right?" he sighed. "You're not in any danger?"

I bit my bottom lip. Cooper had sounded confident that Mark's threats were all bluster. "The detective said the gang the Alvarezes were part of won't care enough to retaliate."

"They think Mark's a snitch," Bill confirmed. "They won't bother with you." He paused. "My flight's tomorrow night. Should I change it and come home now?"

If he had to ask, then no. Bill's workload never ended these days, and while I wanted him here, his clients needed him, too. Nothing would change by tomorrow. I could make it until then to hold him and reminisce about Davena.

My event—I'd almost forgotten. I couldn't miss tonight's Meet and Greet for anything, and if I dragged Bill along, he'd hate every moment.

"I'll be fine," I said. "I have that work event later and a lot to do before it starts."

"I'd say skip it, but at least it'll keep you occupied," he said.

"Beman will be there, so everything has to be perfect." My promotion was riding on every detail of this feature until it published. Focusing on that was much more appealing than wallowing at home.

"What a fucking week you've had, babe. I'll get home as soon as I can." He cleared his throat. "I should get back to work, but I'll call Cooper first. He can be kind of a dick —did he treat you all right?"

"He was great," I said. "He's been very on top of it. You don't need to call him. I know how busy you—"

"He'll want to talk to me, and I should thank him anyway. Your bachelor, too. I'll check in with you in a few hours, K?"

Bill and Cooper were going to talk. Now. I'd suspected they would, but it didn't stop my throat from closing. I forced myself up from the bench, absentmindedly massaging my chest. "Okay. Bye."

Within seconds of hanging up, David—*my bachelor*, as Bill had called him—was at my side. "Is he on his way?"

I rubbed my temple. "Who?"

He nodded at my cell. "*Him.*"

How did David even know who'd called? I tucked the phone back into my purse. "No."

"No what? When's he coming back?"

"He has a lot of work and missing even a day sets him back."

"It's almost the goddamn weekend."

"Do *you* take every weekend off?" I asked.

His nostrils flared the same way they had before he'd exploded during the interview just now.

"I didn't think so," I said.

"I would, if—"

"It doesn't matter," I said. My marriage wasn't any of his business. "What did Cooper want?" I asked, changing the subject.

David glanced away. "To make sure you and I were telling the truth. He said if we lied about anything important to cover up an affair, our statements could be inadmissible."

My cheeks flushed with the word *affair*. "We didn't lie," I said. "And my husband is about to call Cooper. If he says anything—"

"He won't," David said. "He's been around a long time, and he knows how to be discreet."

"There's nothing to be discreet about," I snapped.

Fuck. Why had I been so stupid as to spend the night with David? Why had he come to my office so late? Why hadn't I insisted on giving separate statements and putting distance between us?

My heart pounded so hard at the thought of Cooper saying something to make Bill suspicious, I couldn't even look at David. I turned away and headed for the spot along the curb where David had parked.

"Olivia—"

"We should send Cooper a fruit basket or something for his help."

"He'll *definitely* think we're sleeping together if we send a joint fruit basket."

As I reached the passenger's side of his Porsche, I whirled to face him. "This isn't funny."

"I didn't say it was. I'm just pointing out that a fruit basket would look suspicious."

"*That* would make him suspicious?" I shot back. "Not being together late at night? Not your reaction in there?"

David didn't respond as he opened the car door for me and made his way around the trunk to the driver's side.

I looked at him over the roof of the Porsche. "Why were you so upset?"

"Not *were*, Olivia. *Am*. I *am* upset, and for a lot of reasons. For one, it pisses me off that your husband's not—"

"Wait," I said, holding up my hand. "It's fine. I don't need to know. Let's not drag Bill into this."

"This is *his* goddamn mess. I can't stay silent. Why isn't he on a flight right this minute?"

"He offered, but I'm a big girl. He has work to do, and so do I." I slipped into the front seat, pulled the door closed behind me, and buckled my seatbelt.

David got behind the wheel but didn't start the car. "I saw your face out there. You're in pain. You're scared—and I don't blame you." He gripped the steering wheel. "That fucker invaded your space. He . . ."

I wanted to tell David that I wasn't upset because of Mark. I fought the urge to share Davena's death. Who she'd been to me, and how the world had dimmed in her absence.

How my life had turned upside down overnight, and that I was realizing just how quickly things could change.

But opening up to David wouldn't be fair to Bill.

"This goes deeper than someone threatening you," David said more calmly than I expected, shifting in his seat to face me. "Tell me what's running through your mind. Even if it feels stupid or insignificant."

Cars passed as we sat unmoving. I'd been strong for years, keeping the hurt inside and managing from one day to the next. Couldn't I make it one more night before dissolving? Because that was what I wanted to do. To let someone else take over for a while.

The silence became uncomfortable. I kept my eyes out my window. "I need to get to my office."

"What about after tonight's event? Will you be okay?" David asked. "You can't stay alone."

If he even *considered* suggesting I spend the night again, then he was delusional. I turned to him. "Both Cooper and Bill confirmed we'll be safe."

"That doesn't put me at ease."

"You're in as much danger as I am," I said. "Will *you* be okay?"

He snorted. "I'll be fine."

I tilted my head. "You shouldn't be alone, either. Perhaps you should find someone to stay with you."

"I could find someone faster than you could snap your fingers, honeybee," he said. "In fact, I already have a dinner date. I was going to cancel, but maybe I'll just bring her to the party."

I resisted from clenching my teeth. David's bachelor-hood could make my career, but that didn't mean I didn't *hate* the thought of him with other women. The idea of someone else having his undivided attention, his big, strong hands, his strength and support . . .

"Bring her then." My surroundings focused sharply as I forced a smile. "An event celebrating your single life is kind of a weird first date, but I doubt she'll even notice. She'll be too grateful for just the *opportunity* to spend a few hours with you."

David's knuckles whitened around the steering wheel as he stared forward. "I'm not the one making it seem like I'm some hotshot bachelor. You want me to be some kind of womanizer, either because it's easier for you to handle or because it'll sell magazines—"

"You agreed to this."

"For *you*," he said, turning his beautiful brown eyes on me. "To spend time with *you*. I'm putting my reputation on the line to spend a little time with you, and your shitty husband won't even fly a few hours to make sure you're not murdered in the middle of the night."

I blinked at him. I didn't even know where to begin with that. "You can't say things like that."

"I'll say what I want until you find a way to shut me up. And you haven't yet." He searched my eyes. "You're looking for more. You tell me to slow down while keeping your foot on the gas. If you want me to save you, Olivia, I can. I will. But you can't put all of this on me all of the time."

My throat dried as my mouth hung open. "All of *what*?"

"You act like there's nothing between us, and I warned you, I'm not buying that shit anymore when we're alone. Tell me you haven't fantasized about leaving him for me, and I'll walk away now. For good."

Two words needed to leave my mouth that instant.

I don't.

I don't fantasize about you.

About what our life together would be.

About what would've happened if I'd met you first.

How hard could it be to say all of that, even if it was a lie? My hands shook in my lap. Nobody had spoken this way to me in . . . maybe ever. Nobody had questioned me like this, pushed me, demanded more.

"See? You can't deny it," he said, sitting back. "And that's enough reason for me to stay and try."

"Try what?" I rasped, the words scraping from my throat.

Try to steal me away? I wanted him to say it as I simultaneously wished he'd keep his mouth shut.

He looked through the windshield. "I can tell you right now what's going to happen tonight. There's no way in hell I'm letting you go home alone. So you'd better find a goddamn place to sleep or you're coming back to my place again."

"What do you want from me?" I exploded. "I'm a married woman. I can't spend the night in another man's apartment. I—"

"You already did." His eyes gleamed. "And I warned you what would happen a second time."

"Next time I get you willingly alone in my apartment, even the gentleman in me will step aside."

I ignored the ache his words inspired between my legs and cleared the grit from my throat. "You heard what Cooper said. There's no danger. Mark's in custody. Bill will be home tomorrow night." I crossed my arms over my seatbelt. "I'll be fine."

"I have to say, I'm sick and tired of this 'fine' bullshit. Does he really accept that from you?"

I widened my eyes at David. "What are you talking about?"

"You're always saying everything is *fine*, even though it's not. It's *fine* that you were attacked last night? It's *fine* that you're obviously experiencing some heavy, traumatic shit? Does *anyone* care enough to question whether or not you're *actually* fine?"

"Excuse me?" I asked. "What are you saying? That Bill doesn't care?"

"How can anyone in your presence not care about you? I'm sure he does. What I'm saying is, I don't think that he, or your friends for that matter, know you as well as they think."

"And what, *you* do after knowing me for a minute?"

"It didn't take me weeks to understand you better than them," he snapped. "And I saw everything I needed to in that moment at the theater."

It was the first time either of us had ever mentioned

the intensity that'd passed between us, and the atmosphere thickened with tension.

"You are impossible to read if you're not paying attention, but I am. And I may not know the details yet, but *I know you.*"

I reeled back. "Does that line seriously work for you?"

With a grunt, he sat back, unruffled. "All right, Olivia. If that's how you want to play it. Call me a fucking playboy again because it's safer than the truth."

"What do you *think* the truth is?" I asked.

"If you want a satisfactory marriage with someone who's incapable of loving you the way you deserve, then get out of my car and let's end this for good." He shrugged. "I can't help you unless you meet me at least *part* of the way."

"Satisfactory?" I cried through gritted teeth. "Bill adores me, and everyone knows it." I faltered, completely flustered. "He's an amazing husband who treats me——"

"How?" David leaned in and looked me full in the face. "How does he treat you?" he demanded, his eyes boring into mine. His voice lowered into a rumble. "You have no idea what I'd do with you."

My legs sweat against the car's gummy leather, and I shifted, transported back to the theater, when the red velvet seats had pricked my thighs, David's presence clinging to me.

He was too close.

Too comfortable.

And the way he looked at me and saw everything—had *always* seen everything, from that first glance—was too much.

It threatened everything I'd built. Not just my marriage, but all the little stitches I'd put in place to hold myself together.

"You want to know how it feels to belong to a man like me." David licked his lips. "Admit it, Olivia, and I'll make it happen. We met too late—but we can still do something about it."

I gaped at him. "What—what are you saying?"

"You're made for me, Olivia. And I'm made for you. If you run away like you're about to, you'll always wonder what kind of love we could've had."

"Don't be r-ridiculous." I had love already. And if I didn't, it was because I didn't want it and all the *bullshit* that came with it. I fumbled to escape from the seatbelt. "We're done."

"I assumed as much. Here, let me," he said coolly and slipped his hand down between my thigh and those sticky leather seats. His hand lingered against my bare skin, at the hem of my dress, and my pulse pounded. He bent closer so that I could almost touch my lips to his neck. His faint, earthy scent left me dizzy and pining for more.

His fingertips grazed along my outer thigh as he searched for the release, and it was all I could do not to spontaneously combust from desire. My breath caught in my throat.

Do not squirm, do not squirm. That's exactly what he wants.

He pushed the button and the seatbelt jumped into my shaking hands. David leaned back into his seat and stuck his chin in his hand, looking back through the driver's side window.

I pushed the door open and hurried back out to the sidewalk, but I couldn't bring myself to slam the door. After taking a breath to collect myself, I said, "Maybe you were right yesterday. Maybe any type of relationship is impossible."

He looked over at me with an unreadable expression. "And maybe I'll skip tonight," he said.

I froze. Everything I'd done the past few weeks had been for this article, and David was at the center of it. "You promised you'd be there."

"I did. But you're testing my control, and I can't make you any more promises."

I gaped at him. "What does that mean?"

He locked his golden-brown irises on me. "When you find yourself alone and aching for something nobody around you can give you, when everything feels too heavy, and you want someone else to shoulder the burden—don't you dare look to me."

He *could* shoulder it—and he would if I asked him to. That was the problem. "I won't," I promised.

He cocked his head. "You say that, but you don't mean it. If I see in your eyes all the things you're too scared to admit *one more time*, then it's on."

"What's on?" I asked breathlessly.

"I will fight for you with zero regard for the destruction I leave behind. It will make the war over Helen of Troy look like a child's game. That's why I can't come tonight," he said, "unless you look me in the eye right now and tell me you don't want me. And you fucking mean it."

"Don't flatter yourself," I said and slammed the door.

Oh, *God*. He'd fight for me? At just the thought, excitement pounded my heart as I stormed off—and indignation shook my body. How dare he question my marriage, give me an ultimatum, and assume he'd be the one I'd go to when I felt the most alone?

He'd been lying to himself since the moment we'd met eyes at the theater. This was lust, nothing more. It could not conceivably or plausibly be anything more.

"You're made for me, Olivia. And I'm made for you . . ."

As in *soul mates*?

I nearly laughed. How many other women had fallen for that with the flash of his seductive grin?

That was it. This was done. And, I realized, it had to happen this way. When it came to David Dylan, an explosive fight culminating in an ultimatum I couldn't accept was the only way to finally end this.

Chapter Twenty-Two

Gretchen sat at a pink lacquer vanity table in her otherwise unremarkable bedroom. Empty white walls. Metal bedframe. A straw hamper in one corner. As she did her makeup, I tapped my foot and flipped through an old issue of *US Weekly*, but I didn't register anything on the glossy pages.

I hadn't heard from Bill. But would I, even if Cooper had said something to make him suspicious of David? Bill and I had an understanding. We knew when to communicate and when to sweep things under the rug and move on.

Not that there was anything to sweep anyway. Nothing had happened with David.

All that mattered at the moment was that my event started soon. "I need to get back so I can finish setting up," I said to Gretchen, tossing the magazine on her white paisley bedspread.

"Nope." Gretchen shook her head. "I've put on hundreds of events, Liv. There comes a point where tinkering with small details can make things worse."

"But if my boss arrives and everything isn't—"

"Everything *will not* be perfect. I promise you." She arched an eyebrow at me. LED bulbs lit up Gretchen's smooth, freshly scrubbed skin, illuminating her slight rosacea and the little red bumps that would disappear in moments with a fresh coat of foundation. "You have to let go of the things you can't control and know you did your best. People will pick up on your stress, but if you let loose and have fun, they will, too." Her mouth quirked into a smile. "And if anything gets fucked up, blame it on the event coordinator. That's what they're there for."

Gretchen had lured me to her place with the promise of a closet full of designer wear. What her bedroom lacked, she made up for with sample sales, eBay finds, designer gifts, and Rent the Runway. It hadn't been that difficult for her to convince me to come over, though. Once the sun had gone down, I hadn't wanted to be alone at my apartment.

"That dress looks amazing on you, but it would look even better with your hair up," Gretchen said, holding out a tin of bobby pins. "Show off your shoulders."

I took the box and glanced at myself in her full-length mirror, smoothing a palm over the short, sleeveless leather dress she'd lent me.

I stuck a few bobby pins between my teeth and twisted my hair into a bun as Gretchen used her concealer wand to make two triangles under her eyes. "How was your week?" she asked, blending the concealer with a sponge.

"Good," I said automatically.

Except, it hadn't been good *at all*.

The death of a close friend, a harrowing assault, a trip to the police station, and a blow-out fight with the most infuriating, persistent, and handsome man I'd ever met.

David's accusation rang through my head.

"I'm sick and tired of this 'fine' bullshit."

So far, I'd avoided thinking about all the unwelcome, impudent—and possibly accurate—things David had said by keeping busy with tonight's event.

"What was so good about it?" Gretchen asked.

Filling her in on all of it would only bring down the mood—and invite questions I wasn't sure how to answer.

I focused on pinning my hair into place. "I'll get into it later."

She narrowed her eyes on me as she swiped a makeup brush over the contour palette in her hand. "Well, my week actually *was* good," she said, expertly transforming her face. "Our biggest client called me 'talented' in front of my boss—you know what a witch she can be. Then a head-hunter contacted me today. I'm seriously considering leaving, I mean . . ."

I nodded, but my thoughts wandered. David knew what tonight meant to me. What if he didn't show? I'd convinced Beman to let me throw this event. It had to go smoothly. *Seamlessly.* That included an appearance by Beman's favorite bachelor.

"And, to top it all off," Gretchen continued, "you'll never guess who I hooked up with while you guys were at Andrew's cabin. One of the *hottest* guys in Chicago."

I swallowed, smoothing the top of my hair to ensure every piece complied. Nobody could compare to David. I envied the carefree way Gretchen shared her life. The fact that she put herself out there, had fun, and didn't have to answer to anyone.

It was childish, but if I let myself remember my kiss with David without any guilt, I'd feel just as giddy as she was now. And telling her what'd I'd done would *blow* her mind.

"Liv?" she asked, frowning at me in the reflection. "You look like someone just ran over your dog."

"Oh." I attempted a smile. "Sorry. Who was it?"

She turned in her chair, eyeliner in hand, and glared at me. "What's wrong?"

"Nothing I want to get into now," I said, moving to sit on the bed once my hair was up. "Can I borrow your concealer when you're done?"

Her eyes narrowed. "You're already wearing more makeup than usual."

I'd done a decent job covering the welt Mark had given me since the bruise hadn't fully formed yet. "There'll be photographers at the event," I explained. "Those cameras pick up everything. So, who's the guy?"

Gretchen sighed, no stranger to my deflection. Tonight wasn't about anything except pulling off a spectacular event. I'd tell her everything when I was ready.

"Page thirty," she relented and pointed to the *US Weekly* I'd tossed on the bed. I picked it up and flipped to the "Celeb Sightings" column. "Which one?"

"Graham Broderick!"

My eyes went to the tall, attractive man in a baseball cap and fitted t-shirt with a gym bag over one shoulder. "Whoa. Doesn't he have a movie coming out? He's a *real* celebrity, Gretchen. And so gorgeous."

She smiled and turned back to the mirror. "I haven't even told you the best part. Graham's my date tonight. That should get you guys some good publicity."

It definitely would. I should've been elated, but I could only stare at the page. Graham's chiseled jawline and muscled frame were a good match for David's classic, indisputable beauty. But in my eyes, the two men didn't even compare. It just went to show that there was more to David than his looks. His attractiveness somehow grew the more I got to know him. With his eyes on me, nobody else existed. Not to me, but more importantly—not to him.

"If I see in your eyes all the things you're too scared to admit one more time, then it's on . . . I will fight for you with zero regard for the destruction I leave behind."

It was the first time I'd truly let myself think of his declaration since I'd stormed away from his car.

Because it was an unbearable thought that I couldn't give him what he asked.

I'd already made my choice. Bill had been nothing but a good husband to me. I couldn't leave a kind, loving, and understanding man for someone I'd met weeks ago. Someone with whom I'd already experienced fireworks, a passion that had simmered from the start, ignited with our kiss, exploded in more than one volatile argument. David and I fought in ways Bill and I never had.

Who in her right mind would leave the safety of land and dive headfirst into treacherous waters?

Gretchen whisked on some mascara, glancing back-and-forth between her reflection and me. She screwed the cap back on, got up, and came to sit by me on the bed. "What's the matter?" she asked. "You can tell me anything. You know that. Did something happen?"

I swallowed. I hadn't let myself think of Davena, either, afraid I'd break down before I made it to the venue. She'd said, in her own way, to quit playing life so safely. David had echoed her, daring me to stop hiding behind "fine."

But once I voiced the storm of giddiness, fear, and pressure brewing within me—then my feelings would be real.

Except, they *were* real. They had been since the moment I'd laid eyes on David. And it terrified me that everything I'd worked for could be so easily undone.

If there was one person I could talk to about this, it was Gretchen. Lucy would try to rationalize away my feelings, maybe even scold me for them. But Gretchen never had, and never would, judge me.

I traced the faint paisley pattern of the comforter between us. "I don't know how to say it."

She took my hand and squeezed it. "Imagine this thing that's on your mind is a piece of furniture, like a couch."

I frowned. "A couch?"

"It's way too heavy to carry on your own, right? But I'm here to help, knocking at your front door. If you open it for me, I can come in and lift the other side of the couch."

I half-smiled. "And then what?"

"I don't know. We move it to another room, one with more light. Or maybe we switch out the pillows. Fuck, we can put it out on the curb for garbage day if you want."

I laughed a little. As the tension in my shoulders eased, I blew out a breath and opened the front door. "I—there's this man," I said. "And I'm attracted to him. I'm attracted to someone else."

"Oh, thank God." Gretchen placed her free hand over her heart and exhaled. "You scared me for a second there. I thought it was something really bad, like Bill got you pregnant."

I smiled, though I suspected she was partly serious. "It *is* bad," I said. "What I'm feeling . . . it's more than an attraction."

"Like what? You want to jump this guy's bones?" She rolled her eyes. "That's perfectly *normal*. To be honest, it's more abnormal that you've never experienced that. Just because you're married doesn't mean you can't look."

I shifted on the bed, grasping for the right words. "I've encountered plenty of attractive men. Especially in my line of work," I said. "This is different, Gretch. I'm—I'm *falling* for him. I have feelings for him."

It was the first time I'd let myself think it in such black-and-white terms. And definitely the first time I'd said anything like it aloud. I didn't expect it to feel so *true*.

"Falling for him?" Gretchen's eyebrows cinched before her expression eased with understanding. "For real? Wow."

"Yeah. Wow."

"But, Bill—you guys are happy, aren't you?"

"*Yes*." I took back my hand and placed it in my lap. "It's not even really about Bill at all—it's . . . it's bigger than that."

Gretchen stayed silent, but not in judgment. She gave me the space I needed to hear these things out loud, test them, see them from a new angle.

And something occurred to me. *Was* this more than bad timing for David and me? Could it actually be about *Bill* as much as it was about David?

My nose tingled. I didn't want that to be true. It complicated things so much more if I had to put a magnifying glass to my marriage when Bill and I had created a groove that worked for both of us.

"I love Bill, and I've never even felt the urge to be with anyone else," I said, my throat thickening. "*Ever*."

Gretchen nodded thoughtfully. "But you clearly feel strongly for this other guy. What is it about him?"

My eyes darted over the bedspread. "He and I connected in such a powerful way. The first time I looked at him, something so intense passed between us. That was before we'd even spoken."

"Babe, that sounds like lust."

I nodded. "I know. I thought so, too, at first. Or, at least, I hoped. But our bond strengthens whenever I'm near him, and I can't stop it. I *can't*. I want to so badly, but it's so, so *blinding* that we actually . . . ."

Those Windex-colored eyes grew bigger than I'd ever seen them. "Did you sleep with him?"

"No." I swallowed. "But we kissed."

She blinked at me. "I've never even heard you *talk* about another guy since you met Bill."

"It just sort of happened. One minute, we were talking, and then it's like I just fell into him. I feel so incredibly guilty."

"Oh, Livs." She pulled me in for a tight hug, then drew back, her grip firm on my shoulders. "Listen to me. You're not the first person in the world to make a mistake in the heat of the moment. I'm more surprised that you even allowed yourself to get caught up in *any* moment at all."

I frowned. "What does that mean?"

She sighed, twisting her lips as if searching for words. "Bill has always been—safe. You fell in love slowly and without any hiccups. I saw what your parents' divorce did to you. You stopped taking risks. You stopped knowing how to open up. Bill's always loved you, and he'd never hurt you."

Safe. That was no great revelation—I'd known it from the beginning of Bill's and my relationship. But paired with David's accusations from earlier . . . *safe* became a dirty word.

It implied my marriage was satisfactory.

That I wasn't being loved the way I deserved.

I thought it'd been a kind of safety that had also brought happiness and love. But the more time I spent with David, the less I saw what I had, and more what was missing.

"That doesn't mean you owe Bill anything," Gretchen continued.

"Yes, it does," I said. "I took vows."

"But people fall out of love. And they change. You

know that, but you're so hard on yourself. If you don't change in the ways you think are right or perfect, you resist the fuck out of it. And it will only hurt you, and Bill, too, in the long run."

"So what are you saying?" I asked, a knot forming in my stomach. If she was talking about change, then that meant making decisions I'd thought were already set. Taking action. Hurting people I loved. "Are you telling me to do something about it?"

"You know I can't tell you what to do here. Nobody can. But you clearly need to take some time to think about what you really want. Not what you think *others* want, but *you*, deep down."

I'd let Gretchen in the door, and even though she'd given me a lot to think about, my struggle with the couch *did* lessen slightly.

But it was hard to ignore the question burning in her eyes.

After another moment of silence, I spoke. "I can't tell you who he is, G. Then there's no turning back."

Her face fell, but she nodded. "Whoever it is, I beg you not to ignore this any longer. When we were kids, we had so much *fun*. Remember how we used to spy on Jon until that day we caught him making out with a girl? We were so grossed out."

I smiled. "Your brother nearly killed us that summer."

"You were lighthearted. Fun. Passionate. I know it still lives in you. It was hard to witness all that die during your parents' divorce, and then to watch you suppress anything remotely close ever since."

Her words took my breath away. Months ago, I'd been living the life I'd thought I'd wanted, one I'd carefully constructed, one that proved I could be happy.

I was beginning to realize I may have fooled myself, but

others had seen right through it. Davena. Gretchen. And most of all, the stranger in the tuxedo. *David.*

"My parents fought a lot, but I never expected it to get so bad," I said. "Even at the end, when it was the worst, it didn't occur to me they'd actually split up. I was scared of my mom after the accident, but even then, I thought they'd work it out."

"You thought love was enough. That's not your fault— it's what we're taught. That love conquers all. Then we get old enough to know better."

Exactly. I knew better now, didn't I? Love alone wasn't enough. Passion did more harm than good. So why had I let David get so deep under my skin?

I nodded. "The divorce was for the best. Their highs and lows made everyone miserable, including me."

"It's such a relief to hear you say that. It's been so long since we've had an honest conversation about the past."

"I'm sorry," I said. "It just brings up things I thought I'd moved on from."

"Come on, Olivia. You didn't deal with or move on from anything. You buried it all. You were thirteen, so it's okay. But it's time to grow up and face it now."

I inhaled a breath. It wasn't easy to hear. I thought time would heal the wounds my parents had left, but like the one just below my ribs, scars remained.

Gretchen reached up and swiped away a tear I hadn't realized had escaped. "When was the last time you cried in front of me?"

"I hate doing it in public."

"*Public?* It's *me*. This isn't public."

"Yes. That sounds stupid, doesn't it?" I shook my head, sniffling. "You're a good friend."

"I try, but sometimes you make it hard." She glanced toward the ceiling. "As kids, you told me you were going to have it all. The most successful job, the biggest house, the cutest husband. You said he was going to be the nicest, tallest guy in the world, and he'd love you more than anyone. Do you feel that way about Bill?"

"Everyone thinks that way when they're ten years old," I said wryly.

"Sure, but you carried that into high school, and into your adult life, too. You withdrew from love, but you still expected everything to fall into place the way it should. Not necessarily in a way that excited you."

"I had high expectations because my dad did. I didn't want anyone to ever think that I wasn't good enough."

"Nobody thinks that," she said. "Everyone loves you. And I'll beat up anyone who doesn't. I'll always have your back."

"I never would've survived without you and Jon," I said. "You guys are the reason I made it through."

She gave me a beautiful smile, and I was sure I saw tears in her eyes. "So what about Bill? *Is* he those things?"

"No one can be all of that," I said.

"But is he still 'the one'?" she asked. "You don't have to answer, but you should know you've always got . . . options."

I heard what she didn't say.

Divorce.

I shook my head slowly. "I'm not saying I've always made the right life choices," I said. "But the decisions I made, I made so I wouldn't end up like them."

"There are no guarantees, Liv. You may have to let go of your fears around the 'D' word. Your experience wouldn't be the same as your parents', you know. You don't have kids."

But if Bill had his way, we would—and then I'd never

leave. I couldn't put a child through the heartache I'd lived. How much longer would Bill wait for my answer?

And just like that, the decision ahead of me had nothing to do with David at all. Maybe it never had.

I hadn't considered that my decisions might be reversible. And if they were, I only needed to ask myself one thing . . .

What kind of life did I want?

Chapter Twenty-Three

Gretchen's advice to stop stressing over event minutiae and enjoy the Meet and Greet turned out to be spot-on. The past hour, I'd been all around the event, checking in with the necessary people and mingling with guests. The party, now in full swing, was a success.

I squeezed my way through the dancefloor where Gretchen moved against Graham Broderick with closed eyes and a blissful smile. The Gryphon Hotel's rooftop venue had opened all its sliding doors. The tallest buildings of Chicago's cityscape backdropped the patio's fire pits, a lush, vertical garden of plants that made up one wall, and all-black chairs with overstuffed cushions.

My boss gestured at me from where he stood at a two-top table. Edison light bulbs glowed above him, strung from a lattice covering. "I must say, I'm pleased with what you've done here," Mr. Beman said as I approached. "Not too over the top and an impressive guest list. How'd you manage to get Graham Broderick? There are actually paparazzi out front."

"Oh, I called in a favor with a friend," I said, waving my hand with the slight exaggeration.

He smiled tightly as his gaze jumped over my shoulder. "Here comes one of your bachelors now."

David.

My chest tightened. His non-presence had been almost palpable to me, but if I was honest, I'd known he'd show up. He wasn't the type to let things lie.

And by the way my heart skipped, I was grateful for that. I turned slowly as footsteps approached, but instead of David's warm brown eyes, I met sparkling blue ones and a tan face belonging to one *distinguished beach bum*. Brian Ayers, the surfer and photographer David had recommended I add to the feature, shook out his bleached, shoulder-length hair. "Evening, Olivia."

Mr. Beman started to stick out his hand, but when he noticed that Brian carried two wineglasses, Beman tightened his already taut tie instead. "Thank you for agreeing to do the feature, Mr. Ayers," he said. "I've so enjoyed perusing your photography."

"Call me Brian." Brian turned to me. "And when can I add *you* to my collection, Olivia?"

Almost every wall of Brian's studio apartment had been covered with gritty, intrusive portraits of people from all walks of life. Like David, Brian had a way of looking past people's facades and capturing deeper emotion.

Which sounded *awful*.

"How about on the tenth of . . . never," I said and smiled as he laughed.

"If you'll excuse me," my boss said and hesitated before nodding at me. "Very nice turnout, Olivia. Keep up the good work."

I exhaled a breath of pure relief. With David's help securing the venue at a steep discount, and with strong sponsors and an A-List guest list . . . it was fair to say I'd pulled it off. And that I was squarely in the running to nab this promotion.

Brian held out one of the glasses of white wine. "Cheers."

"For me?" I asked.

He nodded. "Chardonnay. I remember that was what I served you during our interview."

I almost laughed but a pang in my heart stopped me. David would scold me with a look for accepting what others expected of me. Despite tonight's wins, his absence lingered, a dark cloud overhead. As the clock ticked down, it became more apparent that the only man who'd ever thought to question my chardonnay had truly walked away.

Maybe the alcohol would numb the disappointment—and the pain of the last twenty-four hours.

Davena. I blocked the name from my mind and accepted the glass. It wasn't like me to drink on the job, but tonight, relaxing my control even a little felt like a reward for a tough week.

I forced a wide smile, clinked my glass with his, and took a large sip. "I can see why everyone says you're so charming, Brian Ayers," I said. "You always come with alcohol."

"It's nice to see you again." With a grin as he glanced behind me, he leaned in to kiss my cheek. "What is that perfume? It reminds me of Paris!"

I giggled. "I'm not wearing anything."

As I drew away, a voice behind me rumbled in greeting. "Ayers."

My heart leaped into my throat as David's unmistakable presence stopped next to me.

"David. Didn't see you there." Brian winked at me.

The men shook hands with vigor. "I was beginning to wonder if you'd show your ugly mug."

"Careful." David's steady tone hinted at teasing as he started to take a sip of something dark. "You wouldn't even be allowed in the venue if I hadn't pulled strings to get you in this magazine feature."

Brian's chiding response fell on deaf ears as I glanced up and met David's unreadable gaze, locked on me. He'd shown up, but he didn't look happy about it. What was he thinking? His expression remained smoother than his bristly jawline, his dark hair disheveled. I rolled my lips together to keep from gaping.

"How's your date going?" I asked, looking past him for a woman.

David looked into his drink. "Over before it began, I'm afraid."

I concealed a burst of giddiness by drinking more chardonnay. Perhaps it was thanks to the alcohol, but I dismissed any shame over my unwarranted and uncharacteristic jealousy.

"Only a fool would bring a date to a party filled to the brim with beautiful women," Brian said, drawing my attention back to him. "In fact, I was just asking Olivia here when she was going to let me take her picture. You'd look perfect hanging in my living room, Liv."

I blushed. "I don't think so."

"Don't get shy on me." Brian wrapped me in a side hug, looking down at me. "You have magnificent eyes— they really are unusual. The camera would love them. Aren't they magnificent, David?"

"They are," David said without a hint of emotion. He swirled his dark-honey drink in measured circles. A charcoal V-neck sweater over a slate-gray button down showed off the knot of a matching tie, which he loosened as his eyes burned into me. My body thrummed under his dimming gaze. The way he looked at me, like he couldn't control what might happen next, almost brought me to my knees.

"What do you say to that, David?" Brian asked, breaking through our moment.

"Hmm?" With obvious reluctance, David tore his eyes from mine. "To what?"

"I just told you there's a nice-looking redhead over by the railing, twirling her hair, just begging for you to scoop her up. Why don't you run along so Olivia can give me a rundown of available women?"

I followed Brian's gaze to the hotel's event coordinator. After David had connected us, Serena and I had met with her a few times to plan this event. When David looked over, she waved, as if she'd been waiting to catch his attention.

David nodded. "That's Amber. She works here."

"Well, that's convenient." Brian smirked. "She can run one floor down when she's on break."

"Fuck off," David said, glancing at Brian's arm around me. "And why don't you keep your hands to yourself?"

Brian showed us his palms, a twinkle in his eyes as he nodded sideways at David. "I don't know what's up his ass, but he needs a good lay, and he isn't going to get it hanging out with us, is he?" he asked. "She's just David's type, but I like a girl with substance, Olivia. Someone creative and carefree, who's also a little weird."

I bit my cheek to hide my smile at the unsubtle swipe at his friend.

"Let's find me a girl like you—smart and beautiful, but edgy, too," Brian said and sipped his wine. When I started to protest, he took my hand and lifted my arm, urging me to twirl. "Oh, come on, I know you're a little wild. Look at you, in your leather dress."

David's grip tightened around his glass. He didn't like the topic. He didn't like Brian touching me. But so what? He wasn't even supposed to be here, and if he was going to do nothing but brood, why even show up?

"Actually, I'm borrowing this outfit from my friend," I said. "And just your luck—she's here tonight."

It wasn't hard to spot Gretchen, her long, platinum blonde hair like a beacon across the dancefloor. I raised a hand to catch her attention and wave her over. "She's a real catch. Funny and smart, but she came with someone," I said.

"Is she clever?" Brian asked.

"Yes, though she might try to fool you," I said, setting my wineglass on the table next to us. "People always underestimate her, and she plays into that."

Gretchen waltzed over with what looked like a Shirley Temple, her curious blue eyes flitting over the three of us and landing on the sexy surfer. "Hey."

"This is my friend Brian," I said to her. "He's one of our bachelors."

"I'm aware," she said with a killer smile. "I've already had Liv fill me in on the best attendees."

Brian laughed boisterously. "I was just having her do the same for me. But I didn't see you in the feature. Gretchen, is it?"

"Gretchen Harper." Through a tiny straw, she sipped the last of the fizzy red drink I assumed was actually a Dirty Shirley. "And I was in the mag a couple years back."

"Funny, I think I would've remembered." Brian offered her his elbow. "Shall we get you a refill?"

She slipped her arm through his and said, "Always," as he led her away.

"Don't forget," I called after them. "I need Brian single until the issue comes out."

They ignored me. David, on the other hand, didn't. Even without turning to him, I knew how he was looking at me. Penetrating and lusty with a twist of somber, and I suddenly remembered the seatbelt. How he'd leaned over to unbuckle it, his hand grazing my skin, so close to the hem of the dress he'd bought me.

"What are you doing here?" I asked.

"I came for my answer."

The directness of his response made me pause. "I already gave you one."

"Storming off after slamming the door in my face in the middle of an argument is not an answer."

"That wasn't an argument," I said. "It was a finale. With fireworks."

"If you felt fireworks, then I assure you, this isn't over."

"It is," I told him. "It has to be."

"Then give me what I came here for." His eyes drifted down my leather dress and jumped back to mine. "Tell me to back off, Olivia. Say it without pleading me to stay with your eyes, without your body practically vibrating to feel my hands on it."

I sucked in a breath but crossed my arms, even though it wouldn't make a difference. I could close off my body to him, but nobody had ever been able to read the truth in my eyes the way David did. Telling him I didn't want him would be a lie, and he knew that. "Just because I'm married doesn't mean I can't feel attracted to other men."

"Yeah?" he asked, jutting his chin at me. "How many other men?"

None. I picked up my wine for a sip. "You're reading too much into this."

When he set his lips in a line, the angles of his jawline

sharpened. "Why do you think I've pursued you since the moment I saw you?" he asked, glancing at the chardonnay. "Physical appearance has little do with it."

I gaped at the insult. "I never claimed to be your type."

"Don't mistake me. You are the most beautiful woman I've ever met."

I clenched my teeth, arousal and shock mixing with indignation at what had to be a lie. David had his pick of women anywhere he went—and plenty of practice getting them to spread their legs. "And how many women have you said that to tonight alone?" I asked. "Why don't you go see if *Amber* is willing to play, because I'm not."

He ignored me. "Your beauty comes from something inside you. I took one look at you at the ballet, and your eyes told me a story. You were alone. You were desperate, as was I. Your vulnerability struck something deep in me."

I couldn't remember the last time, if ever, somebody had described me as vulnerable, let alone accused me of *desperate* vulnerability. Bill had called me cold. Hours earlier, Gretchen had driven home her point that I'd closed myself off and suppressed emotions since childhood. But I didn't need either of them to tell me that to know it was true.

So what had David seen that night? I closed my eyes briefly, reliving those moments of looking around a crowd that included my best friends—my *husband*—and feeling alone. Alien. My guard hadn't been up in that one, single moment David and I had locked eyes.

Chills spread over my bare shoulders. I looked at him now as the truth struggled to the surface. If David fought for me, it could be game over for Bill.

Was I ready for that? To say good-bye to the life I'd not only known, but the one I'd wanted, the one I'd constructed?

"If you want something, say it out loud."

Out of nowhere, Davena's words sliced through me. Her death had left a wound I was trying to hold closed until I could grieve alone. But it was also the most glaring sign that life was too short not to selfishly reach for my desires when I had the rare chance to catch one.

David took my chin between his thumb and forefinger and lifted my face, inspecting my cheek. "You covered the bruise, but I can still see it."

"What bruise?" Gretchen asked from behind me.

I nearly jumped back as David removed his hand. He glanced from Gretchen back to me. "You haven't told her about last night?"

"Told me what?" Gretchen fixed her gaze on me. "What happened last . . ." She gasped, and her hand flew to her mouth.

Brian approached, brows furrowed. "What's wrong?"

Gretchen's eyes widened as she stared at me. "Oh my God," she said, the words muffled by her hand. "It's *David*? *He's* the one you—"

I grabbed her arm and yanked her away, wine sloshing around the glass in my other hand. "Give us a minute," I called over my shoulder, pushing Gretchen through the crowd until we were in a quiet corner.

Her face, frozen with shock, quickly thawed. "Oh, Olivia. No, no, no. If David Dylan is the one you've fallen for, get up off the ground and run. He's a total womanizer."

I'd accused him of that many times, and it was true. He was a player. But I'd called him that to push him away, not because I couldn't recognize that to him, I was different. What *he and I had* was different. I bristled. "You don't even know him."

"I don't have to. I know enough guys just like him, Liv.

Someone like that can be . . . dangerous. He knows how to make you feel special. Believe me. He's handsome, charming, and sexy. There's no way he's not single for a reason."

"Sounds familiar," I accused.

"Well," she said, seemingly unfazed, "I learned from experience. From guys like him."

"It doesn't matter," I said. "I'm not going to act on it."

"You mean *again*?" she said, pursing her lips. "What was he talking about—a bruise? Last night? Did you sleep with him?"

"*No.* I told you we didn't."

"And?"

"And what?" I asked. "I don't want to get into what happened now—"

"Fine. I'm tired of pulling information out of you." She sighed heavily, backing away. "I thought we made progress earlier, but apparently not. Come find me when you're ready to talk for real. Shit's going to come out one way or another."

I didn't want to think of Davena just then. Or at all. But with Gretchen's warnings, Davena's also echoed through the black hole her absence had left.

"You can't hide from your desires. You can suppress them, ignore them, maybe even kill them off. But they'll stay buried and rotting inside you."

Chapter Twenty-Four

There was nothing in the world like the feeling of bass pumping against my brain, reverberating throughout my entire body. The fast and steady beat pulsed in me, entangling with the chardonnay I'd just pounded, manipulating my limbs and looping my hips. Flashes of red, green, and blue pierced the darkness of the dancefloor. A white spotlight flickered over glowing, sweat-dampened skin.

A man took my hips from behind. For the briefest second I wished it was David, but for all the restraint we'd shown, he'd never grab me out of nowhere. I pushed the hands off and made my way to the bar to order more wine.

As I waited for the bartender, a heavy arm landed across my shoulders. "Hey, babe," a young, stocky blond said, swaying with me. "What's your name?"

"Who are you?" I asked, trying to slip away, but his grip tightened. I'd vetted every name on the guest list, and those I hadn't met face to face were at least of drinking age, while this guy looked barely eighteen. "Who are you here with?"

"I work in the restaurant downstairs and just got off," he said, his words slurring together as he put his mouth to my ear. "My friend and I snuck in."

"Dude, shut up," said another guy in a black button down. "You'll get us in trouble."

They burst into laughter. "What's your name?" the blond repeated. "You're hot."

"You guys aren't supposed to be here," I said. "I have to throw you out."

"Aw, come on. Lighten up," he pleaded. "Let's get a drink. I'll buy."

"The drinks are free. And no." I tried wriggling out from under him. "Please, get off of me."

"Huh?"

"She said get *off*," David's voice boomed a second before he yanked the guy's arm, twisted it, and sent him flying back toward the dancefloor. David positioned himself in front of me and towered over the stocky blond, whose face flashed with a new alertness. "What the fuck don't you understand about *get off*?" David said, shoving him into his friend.

The friend yelled something, holding up his palms, but I couldn't hear over the music. They hurried away and ran right into security.

David turned to tower over *me*. "You need to start paying more attention to—"

"What the hell are you doing?" I sizzled. "I can take care of myself."

"Clearly you can't," he said. "Those guys—"

"Were completely harmless."

"You don't know that."

"Forget it." I pivoted on my heel. "I'm leaving."

"Hang on," he started.

I spun around to cut him off. "Stay here. Go find Amber and have a good time," I muttered, craning my neck to look for Gretchen.

"I've barely looked at anyone else tonight, meanwhile Brian's slobbering all over you," he said. "I didn't think he was your type."

"I don't *have* a type, David. *I'm married.*"

David took a step closer and the thrum he'd inspired in me gave way to a full-body vibration. "So you keep saying," he said, staring me down. "I'm beginning to wonder if you flirt with all of them the way you flirt with me."

I balled my hands into fists on each side of me. "I was trying to set him up with Gretchen. You were standing right there."

David's eyes dropped to my hand as I tugged down the hem of my dress.

"And I don't," I said.

"Don't?" he repeated, riveted as my fingertips grazed against my bare thigh.

I lowered my voice and rasped, "Flirt with them. Flirt with anyone, actually, the way I flirt with you."

He blinked from my hand to my eyes. I had his attention now.

"Goodnight, David," I said and turned to leave.

"Olivia," he commanded and grasped my wrist. "Stop running away."

His touch sent electricity up my arm, threatening to zap any resolve I'd been clinging to not to give in to him. "Don't," I said, withdrawing.

I went directly for the elevator, impatiently punching the button.

"Where are you going?" David asked my back.

"Home."

"This is *your* event," he said.

"I have to be up early," I said. It wasn't a lie. I'd promised George at the local animal shelter I'd spend the day helping him plan their annual masquerade ball. "Just go back to the party, David."

The numbers above the elevator car stayed at the lobby.

David didn't budge. I knew why. I knew what he wanted in order to leave me alone. What he *needed*. I had to tell him I didn't want him, and I had to mean it.

But it was more than that.

I had to tell him I didn't want what he could give me. I had to choose the life I was barreling toward. Lying awake by my husband in the quiet dark, getting myself off in the bathroom, a slower pace, putting a family over my career, a home with a nursery, and a baby to put in it. The decision had been haunting me long before David had come along. Perhaps even before I'd accepted Bill's proposal. And I was expected to decide *now*, once and for all, while every fiber of my being longed to run into the arms of the man behind me?

My chest tightened with panic. With the fucking elevator stalled at the lobby, I turned and bolted for the service stairwell. I burst through the door, slamming it against the wall, and rushed down a flight of steps.

"Olivia," David called from above.

I held my purse to my breast. "I can't do it, David," I said over my shoulder. "I can't. Don't ask me to."

My heart leaped when his hand wrapped around my arm. He was damn near impossible to outrun. Or was I allowing myself to get caught?

"I'm not letting you run again," he said firmly. "Tell me why you're so angry with me. And where's your coat?"

I whirled around to face him on the stark, ugly landing, a much more suitable place to have this conversation. The sleek and smooth party happening above us was too perfect, while this cold stairwell resembled the steel cage around my heart, rattling with the emotions beginning to escape. "Why did you come here?" I asked, seething. "We said this was over."

"I tried." He dropped his hand to his side. "Believe me, I did."

"Tried what?"

"To stay away," he said steadily. "For my own sanity, to protect myself, I fucking tried to stay away, but I can't." He glanced down at his feet, and when he looked up again, his eyes blazed. "Come home with me."

Breath flushed from my lungs. For him, we were already home. Over his shoulder, a sign with the letters *PH* in bold red sat above the door. I'd flown down the stairs and landed right at his penthouse. He'd warned me what would happen if I returned to his apartment. I could almost hear my body buzzing, so coiled with desire from our back-and-forth.

"Why, so I can humiliate myself again?"

"What the hell are you talking about?" he asked.

I watched him closely. "Is this some sort of game for you? You pushed me away in Lucy's office. Then, you told me you never wanted to see me again. That you were finished with me." A fluorescent light flickered somewhere above us, as though channeling my anger. "Suddenly you want me?"

"I have never not wanted you, Olivia. Not for a moment." He swallowed, his brow furrowing. "I left you in Lucy's office because there was too much on the line. Because I couldn't break up a marriage. Because I was afraid of pushing you into something you might regret. But you make it so fucking impossible," he said, pleading up to the ceiling. His breath turned ragged as he looked back at me with stormy eyes. "I can't be around you anymore because you drive me crazy every second of the day." He ran both hands through his hair. "Fuck, if I don't distance myself from you, I'm going to lose it."

I understood. Every word he spoke was true. I wanted to deny it—especially because it made walking away harder. But it didn't change our situation.

"And when I stood there in your office and ended our relationship, you just took it. You didn't even care. Just let me walk out." He stepped toward me. "Tell me you care, Olivia, and that I'm not completely delusional."

How could he think I didn't care? It oozed from my pores all the time, how much I wanted to touch him, how I thirsted for his attention. "You know I can't," I whispered.

"Then show me," he said.

"What do you want from me?" I asked. "You expect me to jeopardize everything—*everything*—for . . . for what —*sex*?" My voice bounced off the empty walls. "My marriage, my work, my life. My *marriage*." My body swayed. "I can't do it, David."

"How many times do I have to repeat myself? Do you hear anything I say? This isn't just about sex," he said slowly, deeply. "And you know it."

"Oh, sure." Sweat formed on my nape despite the cold. My sense of reason began to spin out of control, overtaken by my fear that I wouldn't be able to walk away. I needed him to be the one to do it. "Isn't that why you're standing here now? To see if I'll fuck you?" I stepped up to him, coming right under his chin, my temper flaring. "You claimed to be a gentleman, but you're no different from every other player."

"Even gentlemen have limits, Olivia," he said, above me. "Even gentlemen like to fuck."

My knees weakened. David had never been shy, but he'd always edged the line of polite—until now. And his crudeness melted my insides along with my resistance. "Well, what's stopping you?" I put as much venom as I could into the words, and they tasted bitter leaving my mouth. "Why not take me here? Now?"

"So help me God, Olivia," he whispered, locking his hands under his armpits. "Don't test me. I know what you're doing. I know you're afraid."

"Afraid? I *am* afraid—of losing everything."

"No, of this." He gestured between us. "I am, too, but I want—"

"Stop," I said, covering my ears as I looked at the ground. "We have to stop this."

"Olivia, listen to me." He took an audible breath. "I am afraid. I've never touched a married woman. You might not believe what I said before, but pursuing you goes against the man I try to be. But my fear is nothing compared to the agony of keeping this inside. I can't hide it like you. And if I honestly thought your husband was the right person for you, I'd have walked away long ago."

My heartbeat pounded in my stomach, reverberating throughout my body. He paused, waiting until I dropped my hands, raised my head, and consented for him to continue.

"Come inside and spend the night with me," he said. "And when the sun rises, stay." His angular jaw sharpened with resolve. "I want what he has. All of you. All to myself."

The confession hit me like a blow, echoing through the stairwell. "How can you say that?" I asked, incredulous but no longer yelling. "You barely know me. You're with

Maria, yet you see other women. You're Chicago's bachelor of the goddamn year. Nothing you say means anything. Give up already," I said, desperation threading my words. "You only want what you can't have."

He took a step forward, our bodies nearly flush. "You think I can't have you?"

"Wait," I said, panicked as his nearness threatened my control.

"Is that what you think?" He flexed a hand. "*I* don't. I want you. And I think you want me, too."

He didn't wait, but neither did I. Our mouths collided for a hard kiss, thick whiskey on his tongue. He took my shoulders, and the warmth of his hands on my skin spread through me. Without removing his lips from mine, he whipped off his jacket and wrapped me in it, pulling me closer, drowning me in a mossy blend of pine and aged leather. In *him*.

"Show me you care, Olivia," he breathed. "I need it. I need you." He pressed his lips to the spot beneath my ear that made my knees buckle. Feather-light kisses along my jawbone lit chills over my body, and he stopped at my lips. He stilled there as I became painstakingly aware of the empty feeling between my legs I wanted him to fill.

I looked into his eyes, and for a moment, everything else fell away. He took away the pain, all the things that hurt, that I could never say out loud. Brown eyes pleaded with me to let him take over, to let him ease the hurt.

He squeezed my arms, reminding me with a flex of strength that if he wanted, he could take me whether I agreed or not. "Show me, Olivia. I need you. *Only you*."

"I . . ."

Davena had told me to seize the moment in her own way. Desperation for him filled me to the brim. She'd warned me if I tried to stop it, it would leak out, flood me, pull me under. She'd tell me to swim, to submerge myself in the tide of David's want.

With my slight nod, David engulfed me in a primal kiss —all mouth, saliva, lips, teeth.

Our hands, for the first time, explored each other furiously. His traveled behind my neck, over my shoulders, and along my arms. They grazed the crease of my ass as he bunched my leather dress. He pulled me against his erection, but I was already there, tugging his shirt from his pants, reaching underneath, touching his firm stomach —*oh*, how I'd longed to know what his skin would feel like beneath my fingertips.

He withdrew suddenly, ripping me from my adulation. "This isn't right."

"*What*?" I asked with breathless shock. After everything he'd just fought for—

"Come inside." He tugged my blazer closed, hiding me in it, and put his lips against the curve of my neck. My face burned from his delicious stubble and only more would soothe the sting. "I want you in my bed the first time."

The first time. That implied he'd have me more than once. My eyes nearly crossed with lust, rolling up to the ceiling as if the answer might be written there.

"Choose me," he said. "Walk through that door, and I promise I'll spend every minute, every hour, every day proving you made the right choice."

Before I could respond, he picked me up, and my legs locked around him. His hungry kiss stole my senses, my hands taking greedy handfuls of his soft hair. After a *beep* and a *buzz*, we moved out of the harsh, fluorescent light into a warm, inviting glow. The stairwell vanished. David carried me away as we consumed each other until I was pressed against a wall. Voracious lips locked on mine as his hand found the hem of my dress. Stiff leather crackled, interrupted only by the treasonous moan that escaped my lips when his rough hand moved against the soft skin of my inner thigh.

He was going to take me here, wherever *here* was.

And I wouldn't stop him.

Chapter Twenty-Five

One moment, I was sure David couldn't wait another moment to have me, and the next, we stood five feet apart in the complete darkness of his penthouse.

David shut the door behind us and leaned his forehead against it for a weighty moment. He didn't bother with the lights, just turned to me in the dark as moonlight shone through the living room windows. With his sobering stare, the gravity of the situation set in. After this, there would be no turning back.

"You're so beautiful," he said, as if to remind me of it.

He was a wall of exquisite beauty, rubbing his brow and then pushing a hand through his obsidian hair. He frowned and exhaled. I could just barely make out his expression, full of more than lust and wanting. It held pain, along with adoration, as though I were finally his, something he'd longed for and was now on the cusp of having. Those were the things I thought I saw when I should've been talking myself out of this—but with him, it was easy to get lost, it was right, it was as it should be.

"I . . ." I started, but my voice wavered. "I don't know

how to do this." I could barely form the sentence, due to an all-consuming desire. "David." In that one word, I pleaded with him to have the strength I couldn't and put a stop to this.

He wet his lips and paced forward until my back hit a wall. He stripped his jacket from me, letting it fall in a heap on the ground, then placed his palms on each side of me, trapping my body with his.

After the last twenty-four hours, being cornered should've frightened me, but with David, I was exactly where I wanted to be.

Carefully, he reached down, encircled my wrists with each of his hands, then folded them behind my back, stilling my body with his.

"I've fought to get you here," he said. "But at some point, you have to cross the line to me."

"Choose me," he'd said.

Letting David bring us to this point was not the same as choosing him. I yearned for the burn of his face on mine. I wanted this, I couldn't deny it, but I also knew that it was irreversible. "I shouldn't be here," I whispered.

"So leave."

Restrained by his grip, I moved against his hard body —but despite his words, he continued to fight against me. *For* me.

My chin quivered, and I shook my head, lightly at first and then harder. If he kissed me, I'd give in. But I couldn't be the one to make the final decision.

"Olivia," he pleaded thickly in my ear, the hairs of his cheek tickling me. Nothing rivaled hearing my name on his lips.

I kept my head turned toward the door, knowing that one look into his eyes would be my undoing. After shifting my wrists into one firm hand at my lower back, he reached up with the other and dug his fingers into my hair. He slid out the bobby pins, each one chiming as it hit the floor. My hair tumbled around my face. He tucked a handful behind my ear, gripped my chin, and turned me to him.

With the gentleness of a saint, he kissed my wound.

And with the finesse of a caveman, he shoved his pelvis against me, eliciting my sharp gasp as desire spiraled all the way to my fingertips.

Leaning in, our mouths all hot air and desire, he was careful not to let our lips touch. I squirmed, but he waited, patiently asking me to make my final decision.

I twisted my hands to free them, and he let me.

It was time. Fall into him—or walk away.

Lifting my hand, I flattened it against his heart with a tenderness that surprised me.

I closed my eyes, feeling the hard buttons of his dress shirt through his downy sweater, his heartbeat strong under my palm. "I'm sorry," I whispered, returning my gaze to him.

Agony crossed his face.

But the apology wasn't for him.

I balled the fabric in my fist, pulled, and suddenly his mouth was on mine, his heat and arms enveloping me, his hands under my thighs, lifting me.

He kissed me hard as we moved. I furiously undid his tie before being thrown onto a bed. Our mouths crashed as I landed in fluffy down, and my shoe hit the floor with a loud thud. We ground into each other until he sat back to pull off his shirt.

The apartment's floor-to-ceiling windows continued into his bedroom, and the city's warm glow allowed me to take in, for the first time, perfectly formed muscles that pushed and pulled with every movement—a man both lean and muscled, hard but graceful.

He imprisoned me against the mattress, allowing me the freedom to run my shaking hands along a marble chest coarsened by hair. I leaned up into his earthiness, inhaling a heady pine scent a second before he reattached his mouth to mine. Greedily, I ran my hands over every inch of his warm, naked skin, relishing the firm muscles that detained me.

He yanked my dress up. With a quick glance down, he groaned at the white lace panties glowing against my skin. His fingertips hooked under the elastic, and I sucked in a breath as they dragged along the waistband, sending me into soft convulsions.

He reached beneath the lace to find me slick with longing. I bit my lip when he slid a finger along me. I pulled at his belt buckle, fighting with it until it gave, then threw it. Metal struck the wood floor, ringing through the room.

"You think since the moment I laid eyes on you," he said hoarsely between kisses, taunting me with his finger, "that I haven't wondered,"—he paused, rubbing me harder—"what it would feel like to be inside you?"

His words cut to my core. Scorching eyes fixed on me as he stood, unbuttoned his pants, and shed his clothing with quick but graceful movements. His erection seemed impossibly big. The thought of taking all of him inside me sent a ripple of heat up my aching body to my face.

He disappeared into his en suite bathroom and returned barefoot with a condom.

Disappointment flooded me. David's skin on mine had revitalized me. I wanted nothing between us. "I'm on birth control."

"Trust me, I want to feel you, more than you know . . ." He leaned over the bed and planted a kiss on my pout. "But we have to be extra careful."

He was right, but I pushed the reasons why out of my

head for fear they'd take over the moment. My hair fanned out beneath me. I writhed, impatient to have him inside me as he rolled on the condom.

He took my arms and tugged me into a sitting position. Reaching back to unzip the length of my dress, he inhaled a sharp breath. "No bra," he said, drawing the leather over my head. I pulled my knees to my chest, hugging myself, but he unfolded my arms, drinking in my naked body. "You're incredible."

He climbed over me, guiding my back against the mattress. I lifted my hips as he dragged my panties over my bent knees and down to my ankles, discarding them on the floor.

His mouth found mine again, his tongue hungry and ravaging, and I pushed back, my teeth nipping at his bottom lip. He covered my quivering body as he slid his arms underneath me, pinning me to him. His hips moved, and his kiss matched their pace. I became even wetter under his control—he was so maddeningly rigid against the inside of my thigh, rubbing his length up me, sliding along my opening before hitting my clit.

I thrust my hips up when I could no longer take it, opening my legs wider, steepling them for him. "David." I exhaled. "Please, David. I can't. I can't take it."

He spread my legs farther apart with his, baring me to him, and reached between us to deftly insert the tip of himself into me.

"Olivia," he growled, looking to the ceiling in pleasure. "You're so wet. So ready."

"Please." My voice pitched, impatient to fill the persistent ache David had inspired with one look.

He moved onto his elbows. A small sound escaped me as he eased inside. He exhaled, as if he'd been holding his breath, while I inhaled sharply, clenching the sheets in unforgiving fists as he gave me every last inch. My walls molded around him, and heaven opened inside me. He was what I'd been missing all this time.

I didn't know how my face looked in that moment of pure bliss, but he whispered, "Are you okay?" We remained that way, momentarily immobilized by the earth-tilting sensation, until I managed a quick nod.

"You're so fucking warm, Olivia," he said, his eyes locked on mine. "From the moment we met, you've brought warmth to my life." His breath quickened as he sought my mouth, kissing me as though it were the last thing he would ever do—needy, tender, and fast all at once.

He pulled out almost entirely and drove inside of me with a guttural groan. I gripped his arms and had only a second to put my legs around him before he thrust again, wrapping me up into his rhythm. His pace accelerated quickly, giving me exactly what I wanted and more than I knew I needed. Within seconds he was mercilessly driving into me over and over—*yes yes yes*, he moaned as though voicing my thoughts. He reached for my hair and pulled it, bowing my head to allow him access to my mouth as we fucked.

Our bodies moved greedily after weeks of sizzling tension. I cried out brokenly, heat building within me.

Oh, God. I was actually going to . . . come?

Slowly, but also swiftly in a way, my orgasm mounted, pulling me into a world I'd never been.

It felt so fucking good. So right. So unlike anything I'd experienced with another person.

David kissed that perfectly sensitive spot behind my ear. I licked and sucked the wet saltiness of his neck. I wanted this. I wanted to give him my first time. He whisked my forearms above my head in an iron grip, pushing them into the mattress. Our fingers intertwined, squeezing together as his thrusts became more and more frantic.

"Oh, God. You're so beautiful, so hot," he rasped. "Open up for me."

Open for me. Don't close, Olivia. Don't fuck this up.

Thoughts of opening and closing, heat and cold, inadequacy and flaws began to rush over me. Here I was, underneath the most beautiful man in the world, and I was certain he was the answer to questions I'd stopped asking long ago.

Could I do this for David?

Let him in, give him the orgasm nobody else could draw from me?

As warmth receded, I had my answer. I couldn't do it. David was wrong about me. I wasn't hot; I was cold and too flawed, even for him.

I heard my name and opened my eyes, realizing I'd been squeezing them shut. "Come back," he said, never breaking our rhythm. "Come on, Olivia. Look at me." I met his gaze as he moved into me, slightly slower but with more force. The change in momentum had me gasping for air. "Olivia," he moaned with such intense need that I moaned back and pulled him closer with my legs, urging him deeper.

"That's it. Don't look away," he said, picking up his pace again. "Oh, God. That's it."

He never lost eye contact. Never stopped fighting for me. I'd thought David was the most dangerous thing in my life, but in the eye of the tornado we'd created, I could let go. I was safe here.

"David," I cried suddenly. My bloodless fingertips tingled in his grasp; my thighs shook with the force of an impending explosion. He kissed me with the same force, giving me the push I needed to surrender.

"Let go, Olivia," he commanded against my lips, and I constricted around him as my control vanished.

Pleasure seared through me, and everything around me went white. I gave myself over to the first blissful wave that ripped through me as David called my name over and over, coming fast and hard with me.

When I fell back to earth, our breathing had synced. Sweat began to cool my skin. As our fingers were still linked, David was still inside me, securing his collapsed weight to me.

He drew back and smoothed his hands over my hairline, brushing the strands from my face. He kissed the place the hair had been, then my cheek and neck, lingering with each contact. "I have never," he whispered into my neck, "*never* come that fast. You drive me wild."

Gently, he pulled out of me, threw the condom on the ground, and sat back on his knees. The world slowed when I got up to face him. A heavy pit formed in my stomach as we watched each other.

I'd done it. I'd fucked another man.

I'd broken my vows and the trust that had been put in me.

And I'd used the advice of a dead woman who wasn't even six feet under to justify it.

I looked down at my naked body, opening my adulterous hands. My face contorted as tears threatened. I'd had opportunity after opportunity to walk away, yet I'd fallen so easily into David's arms. How could I have used Davena to defend my weakness? She never would've told me to cheat. She'd be so disappointed.

I shook my head and covered my face, trying desperately to hide from David what was coming. "No," I whispered into myself.

"Olivia, don't," David pleaded.

I lifted myself from the bed. I had to get away now, or I'd never be able to leave his warmth.

But with my first couple steps, my trembling legs buckled, and I sank to the ground.

"No," I wailed as the truths I'd been fighting washed over me. Davena was truly gone. I hadn't even said goodbye. Mack had lost the love of his life. I'd made a mockery of my own marriage and had crossed a line I could never come back from. I'd given David more than I ever had my husband, and even as regret descended, I wanted to stay in David's bubble. "What have I done?"

My entire body shuddered with sobs as I folded over my knees. Tears spilled from my hands and disappeared on the floor. Coarse wood dug into my shins and elbows until David's immense hands grasped my shoulders, drawing me up. When I was on my feet, he turned me to him, hugging me tightly as I shook.

"I'm here," he whispered feverishly. "Let me in. Let me help."

"You can't." Despair squeezed my chest, making its way up to my throat. "I don't know what you think you see in me, but I'm not that."

He placed his hands on both sides of my head, clearing the hair from my tear-streaked face. "I see a girl who wants to let go."

His words struck something buried deep inside, and I shook my head harder, stepping back without breaking eye contact. "I'm not that. I don't want that," I said, pressing my palm forcefully against my chest. "I'm empty inside, David, and I did that to myself. You don't understand. There's nothing left to give." That was why I'd built the life

I had. I'd already opened my heart as wide as it would go, and it wasn't enough. David deserved a woman who held nothing back. "I'm too fucked up. And you . . . oh, God. You're so *beautiful*."

Confessing my ever-present void knocked the breath from me. David had a way of drawing out my closely guarded secrets, charming them from me like poisonous snakes.

David looked equally horrified. I didn't know what to see in the way he stared at me. I only knew that I'd finally managed to drive him away, but not soon enough.

The damage was already done.

Chapter Twenty-Six

I expected David to release me. To make some excuse about having to work early while gathering my things and ushering me back into the night. Instead, he grabbed me to him, kissed me with a heated fury, and picked me up, urging all my limbs around him. Grasping the nape of my neck, his fingers digging into my skin, he charged forward. My back hit cold plaster as he knocked against a nightstand, overturning a lamp.

"I need you," he said through gritted teeth, adjusting my weight with his hips, already hard as stone between us. I flattened my palms and upper back against the wall as he stepped back, my legs still clinging to him, took himself in his free hand, and sank into me without checking to see if I was ready. He slid in easily, but I gasped from the unexpected and delicious feel of his rock-hard and unsheathed cock inside me.

He thrust hard and fast, bouncing me against the wall with his urgency. "You feel so good." He caught my lips in a furious kiss. "*Fuck*."

He slipped his arms under mine and covered each of

my shoulders, bringing me down onto him harder, going so deep that my ass slapped against his scrotum. I grasped vainly at his slick back, trying to hold on as he continued to buck.

My insides seized with each naked plunge, bringing me quickly to the edge. I threw my head against the wall and winced.

"Shit." He backed us away.

"It's fine," I said, panting. "I'm close. Don't stop." I buried my face in his neck as he rounded the bed and stopped at his nightstand. He bent over, cradling my back so I wouldn't fall, and I gasped with new awareness of how deep he was. He drew back to kiss me quickly on the lips, reached into the top drawer, and pulled out a condom. He stuck the packet in his mouth and tore it open.

Still dangling from his body, I gave him an exaggerated pout. He looked me evenly in the eyes and pulsed his hips once with a groan. My lips parted for a sharp breath.

"I can't wait to come inside of you," he said, kissing the underside of my jaw, "once you're officially mine."

I nearly lost my grip at his words. I was so aroused by his determination to claim me that I could've fainted from sheer need. I'd just broken down on his floor, and the guilt would return, I knew—but I would've done anything in that moment to belong to David.

He withdrew from me and set me on my feet to roll on the condom.

As his gaze swept over me in the moonlight, he licked his lips. "Clasp your hands behind your back." He shook his head when I obeyed. "God, you're even better than I imagined. And I imagined a lot."

Warmth rushed up my exposed body. I'd imagined, too. I took in his towering frame and broad, solid torso. Dark curls started at his chest and thinned into a delicious trail. With a six-pack, long, muscled legs, narrow hips, and firm, defined arms, he'd clearly been gifted by the gods with a body he maintained but didn't work to death.

And nowhere was he more gifted than down *south*. My mouth watered at just the sight of his massive, implacable erection.

He turned me around, and I yelped when he smacked my ass. "On the bed."

I climbed up onto all fours, already missing the sight of him.

"You want it that way?" he asked.

The thought excited me, but my first orgasm had happened while looking him in the eye. Perhaps I should've been satisfied to have come at all, but I wanted more.

"Never hesitate in my bed," David said. "I want honesty, always. Turn around. I want to watch your face as I fuck you."

Even wetter with his demand, I faced him, running one foot down my other shin. When he didn't make a move, I bit my lip, failing to keep in a whimper, nearly crazed with aching.

He exhaled a short, forceful breath and took a large stride toward me. "Christ," was all he said as he took an ankle in each hand. In one movement, he'd yanked me and spread my legs so I fell back on the comforter. I shut my eyes with the feel of his lips on the inside of my ankle, making their way up my knee to my inner thigh. His mouth jumped to my stomach, brushing my scar, and my abdominals clenched as I fought from recoiling. *No, no, no. Stay with him.*

He took my breasts in his hands and ran his thumbs under my nipples while I pushed my hips into his torso, desperate to feel him again. His mouth encircled one nipple and then the other. I bowed into the bliss of his tongue, softly crying out as I grasped handfuls of his hair. He let me pull him up for a hard kiss, then shoved a finger into me and massaged, feeling me from inside.

I writhed beneath him as he added another finger, tempting me to the verge of climax. I fought it, arching into his body. I needed to feel him again, to watch him grunt, his face screwing up with pleasure as he hammered me.

"Come for me," he rasped against my neck.

"No." I grabbed his solid ass in both my hands, urging his hips toward me. "I need you inside me."

"So goddamn stubborn," he teased and straightened up, sliding my hips to the very edge. He spread my swollen lips for the head of his cock and slowly swirled his pelvis twice. "Beg for it, Olivia."

"Please," I said. His fingers massaged my clit. "Fuck me, David."

He plunged into me. I put my feet on his shoulders and he leaned on them, deepening his range, gripping my hips, nailing me into the mattress so fast I had to hold on to the sheets.

My ears roared as I squeezed my eyes shut. I'd never experienced the dueling sensations of being wholly filled while fingertips also worked my clit.

"I'm going to come any second." He took my jaw and demanded, "*Look at me.*"

I broke myself from the darkness and opened my eyes for him. The sea of pleasure that had risen in me crashed over my body, throwing me into a violent orgasm that had me coming twice as long and hard as before. He pounded into me through the climax, never losing eye contact. My legs dropped, my spent body sliding up the bed with each thrust, until he seized my waist to pull me back to the brink. With gritted teeth and a punishing final thrust, he came feverishly, shuddering, holding on to me like I might vanish, until every drop had left his body.

It was the most erotic thing I'd ever seen.

David braced himself over me, his massive body propped up by sinewy arms. I ran a hand through my sweat-soaked hair and over my undulating breasts, trying to catch my own breath. I jumped when he brushed my clit while pulling out of me. I hooked my legs on the mattress to keep from slithering over the side.

"You're going to fall," he said and threw the condom where he'd tossed the first one.

"I can't move," I replied between heavy breaths. Hands swept beneath me, and suddenly I was in his arms, being carried to the bathroom where he set me down . . . at the *toilet*.

"What . . .?" I asked with a slight giggle.

"Sex Ed 101. Always pee after sex. Go."

I sat down, more out of exhaustion than compliance. "A little privacy?"

"Just go."

I crinkled my nose at him. "David."

"Fine." He turned his back.

"Really?"

"I just fucked the shit out of you. We're past formalities. Who cares?"

"Peeing is hardly a formality," I grumbled, but in truth, there was something sexy about David's lack of squeamishness. The act was oddly intimate even though I'd peed in front of Bill countless times. And now, I had the advantage of admiring David's toned ass—magnificent, even in the dark.

When I'd finished, he hoisted me back to the bed. "You carry me a lot."

"I'll never take having you in my arms for granted," he said.

I was thankful for the dark that hid my blush. "Aren't I getting heavy?"

He laughed heartily and tossed me a few inches in the air, catching me easily. "No, honeybee. You're not. You think I could've fucked you that long standing up if you were?"

"The wall did most of the work," I pointed out, as he held me over the bed.

"Is that what you think?" he asked, nipping under my jaw with his teeth. "Should we try it again so I can prove you wrong?"

My eyes widened. "*Can* you go again?"

"I could have you till the sun comes up, but you need to rest. We both do." He dropped me, and I laughed as I hit the springs. "But now *I* have to piss."

"What, I don't get to watch?"

"You can if you want," he said.

But as my body settled into the bed, my lids grew heavy.

Did he call me honeybee again?

The sheets must have been a thread count somewhere in the thousands because they were *oh . . . so . . . inviting . . .*

The mattress shook, jarring me awake. David climbed into the other side of his king-sized bed. I reached across the valley between us to touch him. "I'm cold."

"Then come here." He pulled me to him, and I fit myself against a body I wasn't used to. I rested my elbow on his torso and my face on his shoulder.

"How do you feel?" he asked into my hair.

I sighed. "Sore."

"Good. I want you remembering this all weekend."

I nearly shuddered. As if my mind or heart could forget—David had ensured my body wouldn't. "Can I tell you something?" I asked.

"Olivia." He rolled me onto my back, covering me as he looked me straight in the eyes. His body seemed miles long; his legs *had* to be hanging off the edge. "I've been waiting for you to ask me that for weeks," he said. "Please, tell me something that I don't have to emotionally beat out of you."

I swatted his shoulder and snickered. But he wasn't teasing. He wanted my thoughts. My confessions. My secrets.

I cleared my throat, suddenly on the spot. "It—that was . . ." I went to touch my earlobe, but he caught my wrist without even a glance and kissed the inside of it.

"That was my first orgasm with anyone," I admitted. Looking up at the ceiling, I added, "Well, first and second."

"What?" Shock threaded his tone. He moved off me and sat back on his calves. "You can't be serious."

"It's true. Does that freak you out?" I asked, getting up on my elbows. With the loss of his heat, I shivered.

"Sorry," he mumbled, returning over me, tucking each of my limbs into his body. I couldn't quite gauge his reaction until a huge smile crossed his face. It broke only long enough for him to kiss me quickly on the lips. "No, actually, I *can't* believe it," he said. "How is that possible?"

I faltered, wondering how to even explain it. "I've never been able to get there with a partner. I always assumed Bill and I would, but he stopped trying after a while. I don't blame him. The harder he worked, the less turned on I became. I'd just take care of myself later. I could never fully . . ." *Let go.* I took a breath. I kept that confession to myself, since it seemed unfair to Bill. "So I might be on another planet right now."

David kissed the base of my neck more times than I could count.

"I guess it helps that this has been building between us for almost two months," I said.

"Oh, yeah?" He glanced up at me. "Then how do you explain the second one?"

I smiled shyly, and his expression sobered. "You have no idea what that means to me," he said, his lips brushing the hollow of my neck.

"It means you're an experienced lover," I joked, even though I knew it wasn't the entire reason. I had blossomed for him. Beneath him, surrounded by him, we existed in our own world.

"No." He sighed, exhaling against my neck. "It's different." His voice was so soft, that I had to strain to hear.

Is it different for you, too, David?

I wanted to ask, but I just enjoyed the feeling of his lips, his breath, *him*, on my body. For all my fears around David, I was somehow safe here.

He lifted his head, a mischievous look playing over his face. He ground his hips against me softly, alerting me that he was hard again. "Getting your first orgasm might be the sexiest thing I've ever heard."

I squealed. "*David.*"

He laughed, and it was such a playful, wonderful sound that I couldn't help but join him.

"I mean it. You're gorgeous. When you're my girl, I'll have you coming every chance I get."

My laugh melted as reality threatened to creep in, but my mouth watered at his words. When I was his? How could he believe that would happen?

I didn't get a chance to wonder long. He slid down my

body and nuzzled my breasts, sighing into them, his facial hair scraping against my skin. "You're incredible, Olivia. I don't ever want to hear you say you're empty."

I didn't want to think about that, or I worried I'd break down again. "I'm thoroughly worked over, is what I am."

His golden-brown gaze found mine. "You know, when I looked into your eyes at the theater, I was stunned. Nothing like that has ever happened to me. And when I saw you in that gold dress at the restaurant, I knew you were the most beautiful thing I had ever seen. You were glowing. But right now, in my bed, naked and undone . . ." He leaned forward to kiss me softly on the lips. "You are perfect. I never want you any other way."

I ran my hand over his cheek and through his hair. It hurt that I couldn't respond the way I wanted, so I just touched him, memorizing with my fingers.

His gigantic hands splayed over my ribcage. "So smooth," he said, moving his fingers over my skin.

Everything is smooth in the dark.

My body jolted when his index finger ran over my scar. "Except for this," he said. "What is it?"

I squeezed my eyes shut, thankful for the night to hide whatever reaction might give me away.

Why is he asking? Who cares what it is?

I balled the sheets in my fist. I had to relax. It was a simple question, and he'd drop it if I asked him to; he didn't mean anything by it. But my heart pounded.

David leaned closer and examined it. "What's it from?"

"Haven't we covered enough for one night?" I asked, half-joking.

His silence was response enough.

I sighed and pushed his hand away. "It's ugly, and I don't like talking about it."

"Does it have to do with your panic attack a few minutes ago?"

"It wasn't a panic attack," I said. "I was overwhelmed. I'm f—" I stopped myself from using the word *fine* so David wouldn't start another argument over it. "I'm all good."

"You're not. You were hurting just now. Tell me what overwhelmed you," he said, unaffected by my brush-off—a tactic that often worked with Bill.

"I don't want to lie to you," I said, but even I heard the defeat in my voice. "So please don't make me."

He laughed softly and buried his nose in my chest, placing a feather-light kiss between my breasts. "Don't lie. I'm not easily scared off." Suddenly, his body weighed on me, his breath on my skin seeming to hit an exposed nerve with every exhale. I must have moved, because he said, "Stop. Don't pull away. Tell me what's going through your head."

Despite the fact that the scar would forever be linked to my mother, in that moment, it was Davena's memory that made my chest stutter.

I hadn't worked up the courage to tell Gretchen or Lucy yet—I'd barely even spoken to *Bill* about Davena's death. Could I really share my grief with David?

I sighed and looked out the bedroom window. I *could*. I could tell David everything—that was the problem. I could tell him, knowing he would somehow take some of that pain, shoulder it, and comfort me.

"A family friend passed away last night," I said. "I found out this morning while we were at the station."

David stilled beside me. "I'm sorry. I had no idea—you seemed . . . I didn't realize that was what had upset you."

I nodded. "It was cancer."

"And you were close?"

A lump formed in the back of my throat. I kept my face turned away. "She's been there for me in ways my mother hasn't," I said, my voice hitching.

"Ah." David ran the pad of his thumb along my jawline. "I gather your relationship with your mom is strained."

I returned my eyes to his. I was right. There was nothing in his expression but comfort and understanding. And an invitation to tell him anything on my mind without judgment.

"She accidentally stabbed me when I was younger."

His jaw clicked as he jutted it to one side. "Your mom?"

It felt ridiculous to say out loud. I hadn't had to talk about it in much detail since that night at the hospital sixteen years ago.

All that blood.

"My parents fought a lot, but never more than the year leading up to their divorce," I explained. "One night, she pulled a knife. My dad had come home late from the office. I was used to being woken up by their arguments, but this one was especially bad."

"What was it about?" David asked.

"Gina."

"Gina?"

"A client of his. They'd fought over her before."

"If you're using her name all these years later," David said, "then I'm guessing your mom was right to be upset about her."

I shook my head. "My dad wasn't a cheater," I said. "Gina eventually became his second wife, yes, but nothing happened between them until after the divorce."

David shifted. "I see. What happened?"

"That's it. I was spying on the fight, which I sometimes

did in the middle of the night. When the knife came out, I freaked and ran between them. It was an accident, what she did, but it didn't matter."

With the words out of my mouth, I no longer felt cornered. David's body changed from a trap to a shield. I glided a hand over his smooth upper back. I'd said it aloud, and the world hadn't come crashing down.

"Then what?" he asked.

Again with the questions.

"You ask a lot of questions." I moved my hand to his hair, letting the silky strands sprout from between my fingers. "Why? Are you going to rescue me from my past, David?"

He pecked me on the lips softly, lingering there. Slowly, he caressed my tongue with his while running his knuckle along my jawline.

"You're hard," I whispered into his mouth. He nodded almost imperceptibly. He weighed heavy on me and I took it, wanting nothing more than to stay securely underneath him as long as he would let me.

When the kiss grew more urgent, he tore away from me. "I'm getting distracted. What's the rest of the story?"

"Hmm?" I asked sleepily. I opened my eyes, wondering if I could convince him to keep kissing me. "The rest? Screaming. Blood. Hospital. Really, that's all the detail I care to remember. I hate hospitals. Blood scares me blind."

"That's why you were in shock after Mark's attack," he said.

I nodded. "The knife and the blood—it took me back to those moments."

He swallowed. "How old were you?"

"Thirteen."

"Fuck. Does it hurt?"

I cocked an eyebrow at him. "No, of course not."

"You flinch when I touch it."

"A reflex, I guess. I can't control it." The room quieted, the only sound a pair of mirrored breaths.

"Protecting you from your own mother," he murmured finally. "I don't know anyone who could do that."

"It was a long time ago. It never happened again. My dad left her the next day, and we started over without her."

"He sounds like a smart man."

"He is," I agreed. "But she never got over it. She thinks we abandoned her."

David's brows furrowed as my words trailed off. "What is it?"

"Nothing, it's just weird to talk about this in any depth. I haven't in so long. Not since it happened."

"How? What about . . .?" He hesitated. "What about with Bill?"

I let my eyes roam David's face. That might've been the first time I'd heard David acknowledge him by something other than "your husband" and sneer.

"*Now* you can say his name?" I said with a laugh, which promptly turned into a yawn. "No, you're right. I forgot. Of course I told Bill."

I closed my eyes, half-giving in to sleep, half-feigning it so David wouldn't see the truth. I'd just confessed one of my most personal, formative experiences to him—something I hadn't even shared with Bill. How could I admit that without scaring David? Without confirming his earlier accusations that my friends, family, and husband all let me get away with *fine*?

How would he react knowing I'd avoided this topic with Bill for our entire marriage, only to open up for David within a single night?

Chapter Twenty-Seven

I awoke with puffy eyes, soft, unfamiliar sheets under my skin, and raw stickiness between my legs. Hard, strong arms clutched me from behind, locking me to a strange body.

A body that had trapped and devoured and owned me the night before. That had both pushed me to my limits and cushioned me with the warmth and safety I'd needed to give David everything. Guilt flowered as I remembered what I'd done, but my muscles clenched at the memory of all that'd been done to me.

David stirred. He lifted my hair and touched his lips to the curve of my neck, causing my eyes to flutter shut and a moan to escape.

"Perfect," he whispered into my skin.

At the deep voice that I was already coming to know too intimately, my body tensed. My eyes flew open. The dark had lifted and in the cruel sunlight, all that lay there was the truth.

I lifted myself up on unsteady arms, carefully avoiding David's always-penetrating stare. We couldn't have slept more than a few hours. I glanced around a sprawling white bedroom with colorful art that I was too unsettled to really take in. Sleek, black pendants hung from the ceiling on each side of the bed. A wall of gray-shaded stone framed the headboard.

My eyes stung with lack of sleep as I focused on the bedside clock. Only six in the morning.

Bill's plane would land in less than twelve hours.

"I have to leave." It came out harsher than I'd intended, but all I could think was that I'd have to face my *husband* tonight. That, and how every fiber of my being wanted to ignore that fact and curl up next to David. I didn't know how I'd be able to leave him knowing I shouldn't—*couldn't*—ever see him again.

I finally let myself look at him. He'd pulled the crisp white sheets up to his muscled stomach, and his head rested back against his arm as he watched me. My matted hair fell over my shoulder, and I imagined that mascara had smeared around my eyes. Meanwhile, he looked perfectly unaffected—and just plain perfect.

"Stay," he said, no pleading, just flat. If I allowed myself to give in even a little, my worries, my fears, my inhibitions would melt away under his gaze. *I* would melt away.

But this no longer felt adventurous or sexy. It just felt wrong. A dull pain throbbed behind my eyes as I looked for something to cover myself.

David got up and pulled on the same disarming gray sweatpants he had the other night. His sinuous, robust muscles were even more apparent in the daylight. It took every shred of my willpower not to drag him back to bed.

He gathered up the top sheet and offered it to me. I stood, wrapping myself in it as we stared at each other from across the bed. I might've expected the electricity between us to diminish now that we'd given in to it, but if anything, it intensified as my body recalled the night before. I longed to submit myself to him again, to feel the weight of him on top of me. I knew without words that he felt the same—by the way he looked at me, and by his twitching but restrained erection.

God, those fucking gray sweatpants hung low and left little to the imagination.

"Can I clean myself up?" I asked, shifting on my feet.

He nodded.

In the sunlit bathroom, I shut the door behind me. It was just as beautiful and immaculate as the bedroom, with a rock and glass shower that overlooked Lake Michigan.

I sat on the toilet and ran my hands over my face. I'd actually gone through with it. I'd broken my vows. I'd betrayed Bill's trust. And if I kept this from him, I would lie to his face tonight.

Did David normally let his one-night stands spend the night?

Why was I even *thinking* about that?

It didn't matter. He'd gotten what he'd wanted, and so had I. It was a moment I'd furtively fantasized about, yet my daydreams were nothing compared to the reality of his skin on mine, his length stretching and filling me. The reality of him working my body as if he owned it.

I pushed the heels of my hands into my eyes until I saw white.

No.

I'd done so much more than acted out a fantasy. I had a husband and a life to answer to. What had I done? Something profoundly wrong. Something bigger than myself. Something that could never be undone.

As I washed my hands, I stole a quick glance at my reflection. I was right about my smeared makeup and tangled hair. The bruise on my face had ripened. Did I look different? How did adulterers look? Would a scarlet "A" brand my skin?

I wiped the smudges from under my eyes and raked a hand through my hair, starting at the roots. My fingers stuck on several tangles that'd formed from dried sweat. I needed a brush if I was going to fix this. I did the best I could, but it was useless trying to scrub this moment clean.

Wrapped back in the sheet, I opened the door and leaned against the jamb.

David waited on the edge of the bed, his elbows on his knees. "I preferred the bedhead," he said, jutting his chin at me.

I shook my head. "Left to its own devices, my hair would put me in an early grave. It doesn't know how to cooperate."

"Well, I like you that way. Disheveled."

"David." It was part scolding, part plea. He shouldn't like me *any* way. He should keep his mouth shut and not make this more difficult.

"Olivia." No scolding.

"Last night was . . ." I let the sentence hang, wrapping the sheet more tightly under my arms.

"It was," he said, nodding slowly. "I meant what I said."

"About my hair?" I joked.

"No."

"Then what exactly?"

"Everything. That I want you for myself. That my feelings for you are real. That you're incredible." The crease in his brow offset his tousled, inky hair. "I want more. I want it all. I said as much last night, and I brought you here thinking we were on the same page."

My mind raced. The same page? A lot of things had

been said—and done—in the heat of the moment. But he must've known this couldn't be anything more than a mistake I'd live with through every milestone of my marriage.

David's and my connection had only intensified once we'd given in to it, yes. There was no denying our passion —or even that real feelings existed. But did he actually expect me to leave my husband based on one night?

"And *I* meant what *I* said. I'm not right for you," I said. "I'm, I don't know . . . broken. And *married*. Last night shouldn't have happened, but it did. We have to leave it at that. Trust me when I say, there's no other way."

He closed his eyes for a moment and then whipped them open. "You're broken?" he asked with a look of disgust. "And you have nothing to give? How the fuck can you say that to me after everything you just showed me?"

"I understand. Being with you was . . ." My voice hitched as I tried to find the words. "A release, and I don't just mean sexually. I needed it. It opened my eyes to the fact that maybe I can start to heal wounds I thought would never close. But that doesn't change the fact that I belong to someone else."

"*He* doesn't heal those wounds. He probably doesn't even know they exist." David stood from the bed. "And you're going to tell me—"

"Don't." I held up my hands, stepping back.

As his eyes shuttered, and his expression closed, my heart dropped. David had been open about what he'd wanted from the start, but how could he possibly know the extent of what he asked for? He didn't. With his revolving door of women, he *couldn't*. He only wanted what he couldn't have. And maybe that would work for a while, but eventually he'd see the truth—I couldn't break up my marriage for a player, even if it was the best sex of my life.

David took a measured pace forward.

"This isn't how this goes," I explained. "It can't happen again."

"Olivia." This time, it was a command—he must've known what it did to me. He reached for me. "Come here."

It only took one step from me before he'd gathered me in his arms. He kissed my temple, my wounded cheek, my neck. I cherished the feel of his lips on my skin, knowing it would be the last time. With that, I began to weep silently in his arms. This time I cried for what I was losing, not from guilt or regret. He let me, holding me closer, his large hands caressing my back as the sheet fell to my hips. My nipples hardened against his wall of a chest—his equal desire twitched against my stomach.

"Shh," he whispered in my ear. He bent and kissed me full on the lips, pressing my wet face against his and sharing the tears. The slow and sensual tempo of his kiss turned urgent and deep. His hand slid down my back and under the sheet, massaging my ass and inspiring the fervor again.

I'd been with boys before; I'd been with boys I'd thought were men. But this was different. David kissed like a man. He tasted, he smelled, and he fucked like a man. It would take all the strength I had and then some.

I understood now that I was the one who would have to be strong for everyone—for David, for Bill, and for myself. It'd been unfair to ask David to be. It was on *my* shoulders.

"No," I said resolutely and pulled away, drawing the sheet over my shoulders. Looking up at him from under wet lashes, I felt small but with him, never insignificant.

"Olivia." His tone softened, and I could see the struggle within him. "I've waited . . . it's not—I know this is wrong. Don't you think I know?" He ran a hand through his hair. "But I will be by your side every step of the way."

"By my side?" I asked. "For what?"

"You came to my bed knowing this wasn't a fling to me," he said firmly.

"You knew I would," I accused. "Has any woman ever turned you down? What choice did I really have?"

His lips thinned into a line. "Don't pretend you didn't choose this. You have been nothing but vague about your feelings, and I let you have that—but I was always clear about how I feel, and what last night meant to me. And if anything, I'm even more confident this morning."

"Confident about what?"

"That you're mine."

I stared at him. I was . . . *his*. It felt true, and it could be in another life—but in this one, I already belonged to another man. "The only way this works is if I leave my husband."

He crossed his arms. "I understand."

"I—I . . ." Maybe he'd expected that last night, and maybe I'd let myself believe it could happen. But that didn't mean he could snap his fingers and make it so. "You and I have known each other less than two months. We've spent one night together. Bill and I, we have history, years—"

"I don't want to hear that."

"Well, you have to," I snapped. "This isn't something we can try out and see how it goes. Divorce is fucking messy and painful."

"No shit," he said. "Can you honestly tell me you've never considered it, even without me in the picture?"

"*Yes*," I said. "I can honestly say I've never considered it." I shook my head and stepped back. "I don't know why we're even discussing this. We have to forget this happened

—it was a mistake. I knew it would be even before it happened. I take responsibility."

He set his jaw. "Call it a mistake if it helps you sleep at night, but I know that's not how you feel."

"How I feel in this moment cannot be the reason I upend my entire life. I'm going to walk out that door, and we're going to move on with our lives, and very soon, we'll realize this was nothing but lust we shouldn't have indulged."

He waited, his brown eyes searching mine. "You don't believe that at all," he said.

He was right, but it was an argument I couldn't afford to lose, so I didn't respond to it. "You promised you'd leave me alone if I asked you to," I said.

"If you ask and you mean it, I will."

"I mean it." My heart clenched. I had to be the one. I had to make this call for all of us, or things would only get messier. More painful.

I forced any feelings for him aside, straightened my shoulders, and repeated, "I mean it, David."

After a few moments of silence, his expression smoothed. "You can't even say it. If you really want me gone, tell me to get the fuck out of your life."

I stared back at him, urging the final good-bye off my tongue to put an end to us once and for all.

"*Is* that,"—he enunciated each word and stepped toward me—"what you want? For me to walk away for good?"

"I . . ."

"Just say it." He grasped my blanketed arms. "Tell me, Olivia. Tell me that's what you want."

I opened my mouth, but words failed me. I loved his attention, and how it woke me up, how I came *alive* in his presence. But giving in to those passions might just as easily turn against me. Loving someone like David could be the most wonderful experience—and the most painful. Already, his pleas to stay tore me open in ways I'd worked hard to avoid.

He pressed his fingers into my biceps, and my body nearly wilted under his command. "Look me in the eye and tell me you can forget," he said. "If you can, then I promise—we're through."

My knees and my resolve began to buckle. I reached deep inside for a modicum of strength. Any woman would be lucky to have this man standing in front of her, asking her to stay. Any woman would be horrified to know that I was tempted to give up my life for a man I'd just met, who could take me to new highs but even lower lows.

I squared my shoulders. "I-I . . ."

"I can't hear you," he said, stepping into me so I was pressed up against the doorjamb.

"I—you're hurting me."

His grip loosened, though I hadn't meant physically. "Then say it, Olivia," he ordered. "Say it."

"Yes," I yelled, suddenly desperate to hurt him back. "This is what I want! To forget you. To forget this mistake. I don't want you. It's *over*."

His brows furrowed, and his face fell as if I'd struck him.

I ducked away and rushed to grab my things from the floor. I ran out of his bedroom to the foyer, hit the *Down* button, dropped the sheet, and dressed speedily as the elevator ascended.

Thankfully, he didn't come after me this time. I didn't think I could ever look into those chestnut browns again without remembering the agony and betrayal I'd just seen.

Once inside the elevator, I bit my lip to hold back the

tears. I tried, in desperation, to shove David's expression out of my mind.

He'd forget me, though. It would be easy to toss out my memory like he'd surely done with many women. While I feared *my* heart would never forget one detail about him.

The elevator doors parted to a regal, eerily quiet hotel lobby. The click of my heels echoed as I raced through, fixing my gaze on the revolving door ahead as if that would get me there faster. When I pushed through to the other side, I shielded my eyes from the glaring, unrelenting sun.

I stumbled down the block. David had thought I'd choose him. I'd betrayed and hurt both men, breaking promises to each of them. I'd spiraled. I'd snapped. I'd been reckless for the first time since I'd seen the damage irrational love could do.

I couldn't hold myself together for another step. I leaned my back against a scratchy brick wall to pull myself together.

If one night with David could leave me broken this way, what kind of life would ours have been?

Volatile. Unstable. Passionate nights. Explosive *fights*. A mad, combustible lust . . .

Even knowing the heartache David could cause, I wanted to run back to him now. But my past anchored me where I was. That, and the thought of an unpredictable future that could soar to new heights just as surely as it could crash and burn. Getting wrapped up in David, his mouth on mine, his fingers tightening in my hair—it had already made me forget the truth too many times.

I'd chosen Bill for a reason.

And one day, I'd wake up, my lust for David gone, and I'd know without a doubt that I'd made the right choice.

And I realized in that moment what that choice meant.

I hadn't only said good-bye to David. I'd just committed to the life I'd seen inside that two-story suburban house weeks ago. The one on the realtor's postcard currently hanging on my refrigerator door. A commute into Chicago, a manicured lawn, a husband who'd work long hours to make sure our family was always comfortable. And the office that would one day be a nursery.

There was no turning back now.

Alone, where nobody could see, I sank down to the ground, put my head in my hands, and sobbed.

AVAILABLE NOW:
COME ALIVE
BOOK TWO IN THE
CITYSCAPE AFFAIR SERIES

LEARN MORE AT
WWW.JESSICAHAWKINS.NET

Also by Jessica Hawkins

LEARN MORE AT WWW.JESSICAHAWKINS.NET

White Monarch Trilogy

"Exciting and suspenseful and sexy and breathtaking." (*USA Today* Bestselling Author Lauren Rowe)

An enemies-to-arranged marriage series about a cartel princess caught between two feuding brothers who share only one thing —a desire for her.

Violent Delights

Violent Ends

Violent Triumphs

Right Where I Want You

"An intelligently written, sexy, feel-good romance that packs an emotional punch…" (*USA Today*'s HEA) A witty workplace romance filled with sexual tension and smart, fun enemies-to-lovers banter.

Something in the Way Series

"A tale of forbidden love in epic proportion… Brilliant" (New York Times bestselling author Corinne Michaels) Lake Kaplan falls for a handsome older man — but then her sister sets her sights on him too.

Something in the Way

Somebody Else's Sky

Move the Stars

Lake + Manning

Slip of the Tongue Series

"Addictive. Painful. Captivating…an authentic, raw, and emotionally gripping must-read." (Angie's Dreamy Reads) Her husband doesn't want her anymore. The man next door would give up everything to have her.

Slip of the Tongue

The First Taste

Yours to Bare

Explicitly Yours Series

"Pretty Woman meets Indecent Proposal…a seductive series."—(USA Today Bestselling Author Louise Bay) What if one night isn't enough? A red-hot collection.

Possession

Domination

Provocation

Obsession

The Cityscape Affair Series

Olivia has the perfect life—but something is missing. Handsome playboy David Dylan awakens a passion that she thought she'd lost a long time ago. Can she keep their combustible lust from spilling over into love?

Come Undone

Come Alive

Come Together